An Englishman's Guide to Infidelity

STUART CAMPBELL

STUART CAMPBELL

First paperback edition v2i, 2023

Published by Stuart Campbell
Copyright © 2023 by Stuart Campbell

Cover illustration
Image used under license from Shutterstock.com

ISBN: 978-0-6457198-4-0

CONTENTS

Acknowledgements

Many people gave their advice and support while I was writing this book.

My special thanks go to the members of the former *Write On!* writers group in Sydney, and to my beta readers Pilar, Gus, Jonquil, and The Prince of Gozo.

PART ONE: JACK

1: The anniversary

It was a summer Saturday, Thea's day, when she would absent herself from the house while I ran William and Zita from one sporting or artistic activity to another, using the wait times to park the car and jog around a convenient field. The family reformed late in the afternoon on the back lawn, me in my running gear making mocktails on the garden bench, and Zita climbing over Thea and sniffing her neck and wrists, guessing the names of the perfumes she'd sampled at the shopping mall in the New Town. The babysitter was booked for seven, and I had already called my shop assistant three times to make sure that all was well. All fine, she said, not bad for a Saturday. I pushed aside the little niggle of anxiety; I wasn't looking forward to letting her go.

Thea reclined in the deckchair in a white summer dress against her tanned skin, sipping a green drink piled high with orange fruit. Thirty-eight and luscious, she didn't look like any of the university lecturers I'd been taught by. She didn't look like a criminal for that matter.

I'd booked the restaurant and I had a small piece of expensive jewelry tucked into the inside pocket of my linen suit.

We fed the children at the big table in the kitchen, the afternoon breeze bringing the scent of roses from the tiny walled garden that Thea had claimed as her territory. A little plaque on the doorway said, 'No children past this point'. At six, the neighbour's daughter arrived to take over William and Zita, and we retreated to the bedroom.

I never tired of watching Thea getting ready for a night out: Meticulously applying her make-up, dressing and undressing as she approached – by some logic I didn't understand – the final choice of outfit; trying on six different shoes and swirling her hips in front of the mirror. And finally, the laying out of jewelry, matching the pieces with clothes, bag, shoes, make-up, mood, occasion. But tonight was somehow different. She seemed unusually animated and nervous. I showered, lounged on the bed in a robe and watched her begin the ritual at the dressing table, but she said, "Get dressed and come back later. I don't want you watching me." I tried a clumsy manoeuvre, sidling up to her and kneading her shoulders, but she stiffened, raised her palms and said, "Just go".

Downstairs the children were playing with the babysitter's body piercings. She had taken her nose stud out and William was prodding it with a spoon. Zita was trying to get one of the teenager's earrings into her unpierced lobe. "Can we all wash our hands after this game please?" I said. I hung around in the garden reading the paper until it was ten minutes before the arrival of the taxi, and then went upstairs. I knocked gently on the bedroom door. "Not long, Jack."

After a minute I knocked again and pushed the door. Thea did a swirl for me and I was transfixed by the dress – the muted sheen of the fabric, the deep harmony of magenta and charcoal grey, the way it hugged her body like a slinky second skin, accentuating the lines of her shoulders and legs. I must have had my mouth open because she said, "No need to goggle. What do you think, silver jewelry with it?" I recovered myself: "Silver of course, something discreet." Thea said, "Right answer, clever boy," and kissed me deeply.

While she chose the jewelry, I saw the glossy carrier bag. As the owner of a select bookshop in the most upmarket shopping street of a wealthy cathedral town, I know that you don't buy a Jules Hector dress in British Home Stores. "I'll just check whether the taxi's here," I said, sidling into the vestibule and stabbing my phone to log on to our credit card account – no sign of a thousand-pound purchase. Thea caught me up: "Stop fiddling with that phone. This is our anniversary dinner. In fact I want you to leave it at home." I made a face but she gently took the phone from me with one hand and slid the other inside my jacket, caressing my chest. "Just leave it."

We'd chosen The Secret Cottage for most of our special occasions – anniversaries, birthdays, family celebrations – and I'd asked Maxwell to give us the table in the little nook that looked out into the cobbled lane behind the cathedral. Here you were out of earshot of the noisy groups of twenty- and thirty-year olds who seemed to have unlimited funds to spend on eighty quid champagne and mounds of oysters flown in from Scotland. But the hum reminded you that you were still on the fringe of the social ritual of public eating. The nook had a rich velvet curtain, and Maxwell drew it halfway across. We often ate with friends, and so the evening started with the small talk that couples dining alone use to fill the transition from ordinary life to special occasion: Nice tableware, Maxwell's looking well, red or white, what's the fish of the day, you smell nice, gin and tonic to start.

The Cottage was busier than usual; there was a conference at the university and some of the delegates had found the town's worst kept secret – and Maxwell apologized that our orders might be a little slower than usual. In the meantime, he had a waitress top up our G&T's so that after half an hour we were both feeling woozily reckless. If the entrée hadn't arrived at that point we would have closed off the velvet curtain and made love on the table, but we settled down to eat moist scallops glistening against flat pink shells.

We finished a bottle of Chablis before the main course and I was trying to stop my head from lolling. Thea looked determined to stay upright, but I knew that she was as far gone as me. I should say that we have only ever been moderate drinkers. We were in territory we'd seldom visited before. Thea's pink lamb and my veal arrived, along with a leathery red wine. We swapped portions, feeding one another from our forks. Then Thea said, "Well, aren't you going to ask me?"

"Ask you what?"

"How I paid for the dress. I saw you looking at the bag and I know what you were doing on the phone."

"You saved up, I suppose."

"But my salary pays the housekeeping. You know I don't really have any left over."

I was feeling a little nauseous and I tried to drown the sensation with a big quaff of red wine.

"I suppose it's not really my business," I said feebly.

"Don't sodding well beat around the bush," Thea said, smiling.

"So tell me."

"Hold onto your seat."

We both swigged more wine. Thea looked directly into my eyes: "I found a wallet on the ground in the university. There were nine hundred pounds in it. I kept the money and threw the wallet in the pond."

We said nothing. The meat was cooling on our plates. Thea calmly picked up her knife and fork and began eating again, and I copied her, giddy and disoriented, sweaty under my linen suit. I looked at Thea and watched her jaws working. "You look like a hamster," I said, unaccountably, and kept chewing. "You look like a guinea pig," she said, and by some hidden chemistry that fuelled our fifteen years of love and intimacy, we both had an urge to giggle. Maxwell popped his head around the velvet curtain and stared at each of us curiously: "Something I'm missing mes enfants?" We stared back and shook our heads, our mouths ready to burst. As Maxwell withdrew we both managed to swallow our food before breaking down into tipsy laughter. When we'd recovered our composure I looked at Thea, who had taken out a compact mirror and was dabbing at her panda eyes.

"I don't know why I did it, Jack. I was just overcome by this feeling to do something reckless, like skiing off a cliff."

"Did anyone see you?"

"No, there wasn't a soul around. It was on a path between the sports centre and the river."

"Whose wallet was it?"

"Sir Percy Bushmore's."

"The Chancellor?"

"Yes, he was at the campus a couple of days ago for the opening of the new gym."

I thought for a moment. "He's worth a fortune," I said, "God, did I actually say that?"

"Yes, you did, and you can't take it back. By the way, have you forgotten something?"

I fumbled in my suit and gave her the little package.

5

She opened the plush lined jewelry box containing the antique ring: "It's lovely. It's what – Edwardian? See how the stone is set in those tiny gold claws. Thank you."

We shared a dessert like conspirators. Thea's eyes were glistening, and I felt a wave of desire the force of which I hadn't experienced for a long time. We got the bill and asked Maxwell to get a taxi, quickly. At the house I rushed the babysitter next door, giving her too many crisp bills – "No change, don't worry". When I got back Thea was slipping out of the dress. I took it from her, held it to my face, breathed in her perfume, and folded it gently on a chair. We made love with the passion of twenty-year olds and the knowledge of forty-year olds. Later we woke up and surprised ourselves by doing it again.

I opened my eyes to find the bed empty, but I could hear Thea and the children clattering breakfast dishes downstairs. There was no sign of the dress. I felt thick-mouthed and sour-hearted. I stepped into the shower and turned the water on hot, gradually adding cold until I was being drilled by icy needles, and my head began to clear.

The daily routine of breakfasts and tennis packing was under way, with Thea capably directing operations. It was drizzling outside, and the focus was on rain gear.

"Morning," I said.

"Dad looks sick, Mum," Zita said. Thea wouldn't look at me, just kept being capable, although I could see she was pale.

"What time's your first lecture, love?" No answer.

"Why's Mum's taking us to tennis today?" William said. "Is she?"

I went upstairs and hung around the bedroom window, watching Thea bundle the children into the car and drive away. I logged on to the big computer in my study at the back of the house and checked the electronic calendar we shared: 11am First year Philosophy Summer School, Ethics Lecture. I sighed a very big sigh, and looked at my watch: Just time to stroll down to the shop and buy a coffee and a croissant on the way.

Walking through our pretty cathedral town never failed to brighten me up. We lived in a three-storey house, parts of which were centuries old, a quarter of a mile from the cathedral and the knot of cobbled lanes surrounding it. My morning walking commute took me along ancient ivy-clad walls, and dinky half-timbered shops selling quills and parchment, rugged woolen yarns, Italian hiking shoes, antique maps, and all the bits and pieces of expensive frippery fancied by tourists visiting a town where Sir Edward someone or other was hanged during the English Revolution, and where any building worth its heritage contains a good many Roman bricks hauled from the nearby ruins before Chaucer was born.

Around the time of the magenta dress, however, my mood would droop by the time I turned the corner near the market square and caught view of Books by Birdswell.

It's time I explained a bit about myself. First of all, I suppose you could say that I was lucky. I grew up in the cathedral town in the house where I used to live with Thea and the children. There was an imposing brass plate on the front wall announcing our house's name 'The Windings'. The family joke was whether 'Wind' rhymed with 'find' or – the source of lots of flatulence humour – 'sinned'.

My father was a doctor and so I grew up with quite normal expectations that I'd go to university and be another doctor or a dentist or a vet, and marry somebody like my mother, who never worked a day in her life.

Things went only slightly to plan. I became a chemical engineer down in London and not a medical person. I met Thea in my mid-twenties, we married, and we settled down in a rented flat in Kilburn, saving for a deposit on a house – she tutoring in philosophy at one of the better ex-Polys, and me working in a lab designing the next generation of baby wipes. By the time the children arrived we were still in the same flat, wondering when we might ever scrape the last few thousand pounds together.

The change came in the form of a head on crash with an articulated lorry during a night of freezing sleet just near Reading, five years ago. By the time they'd cut my parents out of the Jaguar, both had expired and I was an orphan with an inheritance. Thea and I moved into The Windings. We converted the consulting rooms into a guest flat and still had acres of space for our small family. Thea got some casual work at the local university and I gave up baby wipes while I pondered what to do with the pile of cash and shares I now owned. Thus, Books by Birdswell, named for the little river that threads its way through our town, a shop with a steady tourist clientele, a nice agency arrangement with the cathedral gift shop, and a rock solid annual textbook contract with the university. And that's where my luck began to run out. Having bought BBB I soon learned that I didn't have a clue how to run a business. The previous owner was incommunicado, no doubt laughing kitbags in a farmhouse in Tuscany, so I couldn't ask him why the takings were thirty percent less than they were under his management. Then a couple of years later a London book chain unexpectedly signed up with the university and I lost the core of my business. Anyway, that's enough history for now.

My part-time shop assistant was due in at eleven to help for a few hours with the lunchtime rush, such as it was, but I phoned her and said she wasn't needed. There was silence at her end, and then she said, "I depend on this job. I can't rely on it if you keep putting me off. I need to find something else."

"I have to let you go," I said, almost choking not on what I was doing, but on the trite phrase.

"That's it then."

"I suppose so."

***

At midday Mr. Firth the verger came in carrying a suitcase and looking sheepish. I kept an eye on the midday 'rush' – a few loiterers getting a free read and soiling the book covers with their sandwichy fingers – and greeted him. He had a new shiny plastic badge on his lapel. Next to a discrete cross it said, 'M. Firth Business Development Office'. I knew why he was there.

"I'm so sorry Jack. The Dean had a management consultant go over the Cathedral's finances, and they've recommended we go with another firm." He discretely placed the suitcase by the counter. "No hurry to return the suitcase. All the remaining stock is in there."

Which left me with Major Clive Handwell.

I unpacked the verger's books, shelved them, sold a self-help book to a lunchtime loiterer (he'd left a greasy one on the shelf and paid for a clean one) and then sat down to have a good think about my retired Major.

The mood at dinner that night was dire. The children were silent and sullen, and willingly scooted to their rooms when they had gobbled their dessert. Thea and I filled the dishwasher in silence.

"How was your day?" I said at last.

"How was yours?"

"So so. The usual."

"When I dropped William and Zita off at school this morning, the bursar asked me to come to his office."

I fiddled with a tea towel. "The bursar? Oh, the silly old sod. Was that about the cheque for the fees? I thought I'd phoned him. I picked up an old cheque book for some account I don't use any more and it bounced of course. I said I'd send him a replacement."

Thea looked at me unsteadily: "Jack. What's happened? Are we in trouble? It's the shop, isn't it?"

***

You learn to become invisible after a few months in prison. I fell in with a group of other misfits, among whom the common factor was that we were educated to a level that would be measured in the stratospheric in comparison with the rest of the inmates. The four of us ate together, exercised together and always tried to appear as no more than four smudges on the wall. My three friends had all got shortish stretches for financial fraud of one kind or another. Me, well I was in a different league altogether – on remand for a start, with only the vaguest idea of my trial date. At least I wasn't in the actual remand wing. You heard horrible stories from there – men trying to hang themselves, vicious fights with sharpened toothbrush handles. When I asked why I'd been put in with the sentenced prisoners they said, "Because with a posh accent like that in the remand wing you'd get your brains bashed in, especially after what you've done". We had ten university degrees among us – I say had, because one day my cellmate didn't wake up, died of a brain aneurysm during the night, and we were down to seven degrees and three smudges and me wondering who I'd be sharing the open toilet with.

Here I am then, stuck for presumably quite a few years in prison in a forlorn field in the Midlands, miles from the pretty cathedral town where Thea and I broke the mold cast for us by family, school, university, and the law of the land. Here I am, forty, getting portly on jailhouse stodge, just starting an online bachelor of something or other that I don't need except as an antidote to brain rot, and becoming even more vastly overqualified for my prison job as mopper of floors and duster of handrails.

2: In fine fettle

The detective who interviewed me got it all wrong about Major Handwell. I was outraged to hear that I had 'groomed' the old chap. Disgusting word, made me sound like a gerontophile. Anyway, I'll tell it the way it was and you'll see that my relationship with the Major was based on mutual respect.

The morning after Thea suggested we might be in trouble – and I had reassured her that all was well – I put the 'Back at 10.30' sign on the shop door and locked up. The Major's house was fifteen minutes' drive from the Old Town in a small estate of substantial mock Tudor houses built in the fifties, graced with net curtains, shiny black German cars, mature trees and professionally tended gardens. I knocked several times and listened for the shuffle of slippers and walking stick. The solid timber door slowly opened on its massive wrought iron hinges, and the cadaverous military ancient stood peering from the hallway.

"Dear Francis, do come in."

"Good morning, Uncle Clive. Everything well?"

The Major shot out an arm and a skeletal wrist poked out from the crisply pressed shirt. I shook his hand gently, fearful that I would break a decalcified birdlike bone and cause a fatal hemorrhage. He insisted on making tea and I waited in the parlour for twenty minutes listening to the faint clinking and jets of water. I'd spent quite some time sitting in this room studying the massive tapestry covered armchairs, the sideboard as big as a frigate, the ornate marble mantelpiece that supported a French clock like the Albert Hall laid sideways on a gun carriage.

The Francis and Uncle Clive business had started six months before, but I'm getting ahead of myself.

The parlour door slowly opened, nudged by a long carpet-slippered foot which was followed by a cavalry twill trouser leg, the stick, and then the Major himself maneuvering a little trolley laid out with bone china bearing a regimental crest. I put the proffered cup on a side table, took an envelope from my jacket pocket and placed it – as always – on the tea tray. The Major made a slight snorting noise and waved his fingers at the envelope as if it were a trivial but bothersome matter that was beneath our attention.

"And what news of your family?" Major Handwell asked with the customary conspiratorial inflection. My part in this, I'd learned, was to respond with some similarly collusive gesture, and I'd developed a little repertoire of winks and smirks that seemed to do the trick.

"All in fine fettle Uncle," I said with a trace of arch amusement. "Now you'll be delighted to know I've tracked down the missing 1954 editions, and a man from the Isle of Wight will be sending them up within the week." The Major had told me that he had spent decades trying to compile a complete collection of *Titbits* magazine, which had had a 103-year run ending in 1984, by which time it featured rather more tits than bits. The Major's Holy Grail was the 1900 edition with a P.G. Wodehouse story. The arrangement was a nice little sideline to the business. I bought on eBay and onsold to the Major at a margin that reflected my hard work and persistence.

"Goodness," I said on cue. "That tea's gone right through me. Would you mind if …?", and I trotted up the stairs to the Major's spotless lav. This gave me at least twenty minutes in the upper part of the house while the Major replayed the tea ceremony in reverse, and wrote a cheque in his immaculate italic hand. I stuck to the routine: Flushed the toilet, crept into the Major's bedroom and checked drawers and cupboards, went back to the bathroom and swished some water around, checked the spare bedrooms, swished more water, quietly opened the drawers of the filing cabinet on the landing, looked at some old bills, flushed again and went downstairs. I was tempted to gaze for a moment inside his late wife's jewelry box but a great clearing of throat at the bottom of the stairs indicated that my time was up. The envelope with the cheque was on the hall table. I slipped it into my inside pocket, shook the Major's hand and left.

I'd constructed my own picture of Clive Handwell's life from my monthly twenty-minute excursions to the upstairs rooms of the house. He was eighty years old, ten years a widower, had been retired for decades, and had little family that I could discern, except for his nephew Francis. I found a packet of Christmas cards in a drawer, their number diminishing annually until the last one – from Francis – was dated three years ago. It was a nondescript thing with a rosy-cheeked Santa and the words 'Weather stunning here. Have a great Christmas and NY. Francis'. The only possible clue to Francis's identity was a framed monochrome photograph of the Major and his wife – I assumed that to be the stern female figure – and a small boy on a pebbly beach. The boy would now be about my age.

I was taken aback when, about two months after I'd first met the Major, he addressed me as Francis.

"Excuse me, Major. Did you say Francis? I'm Jack."

The Major looked at me with the faintest hint of irony, and slowly raised a finger to the side of his nose. It hadn't occurred to me that he might be a bit short of synaptic connections, and my querying look must have been taken as acquiescence in his little charade. From that day on, I was Francis and, he made it clear, I was to address him as Uncle Clive. I continued to respond to his little winks and nose taps with my own raisings of the eyebrow and wonky grins. I wasn't entirely delighted when the cheques started to be made out simply to 'Francis', but my discomfort was mollified by the fact that the sums written on them always exceeded the amounts on the invoices I gave him. It slowly dawned on me that he was giving a monthly allowance to a dutiful nephew. I found a barely legal way to bank the cheques in a separate account unknown to Thea, and marked the Major's invoices 'settled in cash'. I paid no attention to the fact that the cheques were written on the account of 'Bathwell Trust'. People's banking business was theirs, not mine.

Does that sound like 'grooming'? I can't see it myself. But the ring business did chew at my conscience. It wasn't that I'd taken the thing from the jewel box, and then artfully rearranged the other items so that its absence would be unnoticed. And it wasn't that on an earlier visit I'd placed a tiny piece of fine metal wire between the jewelry box and its lid and found it undisturbed on the next visit. The dilemma was that my plan to replace the ring with a very similar one when I could afford it had been dashed by the prospect of some unwelcome demands on the 'Francis' reserve savings account. How long could I risk leaving the jewelry box short of an item? As I walked back to the shop that morning I wrestled withugly, half-formed ideas.

At the end of a depressingly inactive trading day, I locked up the shop in the knowledge that the takings would barely cover the electricity bill, let alone the rent. I walked home with dancing visions of the school fee bill in my mind, dreading the prospect of looking Thea in the eye. With my mind distracted I slipped on a patch of mossy pavement and fell towards the cobbled roadway, landing heavily on my hip. On the way down I caught sight of a green bus bearing down on me, and drawing on a primitive store of energy remnant of a time when our ancestors ran for their lives from sabre-toothed tigers, I launched my body across the carriageway. The bus braked, the front wheels locked on the spot where my chest had been, and I lay uninjured among the cars that had pulled up near me. Concerned voices floated around me: "Are you hurt? Does he need an ambulance? What on earth happened?" I looked up and had one of those moments of odd clarity when things slow down and colours get sharp and saturated. I got up tremblingly, waved off the passers-by, and resumed my walk. It sounds goofy now, but my mind was filled with a fairy floss of love and desire for the woman that Providence had saved me for.

Familiar voices penetrated my thoughts: William and Zita staring at me, loaded with enormous sports backpacks, and accompanied by our neighbor and her two children. It was gymnastics night.

"Daddy, are you alright? Why are you all muddy?" I

hugged them stiffly and explained that I'd slipped.

"Better get a move on or we'll be late," the neighbour said, and I waved them off.

My shaky fingers got the front door open. I went through to the kitchen, where Thea was in jeans and a t-shirt marking essays at the old timber table, with a very big glass of red wine at her elbow.

"I was nearly killed by a bus."

She looked up at me curiously, shuffled the essays into a pile, and took a mouthful of wine, which left a little red stain at each corner of her mouth. I bent over her and dabbed each stain with my tongue tip. She wriggled away and ran upstairs. When I got to the bedroom she was putting on the magenta and grey dress.

***

"The kids'll be back in ten minutes." Thea said, rolling naked out of the bed, which smelt deliciously of lovemaking. The dress was rumpled on the floor – it hadn't stayed on for long and a seam had split. The bruise on my hip was going purple and I was beginning to ache as the dopamine wore off. We didn't speak explicitly about what had changed that evening, although when we talked months later about it, we each had our own metaphors. "I felt like we were stunt actors shattering a glass door," I said. Thea added, "For me it was as if we were bungy jumping". Hmm, perhaps. On reflection I think we invented those metaphors, but we both knew that we'd crossed into an unfamiliar land.

"Oh, I forgot," Thea said, pulling on her jeans. "Leave the school fees to me."

3: Clocked

I like to spend time in the prison chapel. I was born without any genetic disposition towards religious faith, and my parents made only token efforts to nurture what nature hadn't provided: A few months of Sunday school, an untouched New Testament on the bookshelf. But, as the prison chaplain says, God's work manifests itself in unexpected ways, and if the chapel provides me with a bit of thinking space, then I'm grateful to Him.

When I was first sent on remand, my meditations were largely rooted in self-pity, remorse and shame. But with time these rambling sentiments gave way to a rather forensic examination of how I drifted off the path of righteousness. I spend many hours reconstructing my childhood, and in particular my relationship with my parents, but to be honest I never come up with anything, because no sooner do I script some little scene ('Daddy, why is hurting animals wrong?') than it fades as I doubt its veracity.

I didn't question Thea about the school fees, and of course that was partly of the thrill of it all; she not knowing the details of my schemes and I not knowing about hers. The whole business was strangely entangled with our sex life, which was warming up rather satisfactorily. We found occasions to pack the children off for unscheduled visits to friends to allow us half a frenzied hour that always somehow included the magenta and grey fetish dress, now torn and stained. These sessions also began to involve more alcohol than we were used to. We existed in a half-world where we were at once strangers and intimates. Of course that all came to end not long after Christmas.

But let me get back to Books by Birdswell. My next visit to the Major was in my diary for a Tuesday in August, which turned out wet. Rainy weather always made me yearn for a holiday in the sun – a nice drive through Provence, a week on an island somewhere in the Aegean – but the shop had stifled anything spontaneous, and I'd have to wait until I could find someone to run the place in my absence. I didn't fancy my luck with my shop assistant, who had blanked me when I passed her in the street.

Thea's confession had shaken me up. I'd had a little plan in mind, but really had no intention of carrying it out – not unlike that feeling you have on a high balcony and you get a fixated idea of hopping over the edge. You'll never do it, of course.

Taking the Major's freely offered stipend was one thing, and filching the odd piece of jewelry while keeping it in the family was not exactly a leap into rank criminality. But raiding the old boy's collection of rare coins was crossing into hazardous territory, especially as portable property had to be turned into spendable cash. But a certain lecturer in philosophy had crossed the Rubicon. Why should I just stand on the riverbank?

I was feeling neither joyous nor confident when I parked two streets away (a precaution I regularly took), walked to the Major's house and knocked on the door. There came faint shuffling from inside the house for a few minutes – no doubt the Major plumping up the cushions and checking the tartan tea caddy – but I was taken aback when a man of about my own age answered the door.

"Do come in," the man said without hesitation. He was thin, shaven headed, and wearing a dressing gown.

"Actually, I think I've got the wrong house," I said. "I think I want next door."

"Nonsense, Francis. Uncle Clive particularly wants to see you," the man said, leaning forward and clamping my elbow with a sweaty hand. I could smell a nasty whiff of unwashed genitals from within the gown. Now, you'll know that as a member of the Three Smudges in Her Majesty's Prison, I'm not keen on violence. I stepped inside and he deadlocked the door as I entered the sitting room.

Curiously, it was the hole in the bottom of one of the Major's carpet slippers that struck me first. I'd never seen the soles pointing at the ceiling, and the little opening seemed ridiculously poignant. It was the first dead person I'd seen. He was on his front and there was a stain on the carpet under his middle that I didn't want to think about. The massive clock from the mantelpiece lay next to his shoulder, and there was a darker stain on the carpet under his face.

"Bit of a shock isn't it?" the man in the dressing gown said. "Let's go into the kitchen."

I sat down at the kitchen table and tried to breathe slowly. I looked up at the man, who was scratching himself deep inside the gown. He raised his eyebrows and proclaimed in cop-show tones, "There was a struggle. Blows were exchanged. The victim died when struck on the forehead with an antique clock". He concluded the performance with a bitter cackle.

I quelled my heart and said, "You're Francis of course".

"Oh, but I thought you were Francis. Aren't you Uncle

Clive's favourite nephew, the one who's been stealing my money for the last six months? Or are you Jack the conman with the bookshop and the big house and the luscious missus and the two lovely kids?"

I took a tissue from my pocket and blew my nose. To my astonishment, Francis leaned forward and snatched the sodden handkerchief.

"Just the jobby," he said. "There'll be some nice DNA in that snot, and then there's all the fingerprints you must have left all over the place." I felt oddly calm, but involuntarily gagged on a throatful of vomit so that a sour warm string of the stuff dribbled onto the arm of the sofa. The man looked approvingly and dabbed it with another tissue.

"That's the way," he said, secreting the muck in the pocket of the foul dressing gown. "Now let me explain what a lot of trouble you've put me to. You see until you came along Uncle Clive and I had a very nice little arrangement. I was his only relative and there was, let's call it, a measure of mutual regard between us ... " I was getting back on balance by now and I began to study the Francis creature as he spoke. He had an earnest expression, seeming genuinely hurt by my intrusion.

"You see, Uncle Clive had no children and I was his favourite nephew. I had no intention of killing him – that was your fault. He thought I was a burglar."

I chanced my luck, more confident now. "You don't just kill people because they think you're a burglar," I said, not anticipating the reaction. Actually, I was barely aware of his reaction because I was laid out on the floor as the words left my mouth, my ear hot and swollen from the slap. I looked up at Francis but all I could see was his veiny ankles and a nasty darkness inside the gaping dressing gown.

"Dear, dear," Francis said. "Lippy. I won't put up with lip. Chat over, I think. Sit here while I get dressed and then we're going to do some clearing up." He disappeared for five minutes and came back dressed in jeans, a nondescript khaki windproof jacket, and leather gloves.

He went into the sitting room and back into the kitchen carrying the clock.

"Right, I'm going to wrap Uncle Clive up in plastic in a minute. Can you just hold onto the clock for a sec?" I must have been in a near catatonic state as I grasped the clock. In one corner of my mind a scene played, in which a forensics officer photographed my fingerprints on the marble base, while in another corner I registered the sheer stupidity of what I was doing.

"Lovely!" Francis said. "More clues for the police. Just like on the telly." He took the clock from me, bundled me into the hallway, unlocked the front door and shoved me onto the front path. I looked up and down the damp street. A woman in walking gear and pink Wellingtons was struggling to discipline a frisky golden retriever outside a house on the opposite side, about twenty yards to the right. I didn't think she'd seen me. Otherwise the street was empty, so I hunched my shoulders and walked as calmly as I could to the car, meeting not a soul on the way.

It was ten o'clock when I got back to Books by Birdswell. I hadn't opened the shop that morning and a couple of old codgers in raincoats rounded on me as I unlocked.

"Flipping nerve," the woman said.

"It says here you open at nine. I've got a good mind to write in about it," the man said.

I snapped, "Oh don't mind me. I'm just a small

businessman trying to make a quid. I do have other important things to do besides sit in my shop."

"That's foolish," the woman said in a quavery voice. "If you have to leave the shop, you should have someone else sit in there."

"Of course! I pay somebody to sit and watch you two keeping warm and putting your grimy old fingers all over my stock until the Library opens and you can get books for free."

The old man came close and thrust his face towards mine: "I was in the war, lad. I know your type – no respect, no decency, no moral stuffing."

They turned and, like a pair of flapping galleons, began to navigate a course towards the Civic Centre. I slipped into the shop and prepared for another dispiriting day. It was then – in the ordinariness and familiarity of the shop – that a wave of shock struck me. This wasn't like the initial impact of seeing Uncle Clive dead. This was cold, sweaty dread.

A murderer. Well not really, but as good as. If I hadn't gone along with Uncle Clive's fantasy, if the real Francis hadn't turned up, if Uncle Clive hadn't mistaken him for a burglar and attacked him, if Francis hadn't brained him with the clock … it all led back to me. The old codger was right: No respect, no decency, no moral stuffing.

Somehow I got through the day, managing to dredge up the minimum of courtesy to deal with the odd customers who came by. I had a few minutes relief when a coachload of Chinese tourists disgorged in the Civic Centre car park, marched down the cobbled street, did a sharp right into the shop and bought up most of my stock of postcards and novelty biros. They all had twenty-pound notes and I had to phone Mrs. Watt at the Farmhouse

Pasties shop next door for change.

"Have you got the flu, Jack? You don't look well."

"Just a touch of something, Mrs. Watt. Thanks for the change."

I was locking up at six when I heard someone whistle from the other side of the street. Even though he was wearing dark glasses and a hood, I knew it was the loathsome Francis.

"Public bogs. Five minutes," he said, and walked away.

I loitered around outside the gents in the Civic Centre, watching the entrance. A policeman gave me a stern look so I walked nonchalantly in, to find Francis facing the urinal, fly unzipped.

"Come on, make it realistic," he said, and I unzipped and stood at the other end of the porcelain wall.

"Right," he said. "I can make all this go away. All you've got to do is a couple of things."

"What things?"

"First of all I want my money back. Tomorrow. Cash. All of it."

"And the other thing?"

"You'll find out."

At that moment the policeman came in, and despite our air of innocence as we both stared into space zipping our flies, said, "Righto lads, I think you're done here. Hop it."

4: Unclocked

"I knew you were up to something. Come on, let's have the rest of it," Thea said after we'd put the children to bed. The evening was unusually warm even at nine o'clock, and we had taken bottles of cold beer into the garden, where clouds of gnats swirled in the last patches of sunlight. Thea didn't look well, and I suspected that her own moral scales were tipping the wrong way.

I'd got as far as my impersonation of Uncle Clive's nephew and told her about the envelopes.

"How much has he given you so far?" I totted up the sum and she made a low whistle.

"And where's the money now?"

I must have looked shifty because she frowned and took an angry swig of beer.

"Let's get this into perspective. I still don't know how you paid the school fees," I said peevishly.

She looked down and mumbled something. I suddenly felt desperately sorry for her and I held her hand. She snatched it away and said, "It was Freda's money," and then dissolved in tears.

"But Freda's dead."

It all came out, in dribbly bits between snuffles and eye dabbing. Freda, one of her fellow part-time tutors at the university, had killed herself six months before during a spell of depression. The body was expatriated to Denmark by her family, who said to Thea that somebody would come back to sort out her affairs in England. Not entitled to desks, Thea and Freda were allocated a shared drawer in a filing cabinet in the Department of Philosophy and Religious Studies. Among Freda's property was a cheque book.

What Freda's parents didn't know, however, was that their daughter was a cruel manipulator who treated her students with indiscriminate dollops of favouritism or hostility depending on her mood, and was – just before her death – in sexual liaisons with the Professor of Sociology and the Professor's husband, the Academic Registrar. Freda was loathed by her colleagues.

"So you presented a cash cheque at the bank?" I asked.

"Yes."

"Which bank?"

"Not here, in that complex near the industrial estate."

"Did they ask for ID?"

"I showed them Freda's university card. We looked alike."

"Could anyone have recognized you?"

"I wore a hat and a pair of your glasses."

"And then you went back and taught a class in ethics."

She gave me a very dangerous look. The neighbours had come outside and the wife called over the fence, "Glorious night. Fancy some fried paneer?" She held a paper plate over the fence: "Enjoy. Goodnight!"

We carried on in a whisper. My remark had obviously enraged Thea and she hissed at me, "Don't lecture me on ethics Jack. I don't even begin to understand what has happened to us. I've spent most of my adult life thinking about right and wrong, and I'm struggling to keep a grip. Now tell me what else!"

"The money," I said, "is in a sort of secret account I

opened. It was meant for a rainy day."

"So you haven't spent any?"

"Let me get to that in a minute. There's something much worse." And this time I told her pretty well most of it, including Uncle Clive's murder and Francis's extortion demand. I say 'pretty well' because I didn't have the heart to mention the ring.

I stopped. She said, "This is just silly. You're making it up. You've gone mad."

"It's true. He's dead because of me."

"Who's dead?" It was William in crumpled pajamas in the doorway. "Is it my guinea pig that's dead? I woke up because I was so hot."

Thea led the six-year old to the garden bench and cradled him. "He's got a terrible temperature. Get the thermometer quickly." Indeed William had a serious fever and, we feared, might be ill enough to suffer a convulsion. I took him inside, gave him aspirin, and sponged him down while Thea telephoned the hospital. Within an hour he was attached to a drip, surrounded by a team of soft toys and plastic monster figures, while we huddled by the bed comforting Zita. At midnight I took Zita home, leaving Thea to sit out the night on the chair watching over William. I collected them at eight the next morning – William apparently recovered – and we put both children back to bed to rest for the morning with promises of chocolate milk when they awoke.

We ate breakfast gritty-eyed and sullen. Thea said, "Jack, the game's over. No more talk of murder, no more of this craziness. Last night was a warning. If we stop now we might just get back" – she searched for a word – "our humanity".

I freshened up and walked to the shop in an other-worldly state, where alternative realities battled for supremacy. Uncle Clive dead, but not for Thea. The real Francis hunting down the fake Francis. An apparently prosperous shopkeeper striding to work on quicksand. I'd had some quite serious surgery once, and I remembered the feeling of resignation when I was wheeled to the theatre. As I walked past the tourist shops I seemed to be on a hospital trolley, my fate predestined, my route predetermined, my volition extinct.

I unlocked, looked around, did some dusting, unpacked some stock, and started putting books on shelves. Now, any bookshop owner will tell you that in the fiction area, the money is in genre. People love to read the genres they are used to and feel comfortable with: Historical fiction, romance, horror, war, espionage, crime. I had a big crime section, and in fact it was one of the genres I liked best. A big seller in my shop (and by big, I mean on a very modest scale of small to big) was the Lincoln Rhyme thrillers of Jeffery Deaver: Lincoln, the wheelchair bound 'criminalist' performs astounding feats of detection through meticulous and complex forensic analysis.

While I was shelving books in the crime section, something was niggling at the back of my mind, like a far-off tune that you can't identify. The niggle grew stronger as I scanned the back covers, with their unlikely plots and even unlikelier detectives. I was disturbed by the door chime. I turned and there, unsurprisingly, was Francis, now ludicrously wearing a false beard.

"Public bogs. Five minutes. Cash in a Sainsburys bag."

"Just a moment, Francis," I said, clarity washing across

my mind.

"Sorry brother. You don't 'just a moment' me."

It was suddenly clear: There was no smell. I remembered that the sitting room at Uncle Clive's house was very warm, and there was no smell. Don't dead people soil themselves? Even if Uncle Clive's corpse hadn't released some solids, surely the wetness under his middle should have had an odour? Francis must have sensed the change in me. He repeated, "Bogs. Five minutes".

But this time there was a faintly susceptible shade of doubt. I looked into his eyes and held my gaze: "I need a week. It isn't that easy." We stared at one another for perhaps thirty seconds and he looked down.

"Four days. No more," he said, and turned on his heel.

I delayed going home. I needed to pore over the events of the last few days on my own.

Apprehensive about the intentions of the thuggish Francis, jubilant at the revelation of the odour and at my defiance, I wandered through cobbled yards and across muddy playgrounds, replaying the ghastly scenes, and rehearsing what I should tell Thea. After an hour I found myself back near the shop and on the doorstep of the Bear and Fox. I slipped in, ordered a double Scotch, and found a seat half hidden behind a timber beam. My meditation was broken by the verger, who had his half of bitter at the bar each evening before going home.

"Not poorly are we?" he asked in social-workerish tones.

"Just a little overwrought."

"I say, don't think I'm being pushy, but you know that even if you aren't a friend of Jesus, the cathedral is a splendid place to just sit and reflect ..."

I could have kissed the verger. The certainty of his faith

shone from his little currant bun face, and I saw at once that I had to go home and tell Thea everything. Well, almost everything. I swigged off the Scotch, thanked him and went home.

The children were eating banana yoghourt and watching the television. Thea gave me a sour look and said, "I saved you some dinner but it's probably ruined." While she put the children to bed I microwaved the limp stir-fry and rehearsed my speech. But when Thea came down the stairs I could tell from her expression who'd be the compere of the show, and it wouldn't be me.

The quality I admire most in Thea is the blend of meticulousness and tenacity, and let's face it, you don't get to be a doctor of philosophy in actual philosophy by being a slacker with no eye for detail. The thing I never really got about philosophy was the vagueness, but I suppose that's the chemical engineer in me. I remember watching her, night after night, poring over articles from learned journals, making detailed notes in different coloured pens, Venn diagrams, timelines, thought frameworks, and inexorably spinning all this formless ectoplasm into razor sharp treatises, so compelling to her blind referees that – if I hadn't dragged her to the provinces – she could have built a stellar academic career in London.

It was plain that I was to receive the same treatment. In a way I welcomed it; Thea is so much better than me at exposing the heart of the fluid problems that beset us humans. Me, I'm good with things that don't talk back – molecules, for example.

We sat opposite one another at the kitchen table with mugs of strong tea, and she took me through one crime scene after another, probing when I veered off the path: The bookshop – out it came, the wounded business, the lost contracts; then the Uncle Clive story again, but this time probing my memory and my revelation that the Major may not have been dead at all, the truth about the anniversary ring: "I'd half guessed something was going on." And then the secret account: How much was in it, had I spent any of it? No, the account was untouched. Throughout the interview (that's how it felt), Thea made no notes, just leading me with cool logic, step by step. But when I had nothing more to give up, she seemed to unwind and I thought I sensed a hint of the guilty excitement we'd shared since the incident of the wallet.

"You know, Jack," she said, solemn again. "Over these last weeks I keep thinking about a student who asked me a question last year that really shook me up. It was in the middle of a lecture and the student suddenly stood up and asked me if I believed in anything. Just like that."

"So why was that a problem?"

"Well, it hit me. I'd spent twenty years studying and teaching philosophy, analysing and weighing up the ways that people believe and reason, developing my own theories by undermining other people's ideas. And when this spotty adolescent asked me if I believed in anything, I couldn't think of a single honest thing to say."

"So what did you say?"

"I just gave her a smart comeback, told her that the answer to the question wasn't the point. The important thing was that the question was asked."

"That was supposed to be smart?" I asked.

"Smart, but pathetically dumb. I felt awful. But Jack, it's the same now. These games with the money, the sex, the drinking – it sounds like a cliché, but we've crossed some line we shouldn't have and I'm scared that I really might not believe in anything except the here and now.

Let's face it, existentialism went out with flared trousers. How do you think it makes me feel to pretend to myself that the Chancellor can afford to lose nine hundred quid, and that it was OK to spend Freda's money because she was a bitch? That's the morality of a cockroach. We've got to stop now, give Francis the money, hope that we've covered our tracks enough not to get caught, go back to how it was. Act like decent people."

"Decent people who are bankrupt. Who've committed serious crimes."

She looked away from me and I knew that there was something else. I said nothing, waited. She knew I was waiting.

"All right. You know that my department shares a tea room with the sociologists? I get on very well with a woman who does research on the military – hierarchy and power and bullying and all that. I asked her if it was possible to check British Army personnel records because I was trying to track down a great uncle. She showed me how to get into the database ..."

" And you looked up Major Clive Handwell?"

The gleam had come back to her eye, I was sure.

" Jack, Major Clive Handwell doesn't exist."

5: The pact

We made a pact that night, Thea and I. Uncle Clive and Francis, or whoever they were, had thrown down a challenge, and we accepted it. They had dangled the money in front of me, tricked me into taking it, and then tried to extort it from me by blackmail.

While we sipped our mineral water (we agreed to cut the drinking down), Thea told me that the anniversary ring was worthless.

"I'd sort of guessed," I said.

Thea said, "I took it to a jeweler and said I thought one of the stones was loose and the setting might need to be replaced. He said it didn't seem to be loose but since it was just costume jewelry it wouldn't be worth repairing."

"The stinkers."

The immediate problem was the family finances. Article One of the Jack-Thea Pact was that Thea and I would join forces to sort out Books by Birdswell. "You've made a bloody hash of it so far, Jack. You need a philosopher on the job." I was elated when my fabulous Thea told me that she would take on some extra classes to get us over the next rent payment for the shop. With the shop assistant's salary saved we thought we might survive for the next three months, and I made some amateurish remarks about 'marketing' and 'promotion' to bolster our spirits.

Article Two was that we would bury Thea's transgressions: Sir Percy's wallet and Freda's cheque had never happened. Thea was such an unlikely criminal that if there were ever a whiff of suspicion, she would simply deny it as ridiculous. In a way, we agreed, I had been punished on her behalf: The shock of Uncle Clive's murder, the blackmail attempt, and the whack around the ear. The stars were in alignment, even if they'd been nudged reluctantly into place.

The basis of Article Three was that we were in jam that we had to fix ourselves. If I went to the police and explained how I'd accepted money from an old man on false pretences, stolen a ring, and left my DNA all over his house, I'd soon be reminded that anything I said could be taken down in writing and used in evidence: "Oh, I see, Sir. You were shown a corpse that wasn't actually dead and you were subjected to extortion threats by a man in a false beard in a public toilet?" No, we had to do this ourselves, whatever 'this' was. Article Three didn't quite get that far, but what we did know was that even if we gave the money back to 'Francis' – we'd begun to use airborne quotation marks when we referred to the two con men – they may not stop there. He's made it clear that my family had been targeted: "Luscious wife, big house, lovely kids." We bristled over our cocoa.

That night the lovemaking was calmer, more measured, tenderer – the deliberate and declarative bonding of two warriors on a quest to right a wrong. The magenta and grey dress stayed on its hanger but it glowed somewhere deep in the crucible of our passion.

In the dark of my cell when sad men snore, fart and thrum inside their blankets, I reinvent those tender hours in my mind until I don't know what was real and what is imagined.

***

Three weeks passed without word from Francis. We carried on life with apparent normality, but paying special attention to William's and Zita's whereabouts, keeping in touch regularly by text message, and securely locking the house. Francis's four-day deadline had long passed, and we assumed that the con men had gone to ground while they planned their next stratagem. Surely they realised by now that we knew that Major Handwell was a fake.

One evening we left the children with the neighbour for an hour and drove to an area a mile or so from the Major's house. We'd dressed in running gear, and we put on beanies before slipping out of the car and jogging in the direction of the house. The place was in darkness and bore an estate agent's sign: 'Executive residence to let furnished'. I saw the woman with the unruly golden retriever and pink Wellington boots coming towards us and the beast leapt at me, flopping its feet on my chest and licking my neck.

"He won't bite. He's quite harmless," she announced in the Princess Anne voice that dog owners of a certain age and class assume. The dog's jaw was locked onto my ankle, and the woman yanked unenthusiastically on the choke chain. A motorcycle puttered past and the retriever hurtled after it, tearing the leash from the woman's hand. "He'll be back for his supper," she said.

"Never mind his supper. My husband's been attacked," Thea said, winking at me. I didn't immediately catch the intent of the wink, but the woman began to bluster about dogs having rights and humans having to respect them. Thea cut into the horsey tirade: Her husband didn't seem to be injured, yes of course dogs have rights, and a lot of dogs are a darn sight more decent than a lot of humans. But that house ... we have a friend who's looking for a decent sort of rental, has it been empty long ...

The lady puffed herself up: "Empty long? It's downright shameful. The fellow just disappeared one day. Up and gone!"

"There's no respect anymore," Thea said, and she glanced at me with a face that said: Just leave this to me. "Probably a foreigner I'd expect."

"No, no, English, but not our sort of English – shifty, not at all nice. Low class. I don't know where they get the money ..."

"It's a big house for a single man ..." Thea pressed on.

"There was an older man, but he came now and then. A woman sometimes. Oh yes, and a chap used to come every few weeks with a parcel." At this, I pulled my beanie over my forehead and stared in fascination at my shoes, but I was rescued by the dog, which cannoned out of the darkness and whacked the woman full in the abdomen with its wet paws.

"So what next?" Thea said when we got back to the car.

"I don't know."

"Don't be silly. We'll ask for a viewing. For our friend."

"What friend?" I asked.

"The one in er ... Uzbekistan who's moving back to the UK and wants to rent a house."

***

And so it was that four days later when Thea had a day off, I borrowed a shop assistant from the Tartan Outfitter's shop to cover while we slipped round to the Major's house.

The place looked much the same. The furniture was all

there, as were the china with the regimental crests and the kitchen implements. But the clock was gone and there were no signs of bloodstains on the carpet. Upstairs some things were missing: The jewelry box, and the little bureau with the Major's papers.

Thea, ever surgically sharp in her instincts, took something from her bag, tossed it under a chair, and called out to the estate agent. "Excuse me. Somebody's lost an earring. Perhaps it belongs to the previous tenant." The agent tried not to sound impatient. It could be anyone's, it probably wasn't valuable.

My diabolically brilliant Thea wouldn't give up: "It might be his girlfriend's. Can't you forward it to him?"

"Madame, I'm reluctant to break a professional confidence, but if I knew where the previous tenant lived I might not be a considerable sum out of pocket. Now, your friend in Uzbekistan ... is this the kind of property he's looking for?"

***

We picked up the children, bathed, fed and storied them, and settled down to a makeshift dinner.

"So," I said, "We've established that Francis was the kingpin and that he's buggered off. What now?"

"The Bathwell Trust of course, the drawer of the cheques. I'll Google it now. Hmm, how odd. It's a charity, named for the Bathwells. Let me just scroll down. They're a big beef farming family and the trust supports poor rural labourers."

It made no sense. A bogus Major writing cheques on a rural charity to compromise a failed bookseller. A beautiful philosopher with the sniff of the hunt in her nostrils. A married couple in beanies sneaking around the scene of a rigged murder scene. Thea brought me back to earth: "The Chair of Trustees is a Marjorie Smith. The office is in Oxford. I'll go and see her next Tuesday."

I fussed with the washing up while Thea checked train timetables. Article Five of our pact had been all about not keeping anything from one another. How long would it be until my remaining messy secret was hauled into the daylight?

6: Adjusting losses

"I want you to take all the children's books off this stand and choose the ones with the best covers. Can you do that?" William and Zita nodded gravely and set to the task. It was the last day of the school holidays, and they would spend the day in the shop.

"Where did Mummy go?" Zita asked.

"To Oxford, to see a friend," I said. "Shall I ask Mrs. Laverty to bring some lemonade?"

And so the day proceeded, with the lady from the shop next door periodically bringing snacks and drinks, while the children made a fair job of point of sale book marketing.

I closed up at five thirty and took the children home. They were tucked up on the sofa sipping cocoa when Thea came in around seven thirty. I caught the gleam in her eye, but I had to be patient. We may have been career criminals but we were parents first, and the children were to have their quota of attention.

It was nine thirty before we were alone, and I was hopping around like a goalkeeper with a full bladder when Thea said, "All right. Let's talk".

"Actually," she said, "Let's just listen". She took a small digital recorder from her bag, and placed it on the coffee table.

I'd only given fleeting thought to Marjorie Smith, the Chair of Trustees of the Bathwell Trust, and had assumed a tweedy two-piece, pearls, a perm, and an accent straight out of a Berkshire thoroughbred stable. So I was surprised at the flat, nasal Estuary voice – and I visualized a professional woman, a company secretary, business attire slightly too tight for comfort.

Thea explained that she'd rung ahead the day before and asked if she could talk to Mrs. Smith about some Charity Commission issues – just a routine call. Marjorie Smith had reluctantly agreed. Thea turned on the recorder.

"Do you mind if I take a few notes as we go along?"

Marjorie Smith made a nasal exhalation.

"Now," Thea continued, "You said that you were glad that it was all coming out. Can you clarify that remark?"

There was a long silence, but the sensitive recorder picked up Marjorie's rough breathing.

"I've wanted to talk to someone about it, but I just didn't have the courage. It's simply too embarrassing," the woman said. "It's not that I'm dishonest. I'm an accountant for goodness sake. It's an affliction … a disease."

"Can we go back to the beginning please?" Thea said.

"Who did you say you work for?" Marjorie asked.

"We are … loss adjusters." I looked at Thea with slavish admiration. Her confident voice went on, "We make discrete enquiries in cases like this to determine whether, er … losses can be adjusted."

"Of course, of course," the woman said, clearly grasping at the notion of a confidential enquiry, and rushing to redeem herself through her confession. "So let me begin five years ago. My husband Neville liked a flutter – nothing big of course – but he opened an online account and he'd show me when he'd won something. He was terribly disciplined of course, and knew when to stop.

'Marj,' he'd say, 'Forty quid a month is all I'm prepared to lose on the gee-gees,' and he stuck to it. When he passed away I never got around to closing all his accounts, and one day I logged on to the betting site."

"And this was five years ago?" Thea asked.

"Yes, yes. For the first few years I stuck to Neville's forty-pound rule, but I started to get brazen. In no time I'd spent most of my savings ..."

"And that's when you started to steal ..."

"Borrow ..."

"Borrow, then," Thea said. "What was your method?"

"It was easy," Marjorie said. "I set up a bogus supplier and invoiced the trust for professional services. The Trustees never read the financial papers properly before the board meetings, so I just bluffed my way through."

"And this went on for a couple of years."

"Yes. I even got it past the auditors." The nasal snuffle again, and the sound of a tissue being pulled from a box.

Thea said, "Mrs. Smith. Do you know a man called Francis?"

"No." The Estuary voice was defensive this time.

"Think carefully. Fortyish, thin, perhaps not ... very nice."

Marjorie said nothing. More tissues, then sobbing punctuated with little honks.

"Perhaps you do know who I'm talking about." This was Thea's 'I know one of you took the last piece of chocolate cake' voice.

The microphone picked up some sighing and more rustling. "Yes, Francis. A ghastly little man. He did some painting and maintenance work here. A cheque book went missing." More honking.

"And you confronted him?"

"Yes. And he knew. I don't know how, but he knew." The voice dipped a register: Pure Hackney. "The dirty little devil must have gone through my files. He just stood there brazenly and said that a couple of cheques was a small price to pay for keeping my secret safe."

"Evil," Thea said. "Pure evil. But we're on his tail."

"Are you really? I've been worried to death."

"Don't worry, Marjorie. He's going to pay. Now can I get a little bit more detail about the loss … that is the loss that we'll have to adjust. How many of the cheques were used?"

"I've got the list here," Marjorie said. "It's a tidy sum. The cheques were presented on a fairly regular basis, and I approved them in the accounts, but I had to do some somersaults to make them look legitimate. Then they stopped coming."

"When did they stop, Marjorie?"

"About three months ago. I would have been relieved but I know that there are still six cheques out there somewhere. At least if they were all accounted for I'd know where I stood."

"Where you stood?"

"Well yes, I had this plan you see, to sell my house and find a way to quietly reimburse all the gambling money to the Bathwell Trust. But I can't do it while I have these six cheques lurking out there."

"And the Trustees know nothing about all of this?"

"Nothing."

"And have you heard from Francis?"

"No."

"Marjorie, you've been very brave in telling me all this,

but I have just one more thing to ask you. What can you tell me about Francis?"

There was a very long silence on the recording, and Thea whispered to me, "It gets worse."

At last Marjorie said, "He's strong".

"Strong?"

"Wiry, doesn't look strong ..."

I raised an eyebrow at Thea, and she shrugged

"I just hate him," the Hackney voice said.

"Of course you hate him ..."

"He wormed his way in, he gained my trust, I was lonely and confused and he used me like a .... dishrag."

"Marjorie," Thea said quietly, "Are you saying that you and Francis had a ... relationship?"

Again, rustling sounds and then a passing airliner in the distance. A police siren – *eyoeyoeyo* – came near and then faded.

Then Marjorie whispered, "Call it that if you like. It was grotesque – he was twenty years younger than me and I behaved atrociously. Oh my God, I'm so ashamed."

"And when did you last see him?"

"See him? See him? I see him nearly all the time. He lives somewhere around here and he drinks in that pub across the road. He makes a point of passing me in the street a couple of times a week. Just walks past and gives me this look, like 'I've got my eye on you'."

Thea stopped the machine: "I'll spare you the rest Jack. Get me a strong drink."

"Before you utter another word," I said, "Was that recorded without the woman's knowledge?"

Thea, looking at her lap, nodded. I took a moment to absorb this, and even to wonder if we were remotely connected with the people we'd been a month before.

"So how did you end things with her?"

"Told her to sit tight, and if she didn't hear from me within a week, assume everything was OK, and she should start quietly reimbursing the Trust."

"And she swallowed it? She's obviously an intelligent woman."

"Intelligence counts for nothing when you're as terrified as that."

We nursed our drinks. Thea said, "Can we give the money back to Marjorie?"

"Very risky," I said, a bit too quickly. I wanted to get off this particular line. "Just let it sit quietly until we know how the land lies."

"The police?"

"Too late. We're in too deep," I said

"I'll check on the children," Thea said.

When she came downstairs she was holding a greeting card with a cartoony clown design and 'A Job Well Done' printed in jolly letters across the top. "It was next to William's bed. He said Mrs. Laverty brought it in with the pizza. Look inside."

Inside the card was written in block letters: 'To William and Zita. Love from F'.

7: The cooling

Healing is a funny word. The prison chaplain uses it a lot, and I've slowly got the sense of what he means when he talks about time healing a spiritual wound. I can almost visualize my wounds, like red raw gashes that granulate around the edges, thin scars forming, but tearing and weeping as the gashes are pulled open again.

It was a bit like that at home. The poisoned money, the evil greeting card, Thea's deception of Marjorie: They all gaped and wept pus until we gradually grew scar tissue over them. They itched and stretched tight, but they became part of us and we learned to live with them.

A month after Marjorie's visit to Oxford I got a call from the University. I drove over, got hopelessly lost in the tangle of one-way delivery entrances, perimeter roads named for Chancellors, buildings with signs for preposterously named research centres (The Martin F. Mooney Institute for Urban Poetics was one I remember), but eventually found a car park next to 'Purchasing Branch'.

"We'd like to propose a new contract with Books by Birdswell," Mr. Khan said.

"Excuse me ... didn't you sign up with the London firm?"

My heart jumped about behind my ribs when Mr. Khan explained that the London firm hadn't met their Key Performance Indicators, and that since Books by Birdswell had been ranked second in the assessment of tenders – "not assessed as ineligible," Mr. Khan said earnestly – he was entitled to reappoint me as the university bookseller. I had visions of piles of chunky prescribed chemistry textbooks, the kind that had revised editions each year which made last year's version as useful as doorstops. My mind lasciviously caressed their glossy dust jackets, and totted up the profit margins. "It's robbery!" Thea used to say, "A cruel trick to extract money from poor students". Well, I thought, watching a group of the lazy spoiled brats smoking in the sunshine outside Mr. Khan's window, I'm no Robin Hood.

My rising business fortunes encouraged more healing, and Thea and I grew cautiously hopeful that the ghastly events of the last year were behind us. We still kept the children closely guarded, locked doors carefully, watched who might be watching us in the streets. I started to harbour a futile hope that Francis had fallen under a train or drowned. Thea told me later that she'd had a similar hope. But we were both too appalled by our private wishes to admit them to one another at the time.

When I recall the events of that time, I find it useful to reconstruct them as eras. When you might be looking forward to many years of jail time, revising your life history becomes an obsession. I had my eras, my newly minted justifications, my moral balancing act, my continual rehashing. These months were the era of the 'false dawn', and when I rehearse them in my dull incarcerated mind for the thousandth time, I link them to memories of an earlier era – the 'cooling'.

The 'cooling' covers a period a couple of years before my parents died. I need to explain that when Thea and I first met, we were, as the trite phrase has it 'on the rebound', she from a couple of years living with an older man, and I from an immature and rushed marriage of about the same vintage. Thea was the daughter of a Greek Cypriot man and an Irishwomen, who slaved in a fish and chip shop. She'd kept the mature boyfriend from her father, but Mr. Dimitriou found out and gave the man a thrashing in an alley way in Camden Town.

"It was humiliating," Thea told me. "But the guy was a bit too free with his fists and I was beginning to wonder why an intelligent woman like me was putting makeup on bruises. My parents had figured it out of course, and Dad just fixed it in his own way."

My story was different. Jacqueline and I had been a dopey pair of childhood sweethearts, joined hip to hip through high school, doing homework together at one another's houses, fortified with apple juice and scones by one another's parents, getting the same A level results and ending up at the same university. Away from our polite and passionless family homes at last, we were able to throw ourselves into erotic froth.

But soon there was no fizz. We'd reached heights of pleasure in snatched moments at home, caressing and stroking while keeping an ear cocked for an opening door, a parental cleared throat. Naked in my frowsy student bed, Jacqueline looked less exciting with her thin sandy hair and watery eye lashes. The feeling was, I think, reciprocated, but we soldiered on, summoning desire from the bottomless biological depths that twenty-year olds are blessed with, our minds making love to brainfuls of sex crazed phantoms while our corporeal selves went involuntarily through the motions.

Catastrophe struck with a missed period. Our prudish homes had made us unprepared to cope with the hot and unpredictable winds of adult life. We procrastinated, another period was missed, we panicked, we secretly married in a damp registry office with a witness called Graham in a Spurs beanie. Jacqueline's period arrived, we confessed all to our appalled parents, we resolved to 'make a go of it'.

So at the beginning of my third year at university I found myself walking through the campus on a warm evening, slightly primed for adventure with a couple of pints of real ale, when I fell in behind a vision of desire, a dark haired student with delicious legs and a bottom that cried out to liberate me from the chains I'd wrapped myself in. Jacqueline and I called it a day. She'd found a rodenty Town Planning student and had in fact been waiting for the moment to quit. We stayed in touch only to arrange the divorce a couple of years later.

In the meantime, Thea and I … well, let me just say that the world changed from monochrome to colour, and we'll leave it at that.

But there was still the 'cooling'. We were by now living in Kilburn with two small children, hard up, short of sleep, and wondering if the conveyor belt we were on had an end. We didn't fall out of love – that never happened and never will – but we fell out of mutual favour. We snapped at one another and often ended up fuming, one in the bed and one on the couch. And, for a short time, I had an affair. How I managed the logistics I still struggle to understand, especially with Thea often staying late at work. My deception was celebrated in my lover's council flat at lunchtimes. She was a pretty West Indian girl, my boss's secretary. The liaison soon collapsed and I confessed, although I never revealed Jasmine's identity to Thea. My wife was surprisingly sanguine and forgiving. We sewed together the threads of our lives and the 'cooling' ended. We just wanted the era closed.

***

It was now three months since Francis's horrible card. The storeroom at Books by Birdswell was drily fragrant with the expensive smell of paper and glue as the textbooks began to arrive. The deliveries were more modest than I'd expected; Mr Khan hadn't mentioned that the textbook market was fast shrinking in the face of online study resources. But we'd passed a financial milestone, Christmas was a few weeks away, and we were set to celebrate. The Secret Cottage was booked for 6pm for us and the children.

At five o'clock the doorbell rang. Zita and William were skating in their socks on the parquet floor of the dining room. "Wait, kids. I'll answer the door," I called out. We still took precautions. As I opened the door, a clapped-out car pulled away from the kerb leaving a trail of blue smoke. A small brown-skinned girl in a padded anorak stood on the doorstep with a scruffy suitcase. She handed me an envelope.

"Who is it?" Zita said.

I opened the envelope, read Jasmine's note, and looked down at the little girl. "I think she might be your sister."

***

Maxwell made up a table for five in the cosy curtained side room. Each in our private universe of puzzlement, we ate pizza. The little brown-skinned girl – her name was Charlotte – picked and poked at her food, making shy peeps at her half-brother and half-sister. Thea was serenely furious, white heat radiating from her. "Just shut up. I've worked it all out. Just act normally. I'll deal with you later on," she had hissed after one glance at the peculiar scene on the doorstep. William and Zita seemed to take it all as perfectly normal; a sister had turned up. Smashing. What's your house like. Do you have a bike. Daddy can we have more Coke.

As for me, I shifted into pre-major surgery mode. I was on the trolley, too late to get up. Horrible things are going to be done to me. Others are in control. No point in worrying. Make stupid smiles. What else can go wrong. The worst is that I might die.

After the meal we zombie-walked to the car. Domestic operations were mechanically implemented. A trundle bed for Charlotte in Zita's room. All go to the toilet please. Bedtime stories for three.

***

"You total bastard." Thea was bolt upright on the sofa grasping a full tumbler of Scotch.

"Swearing at me isn't going to help."

"It's going to help me," she said, and called me – well let's not go into details. We did several rounds like that, me feebly protesting, she dredging the depths of English profanity while the level of Scotch in the bottle went down.

At last she said, "Read your tart's note."

I read:

Jack,

I don't have any choice about this. I have not been able to find another job and I cannot pay my mortgage. If you hadn't stopped sending the maintenance money I would not be in this tight spot and had to sell my flat. I bought it from the council and now stupid me I can't go back and get another council place. I'm sending Charlotte to you while I get on my feet again. My sister has taken me in but she doesn't want Charlotte there. I can have her on Sundays. It is only twenty minutes on the train. Anything you need to know about what she eats and so on text me.

Jasmine.

"How long have you known, Jack?"

"Since the beginning. I'm on her birth certificate. But I never saw her till today."

"And how do you feel about seeing her today?" Thea asked forensically.

And at that I started to bawl like a toddler, great gushes of sobs and howls and hoots of inhalation. Embarrassed, I rolled into a ball on the carpet, hugged my knees and shuddered out six years of stoppered-up grief and missing for my brown daughter.

I uncoiled and lay on my back, wet eyes open looking at the ceiling. I swiveled my head to look at Thea. She was looking pale and shaky, as if she were going to be sick.

"What's wrong?" I asked.

She looked at the ceiling for a long time. Then: "We'll keep her. She's just a little tot caught up in this mess."

"Thea. There's something else. Tell me."

"Tell you what?"

I shouted, "Tell me!"

She swigged more Scotch. "Do you remember that time Jack? The bills, the crappy mattresses, the stinking gas heater, the bloody beans on toast?"

"The overtime, the car breaking down, no money for babysitters ..."

"Dinner parties on two pounds of mince and a litre of

Spanish plonk …" Thea said.

"Tell me, Thea."

She made a bitter laughing sound, not really a laugh at all: "And you shagging your tart in your lunch hour."

"Who was he, Thea?"

"Did you always know?" she asked.

"I think I knew at the time. How long did it last?"

"Not long – as long as you and Jasmine I expect."

"Where did you …"

"Do it? At the university. In the evening. In the reptile research lab. It was his idea of a joke. We did it looking at snakes and lizards in glass tanks."

"You haven't told me who it was."

"Just someone. A maintenance guy."

"Tell me who."

Thea sobbed.

"Tell me who."

"He was called Jez."

"Did I ever meet him?" I asked.

Thea looked away.

8: January sales

My grandfather's cottage often fills my prison dreams. Granddad talks to me in his West Country voice, and I find Thea besides me, and then I am lost in the tiny orchard walking away from the cottage when I know I should be walking towards it, and then Charlotte appears at the top of a hill cradling William, and then I am in a chasm of loss and despair.

My most blissful days as a child were spent at his home in the Cotswolds. My grandfather, a retired fireman, was very different from my father. Granddad had been long widowed and lived alone in a storybook cottage adjoining a small orchard, which he owned. It was a storybook cottage, at least to a child: After what seemed an endless car journey along winding green lanes, we'd crunch into the gravel driveway at the side of the house, and Granddad would sit me down at an oilcloth table with the fire roaring, and serve me cocoa and a slice of off-centre apple pie with the pastry base half cooked. Afterwards he'd put his arm round my shoulder and take me for a ramble around his orchard: "Forty apple trees, aren't they splendid?" I always thought of his West Country speech as a toffee-apple voice – brown and sweet and soothing. My father spoke like a piece of stainless steel medical equipment, when he spoke at all.

When we drove home, my parents would gossip about him in the front seats of the Rover.

"I don't know how he survives on gin and fish fingers

…"

"Did you see the ring around the bath?"

After he died, I went as a teenager to help my parents clear out the cottage. There was talk of a by-pass being built at the top of the orchard, and my parents decided not to sell the property until things became clearer. It was worth almost nothing in the current equivocal circumstances. They had the house painted, and let it to a tenant for nothing, with the condition that he paid the rates and had the right to all the fruit in the orchard in exchange for keeping it in good order. They gave the tenant Granddad's blue Austin Cambridge, the car I used to help him wash in the driveway. It was too much trouble to sell it. With Granddad's things removed and the curtains taken down, the storybook memories were replaced by a more realistic picture of a draughty, damp and charmless dwelling. The ownership of the place passed to me on the death of my parents, but I hadn't given it much thought in the Books by Birdswell era until I received a letter from the council demanding payment of arrears, six months of rates to be exact. My tenant, I gathered, was no more. I paid the bill and forgot all about it.

***

The capacity of humans to adapt to changed circumstances astonishes me at every stage of my life. In no time we were a household of five, with the brown Charlotte a fully naturalized citizen of The Windings and enrolled in the local school. I negotiated a six-month arrangement with Jasmine, renewable by mutual agreement: I'd fully support Charlotte, and Jasmine would forego the maintenance payments. On Sunday mornings

I drove Charlotte to Jasmine's sister's house in London and picked her up at night. Charlotte was my daughter, and the green fuse of kinship triggered in me the same love that I had for William and Zita. Thea resisted getting too close at first, but softened and warmed with time.

In a similar way Thea and I absorbed the revelations of our lovers during The Cooling and, like a nasty splinter, the facts became painful only when prodded too hard. We both knew we were curious about our lovers, and one night as we were dropping off to sleep Thea asked me what it was like with a black woman. I pretended not to hear. For once I was annoyed with her: Was I supposed to ask her what it was like with Jez among the snakes and lizards? The thought made me ill.

***

Thea mentioned the idea of meeting Jasmine one day — not to pruriently inspect my old lover, but to know something of the mother of the little girl she'd become fond of. The children made the decision. One day Zita asked at breakfast if we could all go out with Charlotte's Mummy. William and Charlotte looked at us, little mouths agape, waiting for confirmation of a question that for them was already answered. I looked at Thea, she looked at the children, and then raised an eyebrow in my direction. I shrugged my assent and she said, "That's a wonderful idea! We could go to the sales in the West End".

Two weeks later on a bright January Sunday, we five boarded a morning train to London and took the Tube to Oxford Circus. Thea and Jasmine greeted one another politely, and the six of us now linked hands and proceeded down Oxford Street like a line of mine sweepers, scooping up tourists with bum bags, and Saudi ladies with covered faces, breaking our grip to release them in our wake. Zita and William took turns to hold Jasmine's dark brown hand as if it were a precious artifact. We spent the next few hours in toyshops, dress shops, junk food restaurants, and souvenir kiosks.

Jasmine said, "Can we go in here? I need to get something for the kitchen," and so we regrouped and swung down towards the big department store.

We drifted through the crowds in the kitchen department, and steered round a knot of people watching a demonstration of some gadget. I caught a glimpse of white hair through the forest of shoulders and necks. I stopped and got onto tiptoes. An elderly man wearing a tall chef's hat and white tunic was intoning into a clip-on microphone on the virtues of some electrical choppa-blocka thing which seemed to be turning perfectly good vegetables into useless pulp.

"Thea, I've got to get a closer look!" She frowned, then sensed my urgency, separated a child's hand from mine, reformed the convoy and sailed towards the cutlery section.

I situated myself obliquely behind a Saudi lady so that the Major wouldn't see me directly. There was no question: The lanky frame, the birdlike hands, the same old-fashioned regimental voice: Purees to a fine consistency, ideal for preparing meals for invalids and the elderly, preserves all the vitamins and minerals, easy to clean – and so it went on. I went back to find Thea and whispered, "It's the Major. Can you do without me? Just tell Jasmine that I had an urgent work call to deal with".

"OK, keep in touch," Thea said.

I watched the Major at work for another hour, all the

while sidling behind tall shoppers so that he wouldn't spot me. At 3pm he switched off the display light over the bench, took off the chef's hat and began to pack away the gadgets and tools. He swept the chopped food into a plastic box, wrapped up the plastic tablecloth, put all the props into a wheeled shopping bag, and puttered off through the crowds towards a service exit.

I had no choice but to follow him into the bowels of the shop: Raw concrete stairwells, trolley-battered swing doors, harsh neon strips, stacks of boxes and cartons. Once a woman with an official badge said to me, "Are you staff?" and I muttered something and pressed on, keeping the Major just in sight. Then I lost him in a busy corridor with two constantly swinging doors where people rushed in and out.

But there was his wheeled bag outside the door marked Gents — Staff only. I hung back until he came out buttoning his fly. He bundled the white tunic into the bag and took out a crumpled light raincoat. The chase was on again, and we threaded through a final maze before emerging from a staff entrance into a gloomy alley full of shop assistants having their cigarette breaks.

I was too quick coming out of the greasy-walled exit door. The Major turned, saw me and gaped. He feebly swung the wheeled bag at me. It barely lifted off the ground, but the metal frame caught me on the shin, and I stumbled. As I went down, I saw the broken beer bottle that my outstretched hand was plummeting towards. Then I was on all fours and bleeding badly from a slashed palm. The Major grabbed the trolley and strode stiffly down the alley while I searched in panic for something to staunch the ooze from the flapping skin. A shop girl gave me a silk scarf: "No, I can't take that," I said. "S'alright, I nicked it," she said, and I headed down the alley, binding the scarf deep into the cuts and knotting it with my teeth. My shirt was bloodstained and I thought I could feel something sticky drying on my cheek.

The alley came out into Oxford Street. I swung my gaze left and right, and quickly spotted the white hair just ten yards away. The shopping trolley was slowing the Major's progress and I held back, keeping a good twenty yards away. He disappeared down the steps into Bond Street Underground and I thought hard – Central Line or Jubilee Line?

As it turned out, the pursuit was quite unlike in the movies: No leaping over ticket barriers, no crashing through train doors as they slide shut, no galloping four steps at a time up descending escalators, no knocking over a fruit stall. Instead, the Major sailed calmly on, clearly visible among the crush because of his stature and upright gait, followed a few steps behind by a man in a bloodstained shirt and face, for whom the oncoming rush hour crowds nervously parted. We proceeded to Waterloo where we changed for Elephant and Castle, and within half an hour I stood on the opposite side of a street of run-down flats watching the Major push open the smeared wire-netted glass entrance door.

A grubby curtain twitched in a first floor window. Tightening the silk scarf around my oozing hand, I crossed the street and pushed open the door. A flight of stained cement steps led to a landing of splintered plywood doors, each with a reeking garbage hatch by its side. I guessed at the Major's door, but a large woman in baggy track suit pants and a gym vest backed out of the door opposite yelling, "Fuck off Donna". She looked at me said, "D'you want a soddin' smack in the face too?"

and then plunged down the stairs. I knocked on the Major's door.

"I suppose you'd better come in," he said.

And I found myself in the saddest room I have ever seen.

9: A life on the stage

The room was about fifteen feet by fifteen feet with the only light coming from a horizontal slot of window just below the ceiling. Below the window slot was a chipped metal framed bed, boarding-school style, with the threadbare sheets and blankets smartly tucked in. Above the bed was a wall of framed posters and monotone glossy photographs. Most of the posters bore the name Errol Sparkes, and the photographs were of the kind you used to see in theatre foyers: A man with a pencil moustache and shiny top hat with his arm around a woman in a spangled corset and a feathered headdress; the same man kneeling in tabard and hose with eyes lifted to the sky, the print in dramatic chiaroscuro.

To the left of the room was a makeshift shelf, plywood covered with stick-on waterproof roll, supported by a spindly raw timber frame and mounted over one edge of a square pink bathroom sink with the waste pipe exposed below. On the shelf were a single stacked set of eating utensils: A dinner plate, a dessert bowl, a mug, a knife, a fork and a spoon. Behind them was one small aluminum saucepan sitting atop a non-stick fry pan, and an extra mug. And to the right, a neat arrangement of tinned and packaged food: Baked beans, rye crackers, peaches, eggs, tea, long-life milk. I was moved by the spotlessness and order of the poverty before me.

A very old, plain wooden wardrobe, a small kitchen table bearing a single-burner camping stove, and an easy chair made up the rest of the furnishings.

The Major was sitting bolt upright in the armchair, wrapped in a blanket with a glass of water in his hand. The room was dank and cold. There came a sepulchral chime, and I looked up to see an enormous clock perched on a high flimsy shelf fixed with grey tin brackets. I'd seen it before next to the Major's head on the day of his murder.

"Just taking a pill – the heart, you know. Give me a moment while I get my breath." He pointed to the bed and I sat down.

"Can I use your bathroom?" I asked, looking around for the door.

"Oh, yes, the old bathroom trick – you had a splendid time rooting through the Major's stuff, didn't you?"

"No, I really need a pee and I want to rinse this hand."

"Outside, turn left, second door. Share it with the nignogs next door."

I winced and he must have caught my drift: "Very decent for blacks of course," he muttered.

The bathroom – seemingly improvised from an old kitchen – smelled of stale laundry, and was hung with a line of very large grey underwear. I performed my biological duty with a gigantic brassiere cup next to my ear. My hand oozed nastily when I tried to rinse it, so I made a wad of toilet paper and bound the sticky silk scarf over it.

When I came back to the room the old man was boiling water over the camp stove, his back ramrod stiff.

"So let me get this straight," I said. "You're an actor? You're Errol Sparkes?"

"Let's have a cuppa first," he said, and deftly made two cups with a single teabag.

We sipped in silence and I looked around the room.

Now I noticed a small pile of library books, arranged geometrically on the floor, and a small shelf with a dozen or so bottles and packets of prescription medicines. I glanced round searching for a TV or radio: Nothing, but I did spot a cheap mobile phone.

We finished our tea, and the old man carefully washed the cups. "We can talk now," he said.

"There's only one thing I want to talk about. What the hell does this Francis want from me?"

He lowered himself into the easy chair and his shoulders slumped. He peered at me like a dejected seagull.

"Come on, out with it, Mr. Sparkes or whoever you are." My hand was really beginning to hurt.

"Dear boy, would you mind calling me Major?" he said.

"I beg your pardon?"

"The name, the title, you know. Sparkes was … a long time ago. I rather like 'Major'".

"Were you ever a Major?"

"Not exactly."

"How much not exactly?" I asked.

"Air Force actually, played in a band, Leading Aircraftman, trombone, Dambusters March and all that."

I dragged myself back to cool logic. If calling the old man 'Major' would help get the information I wanted, then so be it. "All right Major", I said and with this Mr. Sparkes' shoulders lifted three inches and his vertebrae straightened and locked into place.

"You're not the only one who wants something," he said.

"What do you mean?"

"Francis owes me eighty quid. I want my money."

At this I burst out in laughter: "Eighty quid? Eighty

bloody quid? I've been conned, blackmailed, beaten up, humiliated, threatened, compromised, and you talk about eighty quid! Here's eighty quid." I emptied my wallet – there was seventy quid actually – and put the notes on the table.

"Very decent of you, sir."

"Good, now tell me what you know about Francis," I said.

In fact, what the Major knew about Francis took only a few minutes to tell. The old fellow took occasional 'artistic' jobs when they turned up – this apparently included demonstrating the choppa-blokka thing – and Francis had found him from the microscopic display advertisement that the Major placed in the local paper each month. The job of conning me was done, the Major asked no questions, and the payments – except for the final one – had been made.

"What did you think it was all about, Major?"

"Not my job to ask, dear boy."

"Did you get any idea from Francis why he chose me?"

The Major frowned and scratched his large ancient ears: "I've been around some shifty types in my line of work, and I've got a bit of a nose for a bad 'un. I regret to say that I got the impression that Francis has an obsession."

"An obsession?"

"An obsession with you."

"Major, did you see anyone else at the house, apart from Francis and me."

The old man put on the old conspiratorial face I remembered from all the Uncle Clive play acting: "Well yes, just once. I made a mistake in my diary and I came to the house on the wrong day. I didn't have a key – I'd knock on the kitchen window at the back and Francis would let me in. On this day I went around the back as usual and knocked, and instead of Francis, a woman opened the door wearing next to nothing. 'Oy' she says, 'Oo are you'?"

"What sort of woman?"

"A bad'un. Loose. Big. Shaved like a piglet down below and got up in a costume with a lot of studs and straps. While I'm gaping she pulls me inside and says, 'I wasn't told 'e was bringing a friend but since you're 'ere.'"

I asked what happened then, barely wishing to imagine the next gruesome instalment.

"Well, there's a fellow on the couch, naked except for his socks and tied up like a baby goat with his arse in the air, striped like a tiger."

"What was striped?" I asked.

"His arse. Great red welts. He'd had a proper beating. And there was some sort of camera on a tripod. Well, I took one look at the scene and thought to myself, 'You're an actor old son. Act yourself out of this!' By the way, I've got fruitcake if you'd like a piece."

"Thanks, but no cake. What did you do?"

"I said I was collecting for the Lifeboat appeal, and could she spare a couple of bob for the brave men who plucked the drowning from the waves, and she said she'd 'ad 'er fill of bleedin' sailors and I could fuck orf before she gave me a dose of what the uvver geezer was gettin'. So I fucked orf with my dignity intact!"

I gave him a little round of applause: "You've got her to a 't'!"

He smiled in appreciation and gave a tiny bow. Other than this single episode I couldn't get any more out of him except for his feeling that Francis didn't live in our town.

I got up to leave.

The Major suddenly spoke in a wheedling Glasgow accent: "Will ye no bide a while?"

"Excuse me?" I wasn't quite sure that I'd heard the question properly.

"Will ye no bide a while?"

"I don't follow."

"Have another cuppa? I don't get many visitors you see. Stay and talk a bit." This time the Major voice was back.

I looked at my watch. "My wife's expecting me, and I need to have a doctor look at this hand."

But the Major was up, boiling the kettle and unwrapping a single slice of vacuum packed fruitcake, which he carefully cut into two, placing each slice on the opposite side of his single dinner plate.

It occurred to me that the Major, or Errol Sparkes, or Jock McBloodyTavish were all guises. He'd done a striking job of the dominatrix. He slipped into character again when he spoke of his old friend Larry, whose name came up when I asked the Major if he'd ever been married. I'd spotted a man in two or three of the photographs: A stocky dark-haired beau leaning on a nineteen sixties car by a beach in old-style swimming trunks with the waistband above the navel, and in a more recent colour snap, two elderly men – The Major and Larry – sitting on a sofa with a large cat curled across their laps. "Nancy boys, they called us in those days," he said in high camp with a crooked wrist raised to his shoulder, and then resumed military discipline.

The Major had been discharged from the Air Force as a young man, and worked for decades as a small-time entertainer in seaside towns and repertory theatres.

"Rattigan – now there's a playwright!" he said, pointing to a poster of a play called 'Separate Tables'. "I played Major Pollock opposite Pearl Rigby as Mrs. Shankland. Lovely skin she had, but ruddy awful breath."

Besides acting he could do magic tricks, play woodwind and brass instruments to some degree, sing, tap dance …

"Is your real name Errol Sparkes?" I asked, but he ignored me.

Larry was an old Air Force chum who owned a car repair business in Tottenham and lived with his mother at Hendon. The Major had moved in as a lodger: "Needed a base you see, somewhere to come back to after a summer season in boarding houses. And of course, Larry was a champion sort of fellow." After the mother's death the Major, now middle aged, gave up touring and settled in with Larry, who was comfortably off. But his old partner became ill and the Major nursed Larry for ten years until "the poor old stick passed on. Riddled he was, top to bottom."

The house, it turned out, had belonged to Larry's sister. Larry left no will. The Major packed his trunk and Air Force kitbag and left in a taxi, farewelled by the 'iron faced harridan' on the pavement. "And here I've been the last twelve years."

"No family then?"

"None. You see I was born in Rhodesia. Did a bloody silly thing when I was a young chap and had to run away from home rather smartish. Came to the mother country. Family never kept in touch."

I was intrigued. Goodness knows who the man really was, but somehow I was starting to warm towards this stiff old phony. I sent Thea a text: "Back within the hour.

May be on to something."

"Major, I have to go, but I want to ask you something."

"Go on."

"You're a man of integrity. I can tell. Do you think Francis should be allowed to get away with what he's done to me?"

"Of course not," he said without hesitation.

I waited, not entirely sure of my direction, and then said, "Would you – as an entertainer of course – be prepared to help me redress the situation?"

"Perhaps ... you mean ... get into some sort of scenario involving Francis, myself and yourself?"

"We can't let him get away with it Major."

"Agreed, absolutely. Now of course, while I understand that you are personally aggrieved, I am myself of course a mere third party, a simple player of a part with no axe to grind ..."

"Fifteen pounds an hour," I said.

"Twenty, cash in hand up front, expenses on top."

"OK, but half up front, half on completion."

"Done," the Major said, and I shook his desiccated hand.

I had one of those foolish impulses, and said, "Would you like to come to Christmas lunch with my family?"

He looked puzzled: "At your house?"

"Yes, with my wife and my children."

"Yes, of course, I'd be ..." he began, and words failed him.

"That's settled then. I'll write down the address," I said.

"No, tell me and I'll write it in my address book." He took a small notebook from his pocket and made a great fuss of choosing from the mostly blank pages.

"I'll meet you from the 11.45 train. My in-laws will be

on the same one and I can pick you all up together."

"I'm very much looking forward to it," the Major said.

"Just one thing," I said.

"Yes?"

"Please don't talk about nig-nogs when you come."

10: The missing guest

Thea sat up, flushed and tousled, and pulled the covers around her.

I lay back and mentally smoked a French cigarette.

"It's got to be more than just the Bathwell cheques," Thea said.

"It's late. I'm tired."

"This is important Jack."

"All right, go on."

"Well," Thea said, "I've been trying to put all the bits together since you went to the Major's place yesterday. But 'm not sure I've quite got it all yet".

"I'm not sure I've got the mental agility for this."

"Hard luck. Just cut the Jean-Paul Belmondo expression and concentrate."

I forgot about the cigarette and listened.

"This is how I think it works: Francis compromises Marjorie Smith at the Bathwell Trust, and steals her cheque book. The cheques are written by a third party of somewhat slippery identity, i.e. the Major, and they are cleared by another third party – you."

"So far so good," I said. I had a nasty feeling of apprehension. "Well, good's the wrong word I suppose. "

"Precisely: You and the Major have stolen the Bathwell Trust's money, and the generous owner of Books by Birdswell is keeping it safe for Francis, who is demanding it in cash. It's brilliant."

"Brilliant? It's downright evil." There had to be a catch

somewhere. "But what about the rented house, the Major's pay, all the paraphernalia involved in setting it up?" I asked.

"Expenses."

"I don't follow."

"OK," Thea said. "We know that Francis has at least two victims – you and the poor sod who was enjoying a spanking. Now let's also make a conservative guess that he's a professional criminal, and has two more victims dangling on his string – blackmail, extortion, whatever. So the house is being used for four scams."

She took a calculator from the bedside drawer: "My very rough estimate is that a quarter of the rent on the house plus the Major's pay come to about twenty five percent of the value of the Bathwell cheques."

"So Francis invests 25p in the pound to offload the risk onto me and the Major? It's more profitable that the bloody bookshop! We should move into full-time crime."

Thea gave me a slippery look: "Let's stick with part-time shall we? Let me go on. Now we've been deluding ourselves with the idea that Francis has lost interest, and that life is back to normal. The reality is that you're one of his savings accounts, and when he wants to make a withdrawal, he'll be back."

"And when you say 'one of his savings accounts' you mean that Mr. Striped Arse and whoever else he has compromised are the others?"

"Dead right. Need a bit of cash? Tell our friend that a shot of his well-smacked bot is about to go online and wait for the ker-ching of the till."

"That's a bit flippant," I said. "We're talking extortion and blackmail here. But Thea, what if I came clean? After all, we all know that the Major was never murdered.

What's the worst thing they could charge me with? Fraud? Extortion? Of course not. All I've done is bank some dodgy cheques".

"You weren't so keen to talk about the dodgy cheques before."

"OK, I was bit reticent, but that's because I couldn't afford Charlotte's maintenance anymore, and I was going to use the Bathwell money. Thea, there aren't any more secrets now. Surely if I went to the police and admitted it, and told them everything I know about Francis, they'd take that into account, especially if it helped uncover all the other stuff he's been doing."

"And where do I stand? Impersonating – what was it? – a loss adjustor?"

"Doesn't sound like a hanging offence to me. You'd just say that you were trying to figure out whether there was actually something suspicious about the cheques. Now it's confirmed we want to help the police."

Thea listened, frowning. I knew she was thinking it through.

"All right lover boy. I'll sleep on it," she said, and snapped off the light.

***

The Christmas day tradition for the last few years was that Thea's parents would join us for lunch. Thea's brother – her only sibling – had followed a job opportunity in Seattle, and married an American woman. His involvement in our Christmas boiled down to a stilted ten-minute video call. Thea's mother's family were in Ireland and in a state of mortification that had lasted for half a century. No forgiveness was possible for a girl who had married a Greek Orthodox, and she hadn't seen them for years.

I liked Thea's Greek Cypriot Dad. At Christmas we'd sink lower into the sofa as the day went on and the cycle of drinks proceeded: An ale to revive the spirits after the train trip from Camden, a champagne to cleanse the palate before canapés, a Martini to revive the appetite after olives and Greek cheese nibbles, an ouzo to neutralise the stomach before the entrée, a retsina to remind Yani of his village in the Troodos mountains. And so the dipsomaniac odyssey proceeded while Thea and Mary toiled in the kitchen and the children chattered over their presents.

By eleven I'd organised the drinks cabinet and polished the glasses. I drove to the station to pick up the guests from the 11.45 London train. Yani and Mary were sheltered under the awning by the kiss and ride, puffing on their fags. There was no sign of the Major.

Yani and Mary gave me big cigarettey hugs and bundled into the car, one on each side of Charlotte.

"Who are you?" Yani asked.

"Jack's my Dad," the tiny brown darling said. Yani said something in Greek.

"You didn't see a tall old man getting off, did you?" I asked. They looked blank. The next train was in an hour. I left them in the car and checked the gents toilet and the other platforms. No Major.

We postponed the Christmas morning ale so I could drive back to the station for the 12.45. Still no Major. I drove home and put him out of my mind.

We shepherded Mary and Yani to the taxi around 6pm and the in-laws sped away. Bloated and seedy, I chivvied up a walking party and we all put on stout boots and thick jackets. The children ran on ahead under the streetlights, rattling the ancient iron railings alongside the Cathedral graveyard with bits of stick. Zita made ghost noises and Charlotte hooted like an owl, while William did a zombie walk.

"Jack. I'm slipping away," Thea said suddenly.

"Slipping away from what?"

"I don't know. From myself I suppose. I can't explain it properly."

"Try," I said. I was worried. Thea didn't say these kinds of things. I looked at her, and her face was white and drawn.

"I thought it was just the stress from all of this, and I could handle it – you know, capable Thea, fix anything with logic and a set of principles. Make a list, review the options. But I've had these grotesque thoughts that make me feel that I'm slipping away. No that's not the word, not slipping away exactly, but as if the thoughts are swamping me so that I can't think clearly."

"What sort of thoughts?"

"Thoughts, weird ones."

The children were heading back towards us.

"Charlotte saw a skeleton walking in the graveyard," William said.

"All right," I said. "Here's what you do. Line up across the pavement – yes, like that. Put your arms out to the front and do a zombie walk past the Cathedral." I made goggle eyes and a slack mouth by way of demonstration, and they veered away, hooting and whooing in the damp night air.

"Thoughts about ... that time," Thea said. "When you and Jasmine ... and I was seeing ..."

"Is Charlotte the problem? Does she bring it all back

to you?"

"No. Charlotte's lovely. And I like her mother. Jack, I'm feeling very sick." She leaned on the railings, her face grey. "OK, I'm all right now. Let's go home."

"You were mixing your drinks," I said, gently rubbing her shoulders as she leaned against me.

"It's not the drinks. It's just too fucking horrible."

"Tell me!" I was panicking.

We walked on slowly in silence for a minute.

"All right. But it'll make you sick."

"Let's get it over. It can't be that bad," I said.

"When we were making love the other night," she said. Her voice hardened: "Actually when we were rutting and shagging and copulating ..."

"Quiet, Thea, please. What's this?" I asked, and grasped her by the shoulders.

"That's it, you're all the same, you don't like what you hear, you grab a woman ..."

"Stop it!" I let go of her shoulders. "Tell me what happened!"

"All right. You asked for it. When you were on top of me and I closed my eyes, all I could see was Francis – yes, Francis." She stood, forlorn and slumped under the streetlight.

"But you've never seen his face."

"I've got an image – a horrible image – from what you've said about him."

This time it was me who leaned queasily on the railing, and I felt her rubbing my shoulder and whispering, "I'm so sorry".

We rounded up the zombies and walked them stiff-leggedly home. William asked if Mummy was ill, but Thea smiled wanly and said no, just tired from all the cooking and eating. I tried to lift the mood by promising deep-fried ice cream when we got back. We walked into the house in higher spirits, Thea hugging and kissing the children, apparently restored. I fired up the wok and produced five bowls of fried goo, and everybody applauded my cleverness.

We were exhausted when we went to bed.

"Forget all that rubbish I said in the street," Thea said tenderly.

***

The other two smudges get regular visitors. Their respectable wives drive up the motorway once a week in their four-wheel drives and expensive waterproof country jackets, and afterwards my two fraudster prison companions spend the day in contented reflection, no doubt calculating on mental spreadsheets exactly how many weeks, days, hours, minutes and seconds they have to serve. Me, I never get a visitor, unless you count Mr. Nussbaum, the whey-faced volunteer pensioner who is foisted on me in the hope that I'll 'open my heart' to him. I don't want a pretend friend, I tell them. He is a trained visitor, they tell me.

Thea won't come. She can't be seen visiting me.

But in March I received a letter from someone called Fiona Salmon asking if I would apply for a Visiting Order so she could come and see me. Why not, I thought, it'll relieve the boredom, whoever she is. On a blowy Wednesday in April, I got my visitor. They walked me down to a room with a table and two office chairs, and there was the beautiful coffee-coloured woman who had arrested me. It was ex-Detective Sergeant Fiona Salmon, and she had come to tell me that she loved me, she couldn't live without me, and she was going to get me out of prison.

PART TWO: FIONA TAKES OVER

11: It's a man's world

"Fiona, see what you can do with this scrote," Boris said, handing me a file with one hand while he rearranged something inside his trouser pocket. Boris – my boss Detective Inspector Boris Rance – had a way with words, usually the wrong way.

"Didn't I read an email last month about using non-sexist terminology?" I said, chancing it.

"A scrote is a fucking scrote. You can quote me on that." End of conversation, gender imbalance reconfirmed. Back to what you're good at Fiona, trying to build a brief of evidence from a file of odds and sods that the blokes handed back because they couldn't make it hang together.

I don't know why I'm not back in Sydney in the sunshine instead of trying to bash my way through the glass plate ceiling out here in the damp Home Counties. You made Detective Sergeant, they tell me in Human Resources. I want more, I tell them. You didn't help your career path by going on a secondment to Australia, they say. I can't help it if people are envious, I say. We're here to talk about you, not other people, they say. They never mention Darren nowadays and I never bring it up.

Actually, the reason I'm not in Sydney is because I couldn't get a visa to stay. I decided I'd resign from the force and not go back to England, but the Australian immigration system wasn't so cooperative. Stuff them and their sunshine and that treacherous golden Gazza, who turned out to be married with two moronic kids and a toothy wife. I'll just have to settle for Boris's scrote – such a vulgar word – here at the nick on the Oxford Road.

It was late in the day and I put the file away. Monday was my night to do battle with the weights machines at the Fit Barn. I'm, well, obsessive is probably putting it rather mildly – addicted is about right. It's been that way for a while, but at least I have periods now. There was a time when I was training so hard that my reproductive system just went on strike for a while. Enough said. Abs and shoulders tonight, my special protein shake when I get home, early night and a fresh start on the files in the morning. Makes me sound like some sort of monster, but how many monsters have a law degree and a masters thesis on the novels of Anthony Powell? Who? Boris asked. Google it, I said, just put in 'Dance to the Music of Time'. Is that by Glen Campbell, he asked.

The police psychologist they sent me to tried her best, but you don't fill a gaping chasm by sitting through twelve sessions of counselling. I'd reconciled myself to the fact that Darren was gone: What I hadn't worked out was how to stop hurling myself at hopelessly unsuitable men. It wasn't just the sex, although that was part of it. It was more the solid physicality, the muscular mass of a man, the closeness, not waking up on my own every morning. At one stage I went eight weeks without touching another human other than shaking hands. Then I fell into golden Gazza in Sydney.

Talking of men, there was a message on the landline when I got home: Hugo. A reminder for Friday, dinner at the Butchers Arms. How does Hugo pick them? Why does he always want to eat at places with carnivorous names? Chops and Ribs, The Beefeater, Le Petit Filet, Kebab City. I'd been looking for an exit strategy: Become a vegan? I let Hugo stew in his own gravy, showered, had a minuscule cognac and went to bed with Olivia Manning, another old literary friend. People sometimes asked me why I read this old stuff. You want me to read chicklit, I ask. You want me to live on pink fizzy drinks and cupcakes? Still, I do slum it on the e-reader now and then, but don't expect me to put that in writing.

Boris's scrote's name was Francis Benton. He had a single minor conviction for shoplifting as a teenager in London, evidently let off with a stiff talking to by a bamboozled magistrate. I'd seen his type before, smirking in the dock when some kindly retired Town Clerk made him promise to pay his fine in instalments. Benton's mother's address was recorded as a house in Islington. He'd come to the attention of the police for the second time a few years ago. A woman in Oxford had reported a sexual assault by a Francis Benton, but the accusation was quickly withdrawn. Even the female police officers who took the woman's statement were very doubtful about whether the sex was consensual or not. Francis was released, but not before leaving a respectable set of fingerprints on file as well as an address in Oxford.

Our detectives, fifty miles from Oxford, caught up with Francis Benton a year later. A local real estate agent had reported to the police that a tenant had abandoned an expensive property on the Sussex Heights estate, to which the police replied that it was a civil matter and not their business. But the real estate agent delivered a little sting: A valuable antique cabinet was missing, and the agent could only conclude that the tenant had stolen it. The police extracted the sting: Since nobody had seen the tenant removing the article, there was insufficient evidence to apprehend him.

But a week later, a lady with a haughty manner and a wet Labrador came to the police station and demanded to see the Chief Constable. The most senior office in the building – Boris – was brought to the counter, and the woman placed a Marks and Spencer bag on the counter.

"Look inside."

Boris peeked inside and fished out a snap lock plastic bag containing a disposable syringe, a credit card, several used condoms, and a balled-up wad of stained tissues. I was on my way out for lunch and I stopped, not because the contents of the bag looked especially appetising, but because the lady with the haughty manner looked like my old headmistress, the person who encouraged me with the 'old stuff' that I still read.

"Where did you find it, Mrs. Mansfield?" Boris asked.

"It was Duke. We were walking past and he stopped, pointed his nose towards the house, and bolted into the garden." I swear that Duke the dog put on a smug look.

"Which house?" Boris asked.

"Twenty-two The Ramblings."

The uniformed constable manning the counter said, "Isn't that the house where the tenant did a runner? We had an estate agent in here earlier in the week with a complaint".

The strands of the story were tied together, and Mrs. Mansfield added the bow: Two car registration numbers. The cars were parked several streets away by men who came to the house from time to time, she said.

"Well done, Mrs. Mansfield," I said, hurrying off for a vegan salad in the Welsh Garden Eco Bar, in training for my Hugo exit strategy.

I settled down to the file after lunch. The credit card had been reported by the bank as reported lost by a Mr. Martin Fitzgibbon. One of the CID blokes had left a file note about a brief phone conversation with Mr. Fitzgibbon. The gentleman had lost his wallet in a pub in Hampstead, and had never visited our town. The car registrations turned up a van belonging to Francis Benton at his Oxford address, and an expensive 4WD registered to one Jack Walsingham, the owner of Books by Birdswell, a shop I'd passed but never been into. Jack Walsingham lived nearby and had no criminal record, I suspected that Mrs. Mansfield's imagination had outrun her observational skills.

No analysis of the syringe, the condom or the tissues had been carried out. At the point at which the blokes had handed the file back to Boris, there was no indication of a crime having been committed other than littering. So why had he given it to me? I'd been given some pretty hopeless quests, but nothing as vague as this. I made a call and arranged to have the contents of the bag examined by Forensics.

There was a buzz in the office as the afternoon wore on, an atmosphere of testosterone-charged anticipation. A few pitiful glances were cast in my direction by some of the less brutish blokes. Then at three o'clock the half dozen or so detectives in the open plan office rushed out to the conference room down the corridor. I went to the ladies and used my peripheral vision to snap a shot of the activity through the glass door. Boris was poking his stubby fingers at a street plan on the wall and the blokes were hunched and tense. When I came back from the ladies I was nearly bowled over by the posse and the miasma of overheated armpits. Was that why Boris had given me the file? Keep the chick busy? A raid on a drug house no place for a woman? Afraid I might see a bit of the rough stuff when it goes too far? Stuff them, I thought. I'll squeeze something out of Francis Scrote Benton's file even if it's drunk in charge of a beer bottle.

***

It was early on a mucky February evening when I put aside an hour to pay Jack Walsingham a visit. I'd been thinking on and off about Francis Benton all week, and while Walsingham didn't seem connected with the case, I needed at least to eliminate him from my enquiry, as they say on the TV. I'd taken a stroll past the cathedral a few days before, and glanced into Books by Birdswell. A tall slim man with thick dark hair – attractive in a rumpled way – was leaning on the counter jabbing a calculator. He looked up, caught my eye as if hoping I was a customer – the shop was empty – and then went back to his work.

I have an extraordinary visual memory: I can walk around a street corner, take one look, close my eyes, and recall every car, every building, every person, as if there is a high contrast monochrome photograph inside my brain. Oddly though, I can't recall colours. I went out once with an internet date who said that I was using so much cognitive capacity on shapes and patterns that I had insufficient working memory to take in the colour detail. The date's internet profile said 'hydraulic flow specialist' but he turned out to be a plumber. I spent the evening on the verge of asking what would happen if he spent all day unblocking toilets and whether he'd have the cognitive capacity to have a pee. Anyway, there was no way those drainy hands were coming near me.

But my memory: It's like an etching, even now: He was

wearing loose jeans, a muted tartan shirt and a linen jacket. I could tell he was tall because he was all angles, legs slightly crooked and his upper body supported by his left elbow on the counter, which was side on to my view. There was a cardboard coffee cup on the counter. Behind him were seven rows of shelves, each with a sign on top that I couldn't read except for the closest one, which said 'HORROR'.

I pulled up outside his house, The Windings: Old red bricks set with creamy mortar in a pattern they don't use nowadays; a slate roof above the porch; a tiny square of garden behind stout iron railings, with snowdrops pushing through the damp wintry lawn; the heavy front door painted to a deep gloss in British Racing Green (God knows where I read about that colour, but it must have been in the 'old stuff'), bearing massive black wrought iron hinges and a knocker shaped like an acorn; leadlight windows with intricate lace curtains, and at the edges the lined backs of heavy drapes held back with tasseled ties. It was raining slightly with a breeze. I knocked.

The door opened a crack and a small brown girl looked up at me.

"Is your daddy at home?"

She disappeared and I waited. A woman – Thea as I later learned – opened the door a little wider and said, "Are you selling something?" She was dark haired, pale skinned, beautiful, no, handsome perhaps.

I held out my warrant card: "Detective Sergeant Fiona Salmon. I'd like to speak to Mr. Walsingham please. Is he home?"

Thea looked thunderstruck. When she'd recovered herself she said, "No, he's working late tonight. What's this about?"

The door opened wider and a man appeared behind her – fortyish, sandy hair, thin face. My memory kicked in: "And you would be, sir?" I said to Francis Benton.

"Just a house guest. Why don't you give us your card and Jack can ring you?"

12: Mr. Norris and me

Boris had me tied up for the next week with one of the endless community policing initiatives that I always seemed to get dragged into. By Wednesday I was visiting my thirteenth primary school with a laptop slide presentation and a stack of brochures, ready to face a class of damp tots. I'd planned my route to save crisscrossing the town with its grim one-way system, and today I was working inward from a battered sixties school in the council estate in the north, through a chic Montessori in an enclave of Georgian terraced houses half a mile from the centre, and finally to the Cathedral school. I parked in the multi-storey across the market square from the Cathedral, and checked my watch: Half an hour early.

I remember giving up smoking years ago, and the way that my mind would play tricks: I'll buy one more packet, have one fag and throw the rest away, and then never buy another packet. Well ... you know the rest. It was a bit like that as I threaded my way through the cloistered shopping arcade to find a coffee: One part of me was looking for coffee, but some other part of me was heading for Books by Birdswell.

My heart started to pound and I felt my face getting hot – luckily I don't really blush in an obvious way – as I opened the door, which set off a little tinkling bell. Jack Walsingham looked up and then back to the two old people in flapping raincoats who were waving their seniors cards in his face.

"We get a discount in Boots," the old woman said.

"And at the electric," the old man said.

"All right, you can have it at cost price," Jack said, checking the back of the book and pressing the buttons on the calculator on the counter. "Two pounds twenty. Best I can do."

"Flippin' nerve!" the old lady said.

"It's not worth a quid!" the old man said. "Come on Flo, let's see if they've got it in the Library."

"Always a pleasure," Jack said as the old couple slammed the door and careered into the cloisters.

I think that first close-up encounter with Jack Walsingham sealed my destiny – yes, I know that sounds like a cliché but that's what clichés are for – stating the obvious with economy. I stood for a few seconds transfixed by his face – the maturity in the premature lines creasing his cheeks, the wisdom in the grey eyes, the relaxed set of his mouth as if he were a man who would think carefully before making a judgment. I looked at his hair – thick, dark, childishly unruly.

"You're after something in particular?" he asked, with a hand gesture that I recorded for all eternity in my mental archive system. The hands were big, evenly shaped fingers, nails like blunt spades, clean. The gesture was generous, self-effacing. The voice was warm and resonant, the accent neutral, cultured. A BBC voice.

I gulped, "I'm looking for some Isherwood." It was the first thing my panicky brain came up with.

Jack Walsingham raised an eyebrow deliciously. "Isherwood – very good. You don't seem like the

Isherwood type."

"What's an Isherwood type?"

"Oh, it's hard to generalize, but older for sure, book clubbish, perhaps a retired teacher."

I recovered myself a little: Was he teasing me? Had I misjudged maturity for cynicism?

"And what type would I be?" I was pushing it, I knew, but I had to be sure.

He looked at me with curiosity, scanned my face from my eyes to my lips and back to my eyes: "You are a reader, and that's all that matters. Let's show you where you can find Christopher Isherwood."

I followed him to the back of the shop, greedily sucking in the discreet waft of an expensively deodorized man in his wake. "Here you are, I'll leave you to it."

I fussed with the books for ten minutes, glancing sideways now and then, but Jack was working at the counter and all I saw was the top of his head behind the Horror shelves. At last I chose *Mr. Norris Changes Trains* – I'd read it before in my Isherwood phase between Margaret Drabble and George Eliot – and walked to the counter.

"Just out of interest, why Isherwood?" he asked while he rang up the sale.

"He's on my list. My Dad was an English teacher and he taught me to love good writing. I've read about Isherwood and I thought I'd better try him."

"You've seen *Cabaret* of course. It was based on Isherwood," Jack said.

"My dad had a copy on video. I loved it. But I've never read *I am a Camera*."

Jack raised that eyebrow again. "The play? Didn't he

write that in forties?"

"Nineteen fifty-one."

"I don't get many like you in here," Jack said. "Mostly it's Thai cookbooks and vampire sex."

"Sounds messy."

"Especially when they're done together," he said, and then looked embarrassed. We both laughed a bit uneasily, and I fluttered in my throat at his sensitivity and concern for my feelings.

"Well, drop in some time again. I'll see if I can get hold of the play," Jack said.

***

I was late arriving at the school, and the tiny assembly hall was dank as a rain forest with the crush of twenty small bodies clad in damp jumpers. I fumbled my way through the talk, said swift goodbyes to the staff. I sat in my car in the bleak concrete car park, breathing slowly and trying to drain the blood from my face. I took the Isherwood from the Books by Birdswell bag and opened it to the inside cover. I wrote 'JW to FS with all my love'. The sensible side of my brain watched this performance with astonishment. I suddenly needed a cigarette – ten years on, the demon still lurked – and I knew I had to get to the gym to pound my body and mind into a condition of temporary equilibrium.

I got home at six with my muscles glowing and my head clear: An hour on a fixed bike and another hour of weights always did the trick. It was my last evening with Hugo – he didn't know it yet – and I got myself ready without enthusiasm. I almost texted to cancel, but I didn't have the nerve. And anyway, I needed to be with a man this evening, even if it had to be Hugo.

He was outside with the old red Alpha at eight, all glossy and sharp in a fine Italian suit and the kind of shirt you don't pick up for less than a hundred quid.

"I've found this brilliant place – they cook the steaks on slabs of superheated volcanic rock," and we were gone, purring and whirring through the evening traffic in his little retro Italian toy. The restaurant was beyond the town limits on the outskirts of one of the quaint villages they have round here – nothing like where I was brought up in Wembley. We slewed into the graveled driveway, and he patted my bum when we entered the restaurant as if it were another piece of meat he'd get around to later. Inside we were seated beneath a huge picture of a cow or a bull or something. The other diners were knocking off stiff-looking cocktails and ordering from a tiny menu. At a corner table a waiter placed two grey bricks onto wooden platters in front of two businessmen, followed by two plates each containing a thick slab of bloody steak. The businessmen flipped their steaks onto the brick and the meat immediately began to smoke. I quietly gagged.

Hugo was pointing at the menu: "It's basically the eye fillet or the sirloin."

"Is there just a salad?" I asked. Hugo looked at me as if I had gone mad. Smoke was rising from more of the tables and my eyes were burning.

***

Hugo leaned back and licked his chops. I'd thought him handsome and refined, but I couldn't get the texture of Jack's hands and his thick hair out of my mind. Hugo's nails were manicured and painted with clear varnish but I could see a fleck of brown meat under a thumbnail. There was a thread of beaded perspiration along his razor cut hairline. My steak was barely eaten. He eyed it but at least he had the manners not to eat it. I suppose stockbrokers who've been to posh schools learn when to hold back.

At his flat, neither of us held back. I juddered under the meaty miasma exuding from his muscular body, loving it and hating myself at the same time, imagining being skillfully loved by Jack Walsingham with his discreet man smell, instead of Hugo ploughing me like a field of spuds.

I quietly dressed as Hugo slept. I was sore down below. One of my school reports said, 'Fiona is prone to occasional showy gestures when under pressure'. I'd seen it done in the movies, the message in lipstick on the bathroom mirror: 'Sorry Hugo. It's not working. Please don't call me again'. As if in reply the sleeping man released a loud fart as I slipped out.

I woke next morning to a filthy February day: Blustery winds and the kind of English rain that doesn't know which direction it wants to go in. Under the duvet I dozed and thought of February mornings in Sydney: The summer heat beginning to build at seven, the jeweled Harbour coming alive with the dinky green and cream ferries bobbing towards Manly and Mosman, coffee smells wafting up from the cafes at Circular Quay, a day ahead full of prospect and hope and shine. Mr. Norris was on the kitchen table where I'd left it. I got up, dancing on the cold floor tiles in my bare feet, took a pair of scissors and an envelope from a drawer and got back into bed. I cut a triangle from the book cover that contained the ludicrous dedication, snipped it into thin strips, snipped the strips into confetti, put the little paper squares into the envelope, and slipped the envelope under my mattress. I allowed myself another ten minutes of Sydney under the covers before going to the bathroom. I stood in front of the mirror and frowned at my tall brown body: Fiona Salmon, Boris's token black female officer and anti-racism trophy girl.

***

"Any progress with Francis Benton?" Boris asked at our Monday catch-up the following week.

"Give me a couple more days to wrap it up. I've got a few enquiries to make about his associates."

"Associates?" Boris asked. "Who are they?"

"Just a few names that came up. It's probably nothing."

"You've got till Thursday. After that you're running a course."

It didn't do to argue. There was the smell of the school bully about Boris. People said he was under his wife's thumb, and took it out on his staff and his clients.

So instead of arguing, I wheedled: "Not anti-racism strategies again. Boris, when can I do some proper work?"

I had two days. By Wednesday I had extracted from the ether some crucial bits of information about Jack Walsingham. I couldn't find a link with Francis Benton, but I did turn up his former Jamaican lover Jasmine, the mother of the nut-brown Charlotte. But there was something else: A bank account with a bad smell about it, and with it a connection to an old man at Elephant and Castle who'd had some previous trouble with the law. I handed the file back to Boris on Wednesday: "Nothing here that'll stick."

13: A blind date

Try as I might, I couldn't get the rational side of my brain to control my urge to see Jack Walsingham again. I wasn't so besotted that I'd log on to the system and find out more about him: They monitor that sort of thing – sack cops who do online searches on their relatives and friends – and having handed the file back to Boris, I had no official reason for snooping on Jack. Anyway, I didn't want to know the kind of thing I'd find in police records. I wanted to get to know Jack Walsingham as a man.

Stalking is a horrible word and it's been used to describe me once before, but I've never stalked anyone. I inform myself, I research, I get my measure of a person. That's what I told Gazza's wife when she flew at me in the café in Sydney and called me that word.

OK, I'll admit that I'd familiarized myself with the places that Gazza went to with his family – the glistening beach at Dee Why, the balmy open-air restaurants at Chinatown, the leafy cycle path at Centennial Park. But it was his fault entirely. When we struck up what you might call an unprofessional relationship at Police HQ in Parramatta, he never said anything about a wife, no mention of toothy Traicee when he was in my bed. It was only when I got sick of the winks and smirks in the office that I clicked that something was amiss, so I followed one of the female cops into the toilets and got it out of her. She must have had her own reasons for shopping Gazza because it only took a second. I told Gazza he could get lost, but who could blame me for wanting to see what his life was really like? He'd taken me for an idiot and I was entitled to know what sort of creature had done that to me.

It was a childish trick really. I went up to their table and pretended to be a waitress: Would they like any more drinks? Anything more for Traicee, I'd asked, and then gone back to my own table. I watched Gazza cringing and gesticulating as Traicee hissed at him before striding in my direction. When she called me a stalker, I said that Gazza had told me she made love like a dead cat. I could see Gazza three tables away with his kids, curling up in his boat shoes, and that was enough satisfaction for me.

The next Saturday I drove to Jack's street – I lived out in the suburbs to the west – and parked on the opposite side of The Windings about thirty yards away from the Cathedral. It was seven thirty in the morning and the shopping crowds were still hours away. I'd done lots of surveillance so I know all the tricks for staying unobtrusive. At eight thirty Jack left the house and walked towards town. I got out and jogged slowly after him. I was in stylish Lycra just like all the other morning joggers coming in and out of the Cathedral grounds: A perfect cover. As I expected, Jack opened the shop. I stood just out of sight, doing hamstring stretches against a cloister. After a couple of minutes, I peeped round the old flint wall in time to see Jack turn around the OPEN sign in the shop.

There wasn't much to be done watching a shopkeeper in his shop, so I jogged back to the car and slipped into the front seat just in time to see Thea, laden with bats and balls, walking the children to sport. I stayed put and watched the front door for ten minutes and, sure enough,

Francis Benton came swinging down the short path lighting a cigarette. He strode in my direction – I had him in my wing mirror – and he did a little hop and skip as he approached my car. I grabbed my mobile and feigned making a call, head down and away from the pavement, and he walked past. He stopped by his van, got in and drove away. I hesitated: Follow Francis or wait to see if Thea came back? I decided to wait for Thea, but after an hour there was no sign of her so I drove home.

***

On Sunday I took up position outside the house at 7am. There was a steady cold drizzle, and the streets were empty. As the car cooled I looked up at the bedroom windows in the street and imagined couples affectionately leaning against each other, propped up on pillows with small children in pajamas spilling toast crumbs on the sheets. That's how it should have been for me if it hadn't been for a man in Watford who bought a small handgun from a man in a pub in Stoke Newington three years before and sold it to another man in a car park in Fulham who wanted to scare a man in Dalston, and who left it in the glove compartment of his unlocked car for a minute while he dashed into a public loo for a pee. And then the teenager who pinched it from the car put it in his jacket when he went with his mates to hold up an off-licence, and when the manager locked the kids into the shop and called the police, and my husband PC Darren Arroyo was first on the scene, the manager opened the door and the kid shot Darren dead.

Darren and I were best pals at school. My mother is from from Jamaica, but my father is half Welsh and half Indian. Salmon was once Salman, my Muslim grandfather's surname. Darren's family were from Antigua but there was a big story in his family about how they had Spanish ancestors, hence the surname. We were bright kids, paced each other in our A Levels and got into Law at London University – lived at home with our parents so we could commute and save money. Somehow, we passed from pals to lovers in that first year at university. It was inevitable really, and we came to it after each sampling what was on offer on campus. I stayed on to do my Masters, the idea being that I'd get a clerkship in a solicitor's firm. Darren went straight into his clerkship but by the end of the first six months he was chewing his fingers off with frustration. He read about an accelerated graduate entry scheme into the police in a part of the Home Counties we knew well. We often had cheap weekends away in a pub near the cathedral that let rooms. Soon he was renting a bedsit in the town while he did his training, and I was the weekend lover. And at the end of the year I signed up myself, and before long we were both clanking around the town wearing tall hats and belts loaded with high-tech hardware. We bought a flat in the budget belt to the west of the town, and looked forward to zooming up through the ranks.

Darren had been in eighteen months when he was shot. They did their best: Counselling, time off, light duties, covering me when I went off on an emotional tangent. I upped the gym work, thrashed out my grief on the cold metal and sweat soaked benches in the Fit Barn, escaped into the minds of my beloved authors where I didn't have to be me, studied and got accelerated into my CID place within a year and a half. They seemed almost obsessed with accelerating my career, sending me on courses, letting me shadow senior officers, molding me as some kind of community relations nanny. But I never got near to any decent crime, always out of the way when something big went down. I grasped the chance for the secondment to Sydney, and came back as an expert (according to them) on ethnic crime gangs. They promoted me to DS before long, but it was made very clear that was as far as I could expect to go. They'd 'invested a lot' in me and now they wanted a particular kind of return.

***

So while the couples nuzzled in their duvets, I put on a black beanie, and slumped in my car seat so that I could see directly onto the house ten yards away. The lights were on in the front rooms downstairs, and after a little while the thick drapes opened. The net curtains were parted for a moment, and two small white faces and a brown face peeked out. They turned away and I glimpsed bright pajamas. Soon lights came on in a ground floor room on the corner of the house, and a window was opened. Francis Benton's face appeared, with an unlit cigarette between the lips. Next a hand holding a cigarette lighter, the hand withdrawn, then appearing again to take the lit cigarette. And then the face withdrew until only the exhalation of smoke from the lips and the hand were visible. The glowing butt was flicked into the garden and the window was closed.

I waited another hour and started to daydream. I was stiff and cold, slumped sideways so that my long legs were coiled in the foot well of the car. I was jerked to attention by a muffled voice, looked towards the house, and saw Thea opening an umbrella as she stepped onto the pavement. I slid down out of view, and gently pushed the window button. Nothing happened. I reached to turn the ignition key to power the window, praying that nothing would beep or flash. Nothing did. I slid the window down an inch, and Thea's voice came clear:

"Go back in. Please, Jack, get inside."

"It's all right, let's just walk around the block. We'll be back in five minutes."

"No, Jack, I don't want the children alone in the house with him."

"But we need to talk, Thea."

"Leave me alone. I need some air. Go back in."

Jack must have turned away because the last thing he said was muffled, but I know that he said, "For God's sake," and then something about "family". The front door slammed, the garden gate clanked and I prised myself up just enough to see Thea striding away in the drizzle.

The episode left me sick at heart and sick at my stupidity. I'd spied on two distraught people, eavesdropped on a woman's anguish for her children, and because of what? An attractive man flattering me over my literary knowledge? A foolish flutter of my heart over a shopkeeper? What if I'd been caught, and what if Thea had reported a prowler? I visualised the scene on Monday morning in Boris's office as I floundered to explain why I was playing Dirty Harry around the corner from the Cathedral, and why I hadn't followed up on the bank account and the old man in Elephant and Castle.

I went to the gym but for once I couldn't raise the enthusiasm – no, that's not the right word – the compulsion to flog my body into exhaustion. I drove towards home, but stopped at a corner shop for a tub of ice cream and a bottle of brandy. It was midday when I got into bed with a spoon, a glass and a Russian novel I'd been meaning to read for years. With alternate shots of brandy and spoonfuls of ice cream I woozed myself into nineteenth century rural Russia, where I dallied with Lermontov for an hour or so before an agitated sleep descended on me.

***

I thought I was being attacked by billiard balls but as I wrangled myself out of sleep I realised it was the clackety clack ringtone on my phone. I rolled over in bed into something sticky; the tub of ice cream had spilled and melted. The phone clacked and I saw it was showing 5pm. I pressed the green phone button and clapped the thing to my ear.

"Fiona?"

"Yes, who is it?" I said, but I knew.

"Hope I'm not disturbing your Sunday afternoon," Boris said.

My insides turned inside out and my mouth turned to sandpaper. Someone had spotted me. I was done. Career over.

At last I said, "Hello, Boris".

"Are you free this evening?" Boris said. What was this? Some sort of softly-softly strategy to avoid Internal Investigations being called in? Call in a favour and let's forget the whole thing? I always felt his eyes on my bum when I left his office.

"I suppose so. Where do you want to meet?" I was running the procedure though my mind: Call the union, get legal representation, make no admissions, agree to nothing.

"My house. Dinner. There's someone I want you to

meet. Seven OK?"

"That'll be lovely, Boris. Looking forward to it."

I closed the phone and lay back in the ice cream. I was looking forward to it like an amputation. Boris had done this once before, trying to fix me up with one of his buddies at a lunch at his place. But then I rewound to two minutes before: Nobody had spotted me, my career was intact, I didn't need a union lawyer, and let's face it – I had nothing else to do on a wet Sunday night.

Boris and his Polish wife lived in a mock-Georgian townhouse a couple of miles from me. I remembered it as being surgically clean and sparsely furnished with desperately modern pieces and abstract paintings that veered between the decorative and the sadomasochistic. I recalled eating pink beef Carpaccio in front of a pen and red wash drawing whose uncertain shapes drew one's thoughts to genital surgery. Boris and his wife had small children, but there was no evidence of their existence, and I fancied that they were kept upstairs in a lab rat facility.

Boris's last offering had been as thick as a roof slate, but my boss had looked confused when I told him on the following Monday that my blind date and I hadn't clicked. That was the kind of expression that would appeal to Boris in his mechanistic world view: Person A clicks with Person B. I think he saw me as a spare block of Lego, and he hated things that weren't clicked into something else. At work he had a reputation for clearing up cases swiftly. If something didn't click he'd force it to fit, sometimes, it was said, with a bit of quiet biffo out of public view.

I still wasn't sober by six thirty, so I called a cab. I'd dressed recklessly – too much showing above and below, and when I got out of the taxi I was pulling my skirt down to cover my thighs. The wife let me in and looked me up and down sniffily. She glared at Boris when he looked down my blouse and gave me a continental hug. Tugging down on my skirt, I followed them into the lounge room and squatted on the edge of a leather sofa as hard as a park bench. I tried rearranging my legs until I achieved a measure of modesty with my knees locked together, my calves angled to one side, and my hands over the belvedere between my thighs.

"Campari and soda, I seem to remember?" Boris asked, and I nodded. Wifey went away and came back with a tall orangey drink. I sipped it and sensed strong alcohol without taste; she'd braced it with vodka.

"My buddy just called. He's parking," Boris said.

The wife went away again and returned with a whole jug of Campari and soda, and an evil look in her Slavic eye. She topped me up.

The doorbell rang, and Boris went into the hall. There was matey banter and a slammed door, and Boris showed a black man into the room. The man turned to Boris's wife and made a curious movement somewhere between a curtsey and a bow, and handed her a gift-wrapped bottle. She took it off him, opened the neck of the wrapping, frowned at the label, and sneered a thank you that sounded more like sink you.

The black man was ghastly. Not physically repulsive like the last blind date. In fact, he was well-built and handsome. And not thick like the other one; this guy was educated and smart, but must have had an advanced diploma in vanity with honours. He lowered himself into the settee, carefully crossing his legs inside razor creased trousers so that a precise strip of brown muscled calf showed above silk socks embroidered with a tiny heraldic device. I did say that I have a weirdly photographic memory, but looking back I can't tell you exactly what was on the little escutcheon, but it may have been a unicorn. I tugged at my stupid skirt. The man – Justin he was called – managed not to glance at my legs. Actually, I think he made a point of not looking, angling his head with a slight upward incline as if he were sniffing a rose at a flower show, so that he could look down his nose at my face. Boris fawned around him.

"Scotch is it, Justin?"

Justin raised a plucked eyebrow. Was he gay? Had Boris's amateur attempt at eugenics gone completely haywire?

"I'm out of the single malt but I've got a Dewars," Boris said, and I heard his wife snigger. Boris glared at her.

"A sparkling water will be fine, thank you," the man said. At this point music began to ooze from loudspeakers on metal stalks, small very hi-tech gadgets that made the sound feel as if it was invading your viscera. I'm not much good with classical music, but the man frowned delicately and pronounced that if he wasn't entirely mistaken it was Rachmaninoff's Piano Concerto No.2.

"In C Minor," Boris's wife barked but the man ignored her.

The music seemed quite loud. It made me think of snowy Russian steppes and sad partings at windswept railways stations, and I wanted to cry. The black man was declaiming about Celia Johnson and Trevor Howard, but I couldn't concentrate. Boris was huff-huffing as if he were a renowned culture buff. My eyes were misting over and I asked for the bathroom. The wife led me to a guest toilet where you could have done eye surgery without fear of infection, and made it obvious that she was standing outside the door. Did she think I might leave a droplet of urine on the mirror-like marble if I were left unattended?

I dabbed my eyes and took deep breaths. Yes, that was it: *Brief Encounter*. My Dad had the video and we had a silly family tradition of watching it every Christmas Eve, and I always cried. It was the Rachmaninoff that had set me off.

When I came out of the bathroom, Anya marched me back to the lounge. I noticed that she was concealing a small remote control in her hand, the way ex-prisoners try to hide the roll-ups they are smoking, and when I sat down again I was sure that she had turned the volume up because the black man Justin was almost shouting, this time about Shelley.

Now, I thought, fully recovered from Rachmaninoff-induced tears, when it comes to Shelley, this Justin had better look out.

14: Shelley as deadly weapon

By the time we were ushered to the dining table at the far end of the lounge, the great sweeping romantic tragic extravagances of Concert No.2 in C Minor were nearing the pain threshold. I was feeling woozy and anaesthetized after refills from the pitcher of fortified Campari and soda and vodka. Boris's wife served fillets of white fish which turned out to comprise mostly small treacherous bones. I poked mine around the plate, but the black man had miscalculated; he'd taken a generous mouthful and was masticating hopelessly, trying to sift the needly bones from fish pulp. He gave up shouting about Shelley.

Now I happen to know *The Boat on the Serchio* off by heart, and I offered to recite it. Boris's wife shrugged, Boris nodded with fake enthusiasm and the black man glowered.

I belted it out, all one hundred and eighteen lines, and the three of them looked goggle-eyed like children who have seen fireworks for the first time.

"What do you think it's about, Boris?" I asked.

"It's about a boat of course. Two blokes on a boat", Boris said. His wife glared at me, sensing a trap. She was no fool. The volume of the music had decreased a couple of clicks.

"Justin, what do you think? What's Shelley on about?" I yelled, trying to stay upright.

Justin expelled a little parcel of mashed bones into his napkin, and said, "Yes, of course, a boat trip. It's a lyrical poem that recalls Shelley's journeys to Tuscany. They've been for a trip on the Arno. If you've ever been to Florence you'll have crossed the Arno to get to ..."

I cut him off. "Well, that's true up to a point, but isn't there a bit more to it?"

The remote control in Boris's wife's hand twitched and the music was lowered a little more. "Say ze lest stenza again," she commanded, and I'm sure that she winked at me.

I began:

"The Serchio, twisting forth

Between the marble barriers which it clove

At Ripafratta, leads through the dread chasm

The wave that died the death that lovers love,

Living in what it sought, as if this spasm ..."

"Boris," the wife asked, "What iss wave that died the death that lovers love?"

"It's a wave on the river. The tide ..." Boris said, confused.

"And vat do you sink Justin"?

"It's clearly metaphorical, allegorical," he said nervously.

"What's it an allegory for?" I asked. Now I could almost feel the wife egging me on.

The two men stared dumbly. Justin moistened his lip with a miniscule sip of mineral water. The wife's fingers twitched and the room was now silent.

"Don't know?" the wife asked, her lip curled.

The men looked at one another.

"Shelley and his boyfriend having intercourse," the wife said.

Boris's face purpled and he glared at her: "That's bollocks. They're fishing, fly fishing, there's a wave from

104

the tide ..."

"Zen zey have orgasm. Shpunk. Fiona, say ze bit about effluence."

"But the clear stream in full enthusiasm
Pours itself on the plain, then wandering
Down one clear path of effluence crystalline ..."

"See?" the wife said.

"Rubbish," Boris said, but he'd realised it was true.

The wife stood up and glowered over him: "You British idiot. I am Polish, I am cultured. From ze country of Chopin. Vat you sink, you bring bleck people to my house and make fool of me?"

Justin stood up: "Lovely evening. I should be making tracks. Thanks so much." He held out a limp hand to the wife, who looked at the ceiling.

Boris handed me roughly into a taxi. I almost broke an ankle on the kerb. He walked slowly back to the house, his shoulders slumped. In the taxi I reran the evening, Jack replacing the hideous Justin. Jack and I would have talked about books, about films, discovered that we liked the same things. Boris and his wife would have been extras on the set, quietly refilling the glasses, occasionally chuckling when Jack said something witty, and then I'd flash a look back at Jack to signal that I'd understood the submessage, got the irony. Then I'd be slightly outrageous – say I'd enjoyed the lesbian scenes in Sarah Waters' books, and Jack would look archly as Boris huffed and sniggered, and then he'd say that the gay scenes in *The Line of Beauty* were quite interesting, and Boris would think that *The Line of Beauty* was a yacht and we'd have to tell him that it was a book, and we'd all laugh grown up laughs. The scene became dim and I sobbed drunkenly and silently the rest of the way home, aching to have Jack Walsingham next to me on the greasy back seat.

The next morning, I arrived at the office at 8am, fortified with an almost lethal mix of analgesics, anti-inflammatories, and digestive scouring agents. Boris's office door was closed, but I knew he'd call me in. I mumbled and scraped through half an hour of pseudo-work, playing various scenarios through my mind: Boris would have a new equal opportunity project for me. Boris would chide me for not getting on with his friend. Boris would embarrass us both by apologising for his wife's behaviour. Boris would tell me to apply for a transfer to the Isle of Skye. He buzzed me at eight thirty, but I was wrong.

"Sit down." Neutral voice. No hint of what would come next. No eye contact. Bad sign.

I sat. Boris rummaged through a sheaf of emails until he found the one he wanted.

"You're always complaining that you never have any proper cases. I've got something for you!"

My heart lifted like a cloud of butterflies. Some miracle of biochemistry turned my drugged haze of sourness into the first morning on earth. I was Eve on a sunlit salt sprayed beach, freshly wrought from Adam's rib, and Adam looked not unlike Jack.

"It's that Walsingham bloke – you, know, the bookshop and that scrote Francis something or other," Boris said. "They've found Walsingham's address in a notebook on a deceased person at Elephant and Castle. Suspicious death. You're to ring this bloke in the Met and get straight down there." The butterflies descended into the pit of hell that was my stomach.

He looked up: "Not gone yet?"

Well, I couldn't really complain, could I? Real

detectives spend half their lives negotiating the boundaries between being an upholder of the law and a human being. You heard things you didn't like the sound of, you saw corners being cut, you saw behaviour that fell somewhere between ethical and questionable. I'd been a pretend detective, a mascot like when footballers trot their kids alongside them as they run onto the field at a cup final. Now I had to grow up and weave a course between the man I was infatuated with and a man implicated in a death.

"Just leaving, boss," I said. "Who's my offsider?" I could summon up a sporty metaphor when I needed to.

"Take Simple Simon. He needs to stretch himself."

DC Simon Simpkin took the wheel while I gazed at the wet cows in the fields alongside the M1 in between the gaps in the solid convoy of lorries hurtling south. He chatted with quiet excitement. He'd made the detectives just a few months ago, and he was wolfing down anything that Boris tossed him: Affrays, drug busts, child molesters, he took them all in his efficient stride. Simon was another one with a law degree, and he revelled in the irony of his nickname. Before long we were crossing Lambeth Bridge and heading for the Elephant and Castle shopping centre. Simon found Walworth Road and I used my phone to guide him to the address.

There was the usual paraphernalia at the grubby block of flats: Yellow crime scene tape, a couple of police vehicles, a knot of gossips standing with arms folded, solving the crime with litres of cigarettey breath. A man in a suit came out of the house, detective written all over him, ducked under the tape and walked straight up to me.

"DS Salmon?" I nodded. He introduced himself but I didn't focus. The bleak reality of the situation hit me. His mouth was moving and I knew he was asking me inside the house. Time froze. Suddenly I felt a sharp pain in my ribs and I was back to clarity. Simple Simon had surreptitiously jabbed me from behind, and he was discreetly holding my elbow and guiding me to follow DS whoever he was called.

"You OK ma'am?" he whispered.

"Bit dizzy for a second. Just had the flu and it's lingering a bit." I guessed the little sod filed it all away for future reference. Boris would have to watch this one.

The squalid hallway led up some soiled cement steps. Sitting on the top step were two women in shapeless tracksuits, clutching one another. The large white one wept and the small brown one stroked her hair, comforting her. In between the sobs the large one was saying, "It was fuckin' orrible Donna, it was fuckin' orrible".

"This is the lady who found the body," my Elephant and Castle detective pal said. "We'll get a statement from her when she's calmed down. Come and have a look. The scene of crime blokes are nearly done."

It was a desperately sad room. Everything was neat and poor. The old pink sink, the spindly shelves, the prison cot, the little bottles of Pan Yan pickle and salad cream. The old glossy theatre posters made a melancholy overlay to the scene. I imagined them in a retro furnishings shop one day, with a cynically high price tag. Inner city couples would buy them to frame at ludicrous prices to hang in the dining nook opposite the Tamara de Lempicka prints.

The photographic memory clicked in. A tall thin man in striped pajamas (Simple Simon reminded me later that they were blue), lay prostrate diagonally across the room, feet to the door. Felt slippers, holes in soles; blotchy ankles; brown stains around the seat of the pajamas; puddle of drying liquid on the floor below the mid-section of the body; pajama jacket rucked up and pinpricks of dark red blood visible on the skin of the stomach; left arm outstretched, no watch, right arm tucked under chest; copious blood now clotted around a large wound at the side of the skull; thin silver hair; eyes open and gazing at an enormous ugly clock next to the head, with hair and blood stuck to it, and dusted with fingerprint powder.

A SOCO man looked up and said, "OK?" The DC said, "Yes," and the SOCO carefully eased the clock into a large plastic bag.

"Blimey," Simple Simon said. "I reckon his time was up." Nobody laughed. The SOCOs packed up and a uniformed constable stepped in: "Mortuary van, gov. Ten minutes." My pal nodded and handed me a clear evidence bag containing a cheap address book held open with a rubber band at the page where in a gracious italic hand were the words Jack Walsingham, The Windings, 29 Cathedral Row and the name of our town. Simple Simon took a picture with his phone and I handed the bag back.

"Cause of death?" I asked my pal.

"Two possibilities," he said. "Number one: The old man took the clock from the shelf, raised it above his head and bashed himself to death. Very elaborate suicide."

"Couldn't the clock just have fallen on him?" I asked.

My colleague looked at me with pity: "The shelf is eighteen inches above our man's height. The falling on head idea only works if he lay face down on the floor and the clock leapt off the shelf of its own accord. So, possibility number two is that somebody picked it up and clocked him with it."

Simon made an obedient muted laugh of appreciation

at my friend's wit.

"Any idea who it might be?" I asked, gulping to wet my dry mouth. The DC and Simon looked at each other with puzzlement.

"Jack Walsingham?" I ventured.

"It's early days," the DC said, "but the lady outside saw a man in the street at seven o'clock this morning who she recognised. She said he's been here before. Fortyish, medium height, dark hair greying a bit – we got that much out of her and we'll have a proper go at her later on. Ring any bells? My old mate Boris said you're familiar with Walsingham's description."

"Could be a match," I said with lead in my chest.

***

Simple Simon and I got back to the office by noon. I lurked in the ladies room and crept to my desk, but Boris spotted me.

"It's your lucky day. It just gets better," he said. How could it get better, I wondered. What bitter luck was this?

"What do you mean, Boris?"

"Looks like Jack Walsingham came straight back from the Elephant and Castle and killed Francis Benton. On your way then. They're waiting for you at his house."

As I stumbled to open his door, Boris said quietly, "You'd better have an explanation when the time comes".

"Explanation?"

Boris's voice was as cold as an aluminum rod: "Why you handed Francis Benton's file back. Nothing to follow up, you said."

I left the office with Simple Simon in tow, watched curiously by three or four of the male detectives. I thought

I saw a sarcastic raised eyebrow.

The scene at Elephant and Castle was repeated outside The Windings: Yellow tape, vans, and onlookers. But these were a different class of onlookers, wearing posh rain jackets and pretending they just happened to be out strolling and came across the scene. There were no clouds of fag smoke, but I did smell the fruity briar of an old gent in thick tweeds that must have dated back to the Suez crisis.

Once inside the house I went into Human Camera mode, sweeping the scene with my eyes – floor, walls, ceilings, objects, people. I stopped two yards into the hallway and took a mental wide angle shot of the frozen aftermath of the violent events that had taken place just an hour ago.

It was a generously made hallway with four dark wooden doors – all closed – and a large polished wood staircase that wound up past a landing to a balustraded corridor on the first floor. Stained glass windows in the front of the house lit the area with a muted warmth, but there were some very modern light fittings subtly recessed high up on the walls, which were papered with a green pastel design. A heating control glowed with a dot of green light and I could hear the low hum of a fan. The hallway was obviously a kind of family gallery, hung with professionally framed photographs of three or four generations of Walsinghams. The most recent picture was of three small children, one brown and two white. The floor was covered with a very old and very luxurious fitted café au lait carpet, and there were faded crimson oriental rugs thrown over the high traffic areas.

Next to the staircase was a massive hall stand of varnished oak, over which was draped the body of Francis

Benton, his head twisted backwards at an improbable angle. He was still in his pajamas, but the bottoms were around his knees.

A uniformed constable stood next to the hall stand looking straight ahead.

"Make sure that nothing is touched, and let me know when the scene of crime mob get here. Where are the Walsinghams?" I said.

"The lady's in the kitchen and the man's in the sitting room."

"And the children?"

"Staying with relatives in London for the weekend we believe. It's half term."

I went into the kitchen and Simon followed. Thea sat at the big farmhouse table looking at her hands. A female constable stood by the cooking range. An Aga, of course. Thea was wearing a sleek grey and red dress – not exactly red, but an attenuated tone of smokey crimson. Funny, I don't normally remember colours but the combination was so striking that it somehow stuck. It didn't look like day wear, more a cocktail dress. The dress had a slight rent in the seam under the left arm. She wore no jewelry, no shoes, no stockings.

I'd thought Thea merely handsome but viewing her in profile I saw a deep beauty that was more than the sum of the parts. She certainly wasn't conventionally pretty – a strong nose, heavy lidded eyes, thick dark uncontrollable hair recently cut in a short style and still under protest. I stared at her and wondered what I was supposed to feel about the mother of Jack's children, the woman who lay in his bed every night.

"Everything OK?" I asked the uniform, who nodded.

And then Thea looked up and said to me, "I'm going

to say this once and once only. I'm not going to make any statement whatsoever," and looked back at her hands.

I led Simon out of the kitchen and back into the hall. My chest began to pump and I felt as if I was swaying, but Simon didn't notice. I stalled, stopped to look at Francis Benton's spiritless face, calculated how it must have happened: Over the top balcony, throat snagged on the top of the dresser while the torso kept falling, the neck bouncing back and snapping, the weight of the torso and legs twisting the flopping head as the dead man crashed onto the table top of the dresser.

"Hadn't we better check on the husband?" Simon, behind me.

I took deep breaths and led the way. This time the room was a blur. All I saw was Jack Walsingham sat upright on a sofa – don't ask me how big or where it was or what else there was in the room.

His face was lined and puffy, eyes dull, clothes rumpled, a shirt tail hanging out his trousers. He looked up and smiled weakly. He said, "It's you," and I knew I was the wrong person in the wrong place at the wrong time, possibly on the wrong planet. I stepped into the hallway, had a telephone conversation with Boris, went back into the sitting room.

"Jack Walsingham," I said with my voice wobbling, "I am arresting you for the murder of Errol Sparkes. Anything you say will be ..."

"Errol Sparkes? Good God, you've got it all mixed up!" Jack shouted and sprang up from the sofa. Simon launched his body at Jack, pinned him to the carpet, spun him round and handcuffed him. I winced to see those bookseller's hands crushed with the metal bands.

"Anything you say will be ..." I tried again to caution

the man I loved and who I knew was incapable of murder.

"No, no, it's all wrong. Errol Sparkes isn't dead – I saw him this morning. But I was here when Francis Benton died. I caught him trying to rape my wife and he went over the balcony."

15: Fifty percent bollocks

With the preliminary formalities concluded, we were ready to go. Jack had tucked his shirt in and run a hand through his hair. I saw that he needed a shave, and I drifted for a moment imagining the rasp of his chin on my cheek. He shifted in the interview room chair to glance at the duty brief next to him, and the movement disturbed the air in the windowless cube. I caught the sharp sweetness of his sweat.

Boris opened: "Mr. Walsingham, can you please run us through the events of this morning?"

Jack stared at Boris and said nothing. His hands were on the desk, the fingers knotted tight, knuckles white. A cable of tension ran up his arms through the stiff shoulders, through the straining neck muscles to his jaw. I thought he might snap, and I willed him to exhale and let the cable ease.

"Mr. Walsingham," Boris said, and looked at the brief. The brief fidgeted. Jack looked at the ceiling.

"Jack," Boris said.

Jack's gaze lowered and he looked first at the brief, then at me, and then at Boris.

"I'm saying nothing until you give up this absurd notion that I killed Errol Sparkes." His eyes turned up to the ceiling again.

Boris exhaled and made a loose raspberry sound with his lips. He nodded to me.

"Mr. Walsingham," I said, looking at his hands. I dared

not look up in case we betrayed each other. "We're at the early stages. We need to establish a baseline."

"A baseline." I could tell from the timbre of his voice that he was looking at me. "All right. I can live with that. We'll establish a baseline." I glanced up and saw that his look was guarded, neutral. I mirrored his guarded look with my own, and we stared at each other like sphinxes for a few seconds. I had an overpowering compulsion to stretch my right leg towards him under the small desk

Boris took over: "Let's begin with Errol Sparkes. How about you tell me how you know him."

"Errol Sparkes is – or was – a client of mine. I got hold of old rare magazines for him and he bought them."

Jack's brief jerked to life and leaned over to whisper to him. Boris craned forward. I had drumsticks in my chest knocking on my ribs.

Jack smiled bitterly and said, "Calm down, they weren't vintage kiddy porn. They were lovely old issues of a magazine called *Titbits*. Arthur Conan Doyle wrote articles for it." I cemented on my sphinx face, all the while seeing Jack in his shop opening an envelope with a schoolboy's wonder, taking out the old magazine, nodding and smiling as he scanned the Edwardian stories, gently turning the pages ...

"But of course Errol Sparkes was a conman," Jack said.

"Go on," I said, and my right foot moved an inch – like a hand on a Ouija board – towards Jack's side of the desk.

"Errol Sparkes was in league with my half-brother. They tried to blackmail me."

"Hold on, hold on, hold on," Boris said. But I knew. Francis Benton was Jack's half-brother. That's what he'd meant when I was crouched in the car and he'd said family. "He's family," – that was it.

I listened with a neutral face as Jack told the story: The cheques written on the Bathwell Trust, the set-up murder scene, the meetings with Francis in the public toilets, the abandoned rented house. I felt as if I were drowning in his distress, wanting to tell him that everything was going to be all right, that we'd get to the bottom of this, that I knew that he wasn't capable of killing an old man.

Boris broke in: "Just, just, just let's backtrack a bit. You say that they set up a murder scene. What actually happened?"

"Francis let me into the house. The old man was lying on the floor face down. Near his head there was a great big ..."

I didn't understand. I felt like a little kid who's lost her mum in the shopping mall. This wasn't happening. Everything would go back to normal in a minute if only mum would come back, if Jack would unsay what he'd just said. I had to tell him to stop talking, not to describe the horrible death of Errol Sparkes. I pressed my shoe against his ankle and hoped against all hope that my brown foot could tell his ankle not to say another word.

And it worked. His mouth closed and he looked at his brief. The brief raised an eyebrow, made a note on a pad and said to Boris, "My client needs a break".

Jack said thank you in foot language. We sat with our shoes in companionly union for a moment, and then the door opened a crack. I withdrew my foot as Simple Simon's face appeared but I was almost certain that he'd seen.

***

"Don't you have a home to go to?" Boris asked. "Go

home, celebrate, you've hit the jackpot".

"I won't be long now, Boris". It was six thirty in the evening. If one of the blokes had made the arrest, the whole gang would be knocking back the pints at the Dog and Goldfish. Instead they'd mostly made awkward gestures of congratulation and scuttled back to their computers.

With Boris gone, I studied the statement. After a half hour break, Jack and the fidgety duty brief had been brought back in, and my innocent lamb had set out the events of the day, frequently interspersing his answers with 'no comment'. This time Simple Simon sat opposite Jack, and I was placed to the side. Boris had asked the questions. Once when I had tried to ask Jack something, Boris had talked over me and Simon had smirked. The statement was sparse and surprisingly well punctuated:

I Jack Walsingham, bookseller of 29 Cathedral Row, make this statement:

1. At 7am on the morning of 23 January I was at home at The Windings at 29 Cathedral Row.

2. In the house were my wife Thea and my half-brother Francis Benton. My children were not in the house. They were staying with my wife's parents in Camden Town.

3. Francis moved into the house approximately two weeks ago, having given me proof that he was the illegitimate son of my father.

4. I have no comment to make on the nature of that proof.

5. I was already acquainted with Francis before I found out that he was my brother, through Errol Sparkes. Mr. Sparkes was a client of mine, and had been involved with

Francis Benton in a plan to extort money from me.

6. I have no comment to make on the nature of that extortion attempt.

7. I state that my wife Thea had no knowledge of my business involvement with Mr. Sparkes or the extortion attempt.

8. I received a telephone message from Mr. Sparkes at 6am. He was in an agitated state and asked me to come to Elephant and Castle immediately. When I asked him why, he said that he couldn't say but that it was an extremely serious matter concerning my family. He rang off and when I tried to call back the number was engaged.

9. Nobody else was awake in the house and so I left quietly, meaning to call my wife once I'd arrived at Elephant and Castle. I walked to the station and took the main line train and then the underground, arriving at Mr. Sparkes's flat at about 8.30.

10. I knocked at the door and heard Mr. Sparkes moving around inside. I knocked again, and heard him ask, "Who is it?" I answered, "Jack Walsingham. You said you needed to talk to me".

11. There was silence and then he said, "It was a misunderstanding. Go home. I'm sorry".

12. I knocked again and asked, "Do you need some help? An ambulance perhaps?" He said, "I'm sorry, Jack. Just go". I did not hear or see anyone else in the hallway of the flats.

13. I walked back to Elephant and Castle underground and went into a cafe where I ordered some coffee and a croissant. I called my wife and told her what had happened and that I'd be back in an hour and a half. I made the call at 9am.

14. I arrived at my house at 10.30 and unlocked the

front door. When I went in I could hear shouting from upstairs. I looked up and saw my wife grappling with Francis Benton on the upstairs landing. He had forced her against the balustrade and was pawing her breasts with one hand and clutching both her wrists with the other.

15. My wife was wearing a red and grey dress, and I noticed a tear under one arm.

16. I heard her shout "Get your hands off me, you sick creep."

17. Francis Benton was wearing pajamas. The bottoms were around his knees and his penis was erect.

18. I shouted to him and ran up the stairs. He released my wife, who collapsed on the floor away from the balustrade. I positioned myself against the balustrade and yelled at Francis Benton to get out. He put his face close to mine and laughed at me, saying, "She's a good fuck that one". I aimed a punch at his face but missed. I lost my footing and fell to my knees, still with my back to the balustrade. He laughed again and got ready to launch a massive punch at my head, but I rolled forward as he flexed his arm, and I head butted his ankles. He tipped forward and flew over my back and then over the balustrade, coming to rest on the hallstand.

19. I dialled 999 and comforted my wife while we waited for the emergency services.

20. The ambulance officers arrived just before the police. They told me that Francis Benton was dead from a broken neck.

***

We reassembled the next afternoon --Boris, Simple Simon and me – take away coffees, printouts, and an air of smug triumph surrounding the two men. I'd had a school visit booked for the morning and Boris had said, "Don't cancel it. Have a morning on something mundane and you'll come back fresh after lunch. I'm going to have a thrilling time catching up on your lot's expenses," pointing at a pile of creased receipts.

But they'd got me out of the way so they could wrap the case up, stick a party label on it saying 'solved', and finish it off with a blue and white checked bow.

"Away you go, Simon," Boris said.

"Thanks, Boris," Simon said, turning his laptop around so that we could see a Power Point presentation. My insides curdled with shame and anger. This overambitious little law graduate who wouldn't know his Shelley from his shoulder blades had been up since the early hours stealing my case from me, and – I knew with certainty – digging a chasm for Jack Walsingham that he'd never climb out of. The presentation started, with the dot points chugging across the screen like Thomas the Tank Engine's carriages being put tidily into the sidings. I loathed Simple Simon.

He began: "Two deaths, a statement by Mr. Walsingham that is at least fifty percent bollocks, utter refusal by Mrs. Thea Walsingham to make any statement whatsoever, one witness, miles of CCTV, and some very compelling forensics."

"Fifty percent bollocks? Which fifty percent?" I asked. I wondered about the forensics and how he'd got anything so quickly.

"Well, let's say it may be a hundred percent bollocks, but hear me out," Simon said, giving Boris a matey nod.

He went on: "Errol Sparkes was killed by a blow to the head with a large ornate clock. The clock found in Errol Sparkes's flat bears the fingerprints of Mr. Sparkes and Mr. Walsingham. Mr. Walsingham admits to being in the flat at what we believe was the time of death. We have some CCTV of him on the railway network and within a few days we will most likely be able to trace him almost from door to door. We have a witness who saw him near the flat."

Boris broke in: "What's the chance of any other forensics that might link Walsingham to Sparkes's body?"

"Not hopeful, but the prints are clear and unequivocal," Simon said.

"Could he have handled the clock at some other time?" Boris asked.

"Actually, yes in theory. Have a look at this." Simon clicked the mouse and the screen filled with a gritty image of a tall old man walking towards the camera pulling a shopping bag on wheels. The man passed under the camera, and another figure came into the frame. It was Jack Walsingham, and one of his hands seemed to be bandaged. Simon froze the picture and blew it up. Jack's hand was wound with a bloody bandage, and his face was strained and grim.

"You see – he visited Mr. Sparkes just before Christmas. To be more precise, Jack Walsingham got into some kind of bloody altercation somewhere in a back alley off Oxford Street, and tailed the old man to the Elephant and Castle. The Met sent this little lot over last night. Judging by the shots we have of him coming out of Elephant and Castle station and back in again, he spent around an hour at Mr. Sparkes's flat. That's when our witness saw him before."

"So he might have touched the clock at that time," Boris said.

"Or he might not. On a glossy surface like this you can't be sure of the age of the print. But sure as shit, he had some bad stuff going down with Mr. Sparkes." Even Boris winced as the young colleague flexed his LA cop idiom.

"Fiona," Boris said, turning to me. "Anything to add?" I shook my head.

"Tidy, very tidy. All the bits click together. OK, Simon, what about our dead scrote?" Boris said.

Simon screwed his face into an expression of heavy irony: "Untidy, very untidy". He'd been practicing that look. He touched the mouse and the Power Point resumed. Three tank engines chugged into place.

"Three possibilities: Jack did it, Thea did it, and nobody did it. The trouble is that apart from this crock of manure in Walsingham's statement, we've got nothing to support any of the three theories."

"Run us through them, Simon."

"OK Jack did it, just like he said. Or maybe not quite like he said. The way he describes it just doesn't add up."

"How do you mean, Simon?"

"Fiona, would you mind?" Simon said, taking my hand and leading me to a chair he'd obviously placed in position by the wall. "I'll be Francis and you can be Jack."

"This is stupid," I said.

"Just do it, sweetheart," Boris growled.

But Simon was right of course. What Jack had described was implausible. With me stooped on the floor with my face in Simon's crutch, it was impossible for him to tilt over me so far that he'd go over the imaginary balustrade. At the worst he might have bashed his face on it and lost a tooth.

"OK, show over, What's the next option?"

Simon pointed at the second tank engine: "Perhaps he caught Thea and Francis about to have a bit of consensual outside the bedroom door, ran up the stairs and flung Francis over the balustrade. The timing fits. We know he got home very close to the time of death."

"Jack's a bit of a grim reaper, is he? Death follows him?" I said. It just popped out.

Boris ignored me. "Go on, Simon".

"So Thea did it. Jack wasn't quite home, Francis fancies a bit of a grope, Thea fights him off and over he goes – maybe loses his footing. Jack comes back, weighs it all up and concocts a confession to save his wife."

"So far so good, Simon. You getting all this Fiona?"

I fumed.

"OK, last theory. Francis flings himself over the balustrade. Ho bloody ho."

"Witnesses in the street outside, neighbours?"

"Nobody saw or heard a thing."

"Forensics?"

"Not good. They're telling me there's sod all chance of getting anything convincing on any of this."

"Drink, drugs?" Boris said.

"Toxicology will be a few weeks but there was nothing obvious."

"Fiona. Last chance. Anything to add?" Boris said.

"Just one thing. Why was she wearing a sexy cocktail dress at ten thirty in the morning?" I said.

"Does it matter?" Simon asked and rolled his eyes up. "She's a woman. Maybe she was trying things on. They do."

Boris let out a big lungful of stale air. He sat back in his chair, let out a sour shirtful, put his hand in his pocket and rearranged something down below. At last he said, "I reckon Walsingham's good for the murder of the old man. That's enough. Let's see what the coroner says about the scrote, but I don't hold out much hope". He nodded at Simon: "OK, hand it over to the CPS. Scram." I waited to be released. Boris eased himself lower in his office chair and I felt his foot touch mine under the desk.

"Alright, Missy. You know what you're doing next, don't you?"

"I'm not going to have sex with you if that's what you think."

He laughed. "You don't get it do you? You're going to write your resignation."

16: An unofficial visit

I didn't go back to work. Got a sick certificate to cover my month's notice, didn't even clear out my desk. I'd paid off the mortgage the year before with the insurance money on the life of my beloved Darren, and I had a decent balance of cash in an investment account, so thanks to a punk in Watford who bought a handgun from a yobbo in a pub in Stoke Newington, I was self-sufficient for a while. No husband and no job, but self-sufficient.

I almost called Boris to thank him for letting me resign, rather than putting me through a disciplinary process that would have led to the same outcome minus the shreds of dignity I still held on to. Well, I did get through to his house one night but his wife answered, and when I didn't say anything she said something about phone perverts.

I thought about my options: Beachcombing in Oz, get my solicitors qualifying exams done, learn sculpture in Venice, have my body pierced in odd places, become a nun, learn Irish, massacre people in a shopping centre, train to be a chef, commit suicide, find a lover, find six lovers, become a pole dancer, become a fitness instructor, do a PhD. The choice was ludicrously wide on the one hand and depressingly futile on the other. All I wanted was to be beside Jack Walsingham in Books by Birdswell, in his house, in his bed, in all of his life. And I knew he wanted that, or he would in time, because it was absolutely clear to me that Thea Walsingham and Francis Benton had been partners in some filthy intrigue to get Jack clapped into jail. And Thea had been the brains, squashing Francis like a beetle when he was no use to her any more. I spent the first five nights of my new life staring at the beams from the street lamps on my bedroom ceiling, picking though everything I knew about the Walsinghams. But I was no wiser at the end about Thea's game.

I packed the car with clothes and books and my laptop, and drove to Wembley, broke the news about my resignation to my parents, and then had some sort of breakdown. Mum put me in the spare room upstairs in the terrace house where you could hear the Bakerloo Line trains rattling out to Watford. She fed me on the peculiar curries she'd learned to make from Dad's aunt in Port Talbot, and Dad read aloud to me while I sat in an old musty armchair I used to play on when I was a kid. Dad was retired now but couldn't stop being a teacher. He read me novels by the Brontës, stopping every few pages to gently ask me a question about the text. Strangely I liked Villette best — it was something about Lucy Snowe that enraptured me. After a week I started getting up before noon, and after two weeks I asked Mum if she could fix me a salad. She was making another lamb and pineapple korma. I found a little gym behind the launderette in the row of tatty shops two streets back from us, and I began to exercise, not obsessively but purposefully and deliberately. I knew that I needed stamina and calm strength for whatever lay ahead.

A month after I arrived in Wembley, I spotted the headline on a news stand: 'Judge throws the book at Walsingham'. I stood outside the Brickmakers Arms reading the paper in the drizzle. Jack had entered a not guilty plea at a preliminary hearing in the Crown Court. I rolled the wet newspaper into a ball of pulp and threw it at a passing cyclist, who skidded and called me something vile that I couldn't hear properly but you can probably guess the general idea. I'd had enough of Wembley.

***

I had three important jobs to do when I got home. The first was to call Simple Simon:

"Christ, Fiona, you shouldn't be phoning me."

"Just thought I'd see how things were going with you."

"Fiona, I had to tell them. You know that. They would have found out anyway. What the hell were you up to anyway? You nearly wrecked the case."

"You're muttering," I said.

"Well, good to catch up. Look Boris is waiting outside ...".

"What prison is Jack in, Simon?"

"Fiona, just drop it. I'm going to cut you off."

"Just tell me, Simon."

"You can find out yourself. It isn't a secret."

"Simon, it was a stuff up. You know that. Boris rushed the job and Jack just let him do it."

"Rushed it?"

"You know what I'm talking about. Jack never did it," I said.

"So who did? The milkman popped in and bashed the old fellow over the nut with a crate?"

"Well, at least you're showing some signs of an open mind," I said.

"It's with the Crown Prosecution Service now. If by some remote chance you were right, it'd never get to trial."

"Don't insult me, Simon. How did it get to a preliminary hearing in the Crown Court if the CPS weren't confident about the evidence?" I said.

"Boris is knocking."

"Where's Jack, Simon?"

I could hear him breathing, and then he said, "Walsingham's on remand at Riswell Park. Now leave me alone".

The second job was to walk past The Windings. The curtains were closed, and the house bore an estate agent's sign: Dignified early Victorian residence, four bedrooms, two reception, library, modernised gourmet kitchen, two baths, self-contained guest quarters, competitive price on application. Good luck selling a death house, I thought.

The third job was to visit Books by Birdswell. Nothing had changed. The two old codgers in their raincoats were arguing with a young man who seemed to be in charge. I wandered around the shop controlling my heartbeat, which threatened to hit a thousand beats a minute. I peeped over the HORROR shelf and squinted my eyes, imagining that the young man behind the counter was Jack. The codgers stormed out.

"The last bloke used to give us a proper discount. He was a gentleman, not a ...." The old man fished around in his brain for a suitably demeaning word, gave up and looked to the old woman for lexicographical assistance.

"He was a gent, not an Orstralian!" she said. "We'll get it in the library for gratis. Good day to you."

"Do you have anything by Isherwood? He wrote *Mr. Norris Changes Trains*," I said to the young man, a silly test really. He chewed a pen and said, "Is it for a child? It might be with *Thomas the Tank Engine*". The accent took me back to Sydney.

I sighed and said, "It's alright. Actually, I read that the owner of this shop has gone to prison and I was wondering what's going to happen to it."

"To be honest I'm not sure. I'm just a PhD student. I ran out of money and the owner's wife took me on for three months as the manager."

"What's your thesis about?"

"It's pretty boring really," he said unconvincingly.

I gave him a fascinated smile, put my head to one side in a grotesquely coquettish fashion. "Tell me."

The boy's eyes were blue as the surf at Manly Beach, filled with naive zeal. "Well, it's a study of the academic legacy of an Australian scholar, a guy called Martin F. Mooney, who founded a field called cultural futures ...."

My phone rang. It was Simon. "Excuse me," I said to the young man.

"Fiona, what you said just now. We need to talk," Simon said.

"I'll be in touch," I said, and cut him off.

I turned back to the scholar, who was preparing to launch into the long version of the synopsis of his thesis about – who was it – Martin Moonwalker? I'd already forgotten.

"Look that was a friend. I've got to go, but can I ask if the owner's wife said anything about selling the shop?"

The scholar frowned and then said, "She might've. There was something about options after three months. Why do you ask?"

"I wouldn't mind buying it – or at least finding out if it's for sale. Do you have any forwarding details for her?"

He poked around under the counter and came up with an address book, and that was the first time I heard of

Forty Apple Trees.

***

I'll admit that I didn't have a real plan. Rather, I had large chunks of plan that didn't really fit together, and I had a feeling that the connections would become evident as I went along. I repacked the car and headed north on a windy June morning.

You could see Riswell Park Prison from the motorway from five miles away. In a bare green valley, it comprised a circular concrete core with grey outbuildings at the four points of the compass. Even on a sunny day it exuded menace, hunkering down like a flattened Dalek inside a cage of steel columns and razor wire. Half a mile before the main gates I drove past a lay-by where a bus was spilling a clutch of women and children onto the concrete pavement. I looked in the mirror and watched them staggering into the wind towards the prison with their plastic bags flailing around them. I parked the car next to a brand-new Range Rover. A blonde, well-groomed Home Counties mother got out, looked at me and looked away. She took off a Hermès scarf and a gold bangle and put them in an expensive handbag. I followed her to the gate, where we each showed our documents before being led to a lobby in the main building. We were scanned and patted down, our bags inspected, our papers checked again. We didn't speak.

Jack frowned when he saw me, then recognition passed across his face. He leaned back in the chair and said, "I just didn't connect, but now I remember your surname. I thought you'd be someone with a Bible come to save my soul."

I sat down and clutched my bag to conceal the tremor

in my fingers. He looked plumper, paler, more lined in the face. I was stricken with sorrow to see him in this grim place, to see his big fingers flat down on the steel table, to see the grey-flecked chest hair against the baby blue of his V-necked prison skivvy. I couldn't make any words come.

"Read any good books recently?" he asked.

"Villette," I managed to croak. The querulous eyebrow was raised in irony: "Yes, I come back to the Brontës every few years. I love Haworth. Have you been there?" I shook my head.

Then: "Why are you here?"

"I love you," I said. The ironic expression again.

"I can't live without you," I said, cringing at the awful cliché. The expression was unchanged.

"Is this an official visit? That wasn't what I understood," he said.

"I resigned from the police. I'm here as a private citizen." This took him off balance. The expressive eyebrow lowered.

"Why did you resign?"

"It doesn't matter."

"It does to me. Was it because of me?" he said.

"Yes, in a way."

"You shouldn't have resigned, not for me." The irony was gone, his demeanor was neutral, cool, flat. I suddenly felt a shaft of doubt piercing me. A sickly yellow light threw my feelings into bilious relief. This man had been accused of a horrible killing, committed to trial for murder. I had seen the wretched old man with his brains stuck to the clock. I knew about sociopaths. Innocent people are hardly ever convicted of horrible crimes. Had I been the victim of a gruesome self-delusion?

And then he smiled and said gently, without irony, "I'm

sorry, you've taken me by surprise. I need a bit of time to absorb what you've said. You get emotionally neutered in a place like this. Will you come to visit again?"

My emotional jangling sorted itself back into familiar categories.

"Yes, Jack, I'll come again. And I'm going to get you out of here."

As I walked back to the car the Hermès lady caught me up. "I've got a flask of coffee. Join me?"

She opened the back of the Range Rover, opened a pricey-looking picnic hamper, and poured two cups of coffee from a tartan-covered flask. We got in the front of the Range Rover and looked down at the toy cars streaming along the motorway a mile away. The taste of the warm flask coffee reminded me of seaside holidays when I was a kid. I thought Thermos flasks had gone out with Abba.

"You can't talk to people about it, can you?" she said. "The neighbours think he's gone to Dubai on a contract, and the children are sworn not to tell anyone. I had to move them to different schools and now they're on medication. Ridiculous. I line them up each morning and give them powerful drugs and make them repeat their cover story."

The clutch of women and children were spat out of the prison gate, and walked past the Land Rover, the squally wind at their backs this time. The smaller children were crying and the women were sullen. One women tried to light a cigarette in the wind, gave up and threw it away. Her lips said, "Fuck".

"Look at them," the Hermès lady said.

I looked but I wasn't sure what I was meant to think:

Pity, contempt, inspiration?

"How long?" I asked.

"Another year. He's been in for eighteen months. He was only doing what every other accountant does. They wanted to make an example of him. How about your chap?"

"Waiting for his trial," I said. "Murder, but he didn't do it."

"I'd better go," said the woman, and I got out of the car.

***

I needed clear air, vistas, places where I could scream my head off without anyone hearing me. I headed north and in three hours I was in Brontë country.

17: Not the packet rubbish

I took one look at Haworth and kept driving. I needed something other than tourist coaches, tea shops and the kind of tacky souvenirs that only the British can make. Sorry, Charlotte, Emily and Jane, I'll be back when I'm in the right mood. I meandered south through Oxenhope and Pecket Well. It was raining, the lanes were empty, and the light was milky grey. I slowed down to look at the soft mossy grey rock, the blackened angular cottages with dripping slate roofs, the undulating moorland in pastel greens and washed lilac. I stopped at the dinky townlet of Hebden Bridge, where stoic locals were sweeping liquid mud from flooded shops, and the river roared along its stone culvert, swollen by the rains oozing off the soggy moors.

I found a public loo and walked back to my car. A woman smiled at me and said, "Are you lost, luv?" I asked her what was worth visiting and where I might find a room, and she pointed out a snug Yorkshire pub that had a B&B. "Heptonstall's worth a visit. It's just up that way." I booked in at the pub and ate a hearty meat pie at the bar. The crystal moorland air seemed to be recharging my body but my mind was flat as a dud battery.

Late in the drizzly afternoon I stopped near Heptonstall, and followed the finger posts to the village centre along a path of tufted grass and luxuriant weeds. The path ran along the back yards of a lane of damp cottages full of kids' bikes and toy trolleys, plump cats, plastic pots of dead flowers, drooping washing, and old building materials – bricks, bits of two by four, toilet bowls. The yards exuded an air of cosy ramshackle domesticity, and I suddenly yearned to be in a battered chair in one of the cottages where a favourite neighbour would cut me a wedge of cake while I flicked through a magazine and stretched my toes in front of the hearth.

I heard a man's voice in one of the cottages say, "Fookin' shut yer fookin' gob". A woman's voice said with a warm chuckle, "Fookin' shut yer own fookin' gob," and they both laughed. I smelt cigarette smoke and the man coughed. My hair was getting heavy with the drizzle and I wrapped my thin jacket more tightly around my shoulders.

I found a place to scream. Heptsonstall Old Church is roofless and gaunt, a pitted stone-floored rectangle surrounded by blackened arches and low stone walls, all streaked with green lichens and mosses. Its silence is unnerving. The lack of clear sightlines as you circle the outside of the arches is unsettling. As I wove a path towards the sacred interior space I felt a scream forming in my throat, felt my fingers gripping tight round my thumbs, my diaphragm taut. I took a step forward, braced myself and opened my mouth.

But no scream came.

The woman was leaning back on a wet slab of masonry, white, completely naked, streaked with rain, eyes staring at the clouds. Her feet were muddy and there were green smudges on her knees. Eight anoraked figures surrounded her, each silently peering through the viewfinder of an SLR camera on a tripod and clicking. Some of the photographers had umbrellas, some big rain hats. The naked woman must have caught my movement in her peripheral vision because she lowered her head slightly and frowned at me for a second. The camera club were too engrossed to notice me.

I walked quietly away. It took me just a few moments to find Sylvia Plath's grave, where I lingered for half a minute trying to form some kind of emotional response to the headstone and the wretched plastic pots of biros next to it. I couldn't manufacture a reaction other than scorn for the people who had honoured a poet with 20p pens.

The day was saved by a lawyer from Halifax.

I checked into the pub, showered, ironed ninety percent of the moorland water out of my hair, put on some jeans and a comfy old jacket, and went down to the bar. There was the lulling English pub hum that makes the loneliest drinker feel part of humanity. Well, except when the lonely drinker is looking out to buy an illegal handgun, but let's not keep on about that.

I found a bar stool and ordered a red wine, which I drank quickly. I was fishing in my purse for change when the barman slid another glass of Bordeaux towards me. "Complements of the gentleman by the door." I laughed out loud. I'd seen this done a hundred times in the movies.

"Would you please buy a pork pie and a pickled onion for the gentleman on my behalf?" I said.

Five minutes later the man eased himself into the barstool next to mine, and put the plate between us. The pork pie and pickled onion were neatly cut into two. He was youngish, thirty-five, with well-cut fair hair, good looking and as slim as a sprinter. He wore a deliciously cut light grey suit with a cream shirt and a shimmering pinkish tie.

"My dinner partner's had to pull out at short notice. What say we have this for the entrée and then have mains in the restaurant?" He was local, spoke Yorkshire with the rough edges worn off. "Ray." He extended a hand and I shook it.

"I can't think of a single reason why not," I said.

He was a Halifax solicitor, working out of what he called 'the family dungeon' in one of the grand Victorian mercantile buildings in the town centre. His father had been a solicitor, and the family were part of the professional establishment of the town – accountants, doctors, businessmen, lawyers.

"And how about you?"

"Ex-detective, unemployed, widow, taking a driving holiday. That's about it. I'll have the fish."

Ray said, "The fish," and studied the menu.

After a minute he looked up and said, "Now let's think about that. Ex-detective, unemployed, widow, taking a driving holiday. The trout might be nice".

"There's monkfish, but I always think it's overrated," I said.

"That's what my ex used to say. There's the Yorkshire pud of course. Have you ever had a real one? Not the packet rubbish. You don't seem the driving holiday type."

I widened my eyes and challenged him. "So what type am I?"

"Never mind, I'm teasing. My mother says it's a dreadful habit and it'll get me into an awful pickle one day."

"Was your dinner date a man?" I asked.

He nodded.

"I'm rather relieved actually," I said.

"Me too," he said, and we both laughed.

I laboured through a Yorkshire pud the size of a trilby hat, dabbing at the gravy on my chin while Ray ate slivers of monkfish on a tiny nest of seaweed salad. He insisted that I had a pint of Black Sheep Ale: "It's the perfect companion to the pud." He sipped a Prosecco. At last I leaned back, gassy and woozy, feeling as if I'd eaten a medium sized ruminant and washed it down with a bathful of soap suds.

"You said you didn't think I'm the driving holiday type," I said, decorously holding back a burp.

"That's right. I think you might be looking for something, something rather serious given what you've told me — an ex-detective after all. Were you sacked?"

"Shoved with an earthmover. It was that or the sack, but my boss let me resign — probably to save the paperwork."

"Tell me more. I'm a stranger after all." I gave him a lopsided smile. "Why not?" I said, and told him the lot, or so I thought.

When I'd finished, he made his hands into steeple and said, "So let me see if I can pick out the important bits. The rhubarb crumble's lovely by the way. You must have it." 'Croomble' was how he said it.

"No rhubarb crumble. Just tell me what you think are the important bits."

"OK." Ray held up four fingers and began counting them off. "One, this Jack character's been set up for the murder of the old man and he's going to plead not guilty even though — according to you — he didn't do it, despite some compelling forensics. Have I got that right?"

I nodded.

"Two, Thea and Francis have conspired to pin the murder on Jack. Thea has then decided that she doesn't need Francis anymore and has arranged his death. However, Jack has confessed to killing Francis but the police don't believe him. Three, you are in love with Jack, and you've lost your job because you've been caught coaching him in his interview."

"You make me sound like an idiot," I said. "Can we just drop it now?"

"You missed something," Ray said.

"Missed what?"

"Thea – what she's like. Why she wants Jack in prison. You just skirt around her."

"I've only met her twice and we barely spoke. She's refused to give a statement. I don't know her at all," I said. I was feeling peeved with this line of questions. The Yorkshire pudding and ale repeated on me.

"And yet you are convinced that she's got Jack arrested. Are you sure about all this? I can't resist the crumble." Ray got up and went to the bar. He looked back and made a spooning motion and mouthed 'sure?'

I stared sullenly into my lap. Ray had made me feel like a school kid who didn't know her eight times table. I got up and went to the loo, sat there for five minutes reading the graffiti and grinding my teeth. Someone had written 'wank you very much darling' in white correction fluid, and beneath it somebody else had carved 'leeds uni dykes spank best'. I wanted to sneak up to my room but I'd left my jacket on the chair. I went back to bloody gay Ray from Halifax.

He was surgically dissecting a slab of rhubarb crumble atop a pool of light lemony custard. "It's not packet, this custard. They bake it in a *bain marie*."

"Thanks, Ray," I said.

"For what?"

"Putting it all under the lamp for me to see. You're

right. I'm missing the most important bit."

"So you didn't come north just for a driving holiday?"

"Obviously not. I came to clear my head, to make some sense of all this bloody jangling," I said.

"And to circle back via the west country ..."

"Yes," I said, "To talk to Thea".

***

Next morning, thin high clouds streaked across an eggshell blue sky. Two vapour trails crossed and I squinted to see the tiny aircraft at their points. It was still cool, and the moist air filled me with optimism and hope. I said goodbye to Ray in the car park. We'd gone to my room after dinner and got half undressed – me in chaste T-shirt and panties and he in his undervest and silk boxers – and lay side by side on the bed chatting, my brown legs pressed against his white legs. He told me about the stodgy family firm and how he'd never been able to come out. "But everyone knows of course. We have elaborate fictions to avoid social embarrassment. Lovers are introduced as old school pals, female cousins enlist friends to make up a couple with me when necessary. My ex just couldn't stand it anymore. So there's no one right now. If I want a fuck I just go up to Leeds where nobody really knows me." We fell chastely asleep and were woken up in the morning by the landlord's wife with breakfast on a tray. "This'll be all round West Yorkshire: Confirmed bachelor solicitor in love tryst with mystery woman," Ray said.

I took the motorway west and skirted Manchester to the north, locking into the phalanx of dirty trucks until I was spat out onto the M6 and locked into another phalanx streaming south through Crewe and Stafford. It began to rain near Birmingham and by the time I left the motorway at Worcester the sky was black, and the windscreen wipers were losing the fight against the deluge. I pulled into a side road and parked under a tree, turned off the engine and pushed the seat back into the reclining position. Within a few minutes the rain stopped, and all I could hear was the dripping of the tree. I opened the window to refresh the fug in the car and laid back with my eyes closed. As I relaxed I focussed on the sounds around me – a small bird, the drips on the car roof, the distant hum of the motorway. And then the ticking of the hot engine cooling.

My heart and my brain jumped violently at the same time, as my memory suddenly sorted and resorted impressions, images, smells, sounds. I sat bolt upright and squeezed my eyes shut, recalling the day I'd arrived at The Windings to find Francis's pajama-clad body: Parking the car, walking the ten yards to Jack's house, past the white van with Francis's registration plate, the hot engine ticking. The ticking hadn't registered in my conscious mind; it must have been swamped by my anxiety about facing Jack.

Francis had just got back from a long drive.

I lay back in the seat for half an hour, dead still, watching the squirrels and the sparrows, an ant walking boldly across the windscreen, a breeze unsettling the leaves on the tree, the sun emerging, the nettles steaming as the rain dried off. I called Simple Simon.

"Where are you, Fiona? We have to meet."

"Not yet. First you need to do something."

"What?"

"Francis. His van engine was hot that morning. I think he drove to Elephant and Castle – early. There's got to be

ANPR data."

"ANPR?"

"Automatic number plate recognition. It's kept for two years," I said.

"He was in his pajamas."

"Yes, by the time we arrived."

"Oh shit," Simon said.

"Yep. Oh shit. So you'll check the ANPR? Talk to Boris? Talk to the CPS if I'm right?"

"Shit shit shit shit."

"Concentrate, Simon. Will you do it?"

"One condition," Simon said.

"OK, let's have it."

"We meet next week. Discreetly."

"Do you run?" I said.

"Every morning at seven."

"OK, back of the cathedral, Tuesday at 7am. We'll run across to Parson's Wood and back along the Birdswell. We can go our separate ways where the Oxford Road crosses the river."

18: Forty Apple Trees

It was a bare ten miles to Forty Apple Trees from the lane where I'd parked. I took the winding road slowly, trying to formulate some kind of approach in my mind. If she wasn't home I'd drive around for an hour and check again, and perhaps find a B&B for the night if there was still no sign. The children must attend a school in the area, and Thea would have to be home to feed them at some point in the afternoon.

I stopped the car twenty-five yards from the cluster of cottages. There were four, each with disintegrating pebbledash exposing the Victorian brickwork below, each with buckled wooden windows and weedy front gardens. The last cottage on the right stood slightly apart, adjoining an overgrown orchard. A rusted out blue car with no wheels stood on bricks at the edge of the trees. A woman came out and stood by the garden gate, staring in my direction. Thea.

I got out and walked along the rutted lane, avoiding the muddy puddles. It was humid, and as I passed through the shade of a scruffy privet hedge, a cloud of gnats swarmed around my face. I felt calm, self-possessed, watchful.

"I thought it was you," she said as I came close. She looked unkempt. The smart choppy hairstyle had grown out into clumps with split ends. The track pants had food stains. She had put on weight around the middle. She turned and walked back to the front door. "Go back to where you've come from," she said over her shoulder,

"I've told your people that I'm not making a statement".

"Wait," I called out. "I'm not the police. I resigned."

She stopped and stared back at me. "That's your problem, not mine."

"Your husband's innocent. He won't go to trial."

"That's my business. Now get out and don't come back."

I held her stare, weighed up what I had in my arsenal. Not much, I knew, but I recalled the Francis Benton file that I had handed back to Boris. Thea hadn't got a mention, but I took a chance:

"The Bathwell Trust. I know all about it."

Thea's stare slid from hostility to alarm. She looked down and mumbled, "You'd better come in".

The cottage was shabby. We entered through what would once have been called a scullery, with an uneven flagstone floor and a large cement sink. Saucepans and plates were stacked on sagging open shelves, and there was a cardboard box of vegetables on a gas stove that must have dated back to the second world war. Thea led me into a sitting room with two ancient deep armchairs covered in threadbare tapestry, and an ironing board. At one end was a basket of washing – mostly school uniforms – and at the other a stack of stapled paper booklets. They were university examination scripts.

Whatever I'd felt for Thea – hostility, suspicion, even hatred – ebbed away at the sight of the squalid interior. She dropped into an armchair and covered her face with her hands, rubbing her eyes. I sat down in the other chair.

"Who asked you to sit? I only asked you in because I don't want the neighbours hearing my private business. You've come here to blackmail me, so get on with it. What do you want?"

Despite the venom in her voice I was stricken with sympathy for her. Taking a stab with the Bathwell remark was fair game for a cop trying to trip up a suspect, but it felt like a low trick with this troubled woman in her dirty track suit pants, marking exams to feed her children. For the second time in a week I suspected that I'd got the whole story wrong. If I was right about the hot engine, Francis had driven to Elephant and Castle in the early hours, forced the old man to telephone Jack and ask him to come. The old man had then – under duress from Francis – told Jack to go home. Francis had then killed him, driven back to The Windings at high speed and got back into his pajamas before Jack arrived home. Perhaps in his excitement Francis had decided to rape Thea in some grotesque finale to Jack's destruction, and Jack had killed him. But how did Thea know about the Bathwell Trust? Had she been part of Francis's plan to implicate Jack in the fraud? Or had she and Jack been partners in laundering the old man's cheques?

I didn't get up. I didn't know why I was there. I didn't know what I wanted to know. I cursed gay Ray from Halifax. How had I let myself get talked into a planless plan after a night of sentimental cuddling with a screwed-up queen in lemon boxer shorts?

"I just thought you should know that Jack will be getting out," I said.

Thea slitted her eyes. "I thought you said you'd resigned from the police. What do you know?"

"I arrested Jack. I saw Francis Benton's body."

"I remember you. What's this 'Jack' business? Bit familiar isn't it?" she said.

"Your husband. I arrested your husband Jack

Walsingham."

"No, hold on. There's something else here," Thea said, and looked at me as if I were a frog on the dissection slab – clinical, inquisitive, searching.

"There's nothing," I said and looked away, and she had me. We'd been taught at the police college how to recognise the lie, the eyes sliding to one side.

"You cow. Christ, he always had a thing for black women. I suppose you know about Charlotte?"

"Jasmine's daughter?"

"Jasmine's and Jack's daughter. God, how I had to clench my teeth over all of that," Thea said. "How long was it going on – you and Jack?"

I said nothing. Nothing had been going on.

"Anyway, are you getting a thrill out of all this? Your fancy man's wife in poverty, you the disgraced rogue cop on some sort of crusade to free her husband? And you're going to send the wife to prison for the murder, and then take up with the husband? It's so bloody corny. Hang on, rogue cops are supposed to have a drink problem, aren't they? Don't they go home to their lonely bedsits and listen to jazz and drink scotch? No, that's the men, isn't it? Let's see, women rogue cops – some dark event in the past, some thirst for revenge, tragic event. I've got it, your partner was shot on a stakeout and you've blamed yourself ever since!"

I'd seen human beings at the deepest reaches of despair and misery: Abused wives with broken teeth and blackened jaws, young alcoholics drowning in vomit in garbage strewn back lanes; dazed drivers at a crash scene slowly realising that they've killed a kid. Cops see things that ordinary people can't imagine, and deal with it by growing a kind of emotional carapace. Thea's sarcastic words slammed me into the gutter with all those poor sods I'd seen. The shell I'd slowly built to protect me from the memory of Darren's death was shattered. I slumped in the old armchair and shoved my wet face into the saggy cushions, my tears mingling with the sour smell of old perspiration and tobacco and dogs and stew.

After perhaps five minutes I felt the cool of glass on my hands. I opened my eyes and Thea was kneeling on the floor holding out a glass of brandy.

"You've never bedded my husband, have you?" she said.

I shook my head.

"You're a sad one, aren't you?" The voice was cool, the look clinical again.

I nodded.

"I hit a really big nerve, didn't I?"

"The biggest. My husband was shot dead. He was a policeman."

"Christ, I'm sorry."

"You weren't to know."

"What a pair we are," Thea said. "Now tell me what you know. Why is Jack getting out?"

"Francis Benton killed the old man. He drove down early to Elephant and Castle, lured Jack there, got the old man to send him away, and then killed him. He drove back, beat Jack home and then got into his pajamas."

Thea's eyes slitted again. I was getting wary of that look. "Is that right? And then what happened, do you think?"

"It doesn't matter. They don't have enough evidence to make a case against anyone for Francis's death. What matters is they drop the charges against Jack for the old man's murder. You could help. Maybe you saw Francis come back in his day clothes. Give them that at least."

Thea went into the scullery and came back with a glass of brandy for herself. "OK. So Jack is released. What then? What happens to you? Do you just disappear?"

I said nothing.

"Something else in mind? You and I share the prize? Jack has a nice bit of white and a nice bit of black? Separately or both at once? Chocolate pud with vanilla ice cream? He'd love that. No thank you very much. Grow up, will you?"

"So you wouldn't give a statement?" I said.

"I wouldn't give you the time of day if I'd invented the clock. But I'm curious. What's the fascination with Jack?"

"Books."

"Books?"

"Fiction. Good stuff. I've always been obsessed with books. I first met him in the bookshop."

Thea sipped her brandy. She looked at me and then at the ceiling.

"What?" I asked.

"Just thinking," she said. I looked at the ceiling but all I could see was a dusty lampshade and scrolls of peeling paint.

"I think I'd better go," I said.

"No, not yet," Thea said. "Have you got a job?"

"No."

"And you're obsessed with books?"

"Yes."

"Got any money?"

"Some."

"Do you want to buy the bookshop? I need to sell it. Cheap."

Thea got up and came back with an address book. She

copied a name and number on an old envelope. "This is the business broker. If you're interested, give him a call. I've got to cycle down to the school to meet the children."

"Thanks for talking to me," I said.

Thea held her palms up towards me. "Go."

***

On Tuesday morning, Simon was limbering up behind the cathedral in microscopic shorts that left only the anatomical specifics to the imagination, and two-hundred quid trainers. His vest said 'Nizhny Novgorod Hash House Harriers'.

"Gorky fan, are you?" I asked.

"Isn't that a park in Moscow??"

"Maxim Gorky, born in Nizhny Novgorod. Soviet author."

"Oh, that. I found it in a locker in a gym in Hull."

"I give up," I said. "Doesn't anyone read books anymore? Do you read books, Simon?"

"I like self-improvement books, and biographies of great leaders."

"You're taking the piss," I said.

"Did you know Gorky lived in Sorrento and Capri for a while? I like his early stuff better of course," Simon said.

"OK, stop showing off. Let's run."

Simon was bloody fit, but I eased into his rhythm and loped across the parkland at a speed that left most of the morning joggers in our wake.

"It's on," Simon said. "You were right about the ANPR. It places Francis Benton's van all the way to Elephant and Castle and back."

"Timing?"

"Spot on. We know what train Jack was on, and Francis

would have got home five minutes before Jack arrived at the station."

"So, ten minutes walk home gives Francis time to get changed and do whatever he did with Thea." I said. "What next?"

"It's early days," Simon said. "Let's stop for a minute."

We were approaching the edge of Parsons Wood. We stopped and bent over to catch our breath at a dewy clearing in a copse of beeches. There were the remains of a campfire in the middle of the clearing, six blackened beer bottles, a couple of charred sausages and a used condom. I heard a car engine and looked around. There was no road around here. The engine got louder.

"Let's get moving, Simon," I said, uneasy. He kicked me behind the knee and I fell down. A four-wheel drive appeared at the crest of a rise, and trundled down towards the copse. Boris got out. He had a golf club in his hand. I started to get up but he whacked me on the knee with the club, not hard enough to break anything but enough to send shards of white pain up and down my leg.

"I suppose I should say thank you, Missy," Boris said. "So thank you for working out where Benton went," and he whacked me on the other knee. "And thank you for making me look like a fucking twat with my men." Down came the club, catching me on my hip. "And thanks for all the work I've got to do now grovelling to the CPS." Whack on the same hip. "And thank you for humiliating me in my own house with Serpico and his spunk," and this time he handed the club to Simon, who gave me a gentle tap on the other hip.

"Serchio," I groaned.

"Whatever. You made a bloody fool of me in front of my wife. For Christ sake, Simon, put some energy into it,"

Boris said. Simon half closed his eyes, winced and brought the club down fast, just as I rolled over and tried to scramble to my feet. The club smashed the beer bottles and Boris wrestled to grab it from Simon.

"That's enough, Boris. We don't want her turning up at a hospital and people asking questions."

Boris stood over me, sweating in his suit. I could see his paunch pulsating as he gasped for breath.

"Look here, Missy. You will never ever do anything or say anything about this case again. You will keep away from Thea – oh yes, we know you were there – and you will keep away from Walsingham, even after he gets out. Is that clear?"

"Or what?"

"I'll come back and do the job properly."

They drove off in the four-wheel drive. I eased myself down onto the dewy grass and yanked a handful of wet weeds to cool my throbbing knees. The hip would wait, but I had to get the knee joints moving and stop the swelling. I stood up, straightened my legs and slowly hobbled towards the Cathedral.

I drove home, kicked off my trainers, unstrapped my phone from my armband, peeled off the Lycra and tied a bag of frozen peas to each knee. I looked at myself in the hall mirror. With my yellow sports bra and panties and my swollen green kneecaps I looked like a large rainforest insect.

Sitting at the kitchen table I transferred the sound file from the phone to my laptop and clicked the play icon.

"Gorky fan, are you?"

"Isn't that a park in Moscow?"

"Maxim Gorky, born in Nizhny Novgorod. Soviet

author."

"Oh, that. I found it in a locker in a gym in Hull."

I pressed the stop icon. This insect had a sting in her tail.

19: The book lover

The first thing I did was take down the display of books by the temporary manager's academic hero Professor Martin F. Mooney. Somehow the Australian PhD student had got hold of sixty copies of *Culturing Futures and Futuring Cultures* from an unpronounceable university press in Poland, and made them into a Hadrian's Wall in the shop window. Sixty images of the flop-haired professor staring dyspeptically into the eyes of shoppers had kept the plundering hordes out.

Thea was right: Books by Birdswell was virtually going for loose change. Like The Windings, the taint of murder was a terrific price deflator. The For Sale sign on the house had been joined by For Lease.

By mid-August the paperwork was signed, the money paid, the temporary manager let go. On a warm Saturday morning with the first tourists already snaffling Cornish pasties and take-away megaccinos on the cobblestones, I opened the shop and spent the morning rearranging the window and building cardboard display stands. There were reminders of Jack everywhere I looked: Yellow stickers with his handwriting, a linen jacket hanging on the stock room door, his mug on the tiny sink. And it wasn't just things, but the absence of things. I searched for travel guides and barely found any at all. Shouldn't there be a rack of the things on the pavement outside? And cookbooks — none! I found myself having imaginary conversations with my missing would-be lover. I'd teasingly chide him for being an absent-minded bookworm, and he'd chuckle and concede that he might stretch to ordering a couple of Lonely Planets. I'd laugh and tell him to go for a walk and come back in half an hour, and he'd come back and pretend amazement at the new stand of travel books. Why Kabul, he'd ask. Silly, I'd say, people buy travel books for places they won't necessarily go to. But why Armenian cooking? Dafty, people are always looking for something new for dinner parties.

And then I'd look at the takings and wonder if I'd had made an awful mistake, and acknowledge how pathetic my secret conversations were.

The truth was that I'd slowly come to separate the legally trained mind that ticked away in the back of my head from the Jack and Fiona show playing out front. As I made the shop my own, and Jack's presence faded, I had more grown-up reflections on the whole business. Admit it, I'd say to myself, you know almost nothing about him. You only met him a couple of times. As the first month of my bookselling career closed, I was having only occasional conversations with the absent Jack, mostly on the lines of why is there so much Isherwood stock when nobody reads him anymore.

One day a local author came in, older than me. I carried some of his titles, and had read two or three of them – quirky, unsettling novels that didn't end in a satisfying way, but left a precious but indistinct aftertaste. He was published by a small firm that didn't have the marketing power to promote their books widely, and they left it to their writers to find ways to publicise their work. The author wanted to have a book launch at my shop.

"What's involved?"

"Not much. Wine, cheese and biscuits, someone good to MC the event, and some advertising. I sign books at the end and you sell them. I should confess that I've launched it three or four times already. If you can live with that, we both win," my author said.

We met for dinner a couple of times in the following weeks and learned something of one another. He was an architect, working part-time so that he could write, and divorced with teenaged children. He knew who I was. Everyone in town did, but he was courteous enough not to talk about any of it. I wondered if I could possibly have a normal relationship with a normal human being. So far, the record was grim: I was in love with the memory of my dead husband, I'd dallied with a Sydney cop and the narcissistic carnivore Hugh, and then become smitten with an accused murderer who I barely knew. One evening the author and I found ourselves in his bed: No fireworks, but a tender exchange of passion.

And the launch of his novel *An Englishman's Guide to Fidelity* was a surprise. My life as a widowed gym-addicted police officer hadn't left time for anyone outside professional contacts, let alone friends or casual acquaintances. But my author's book launch crowd were a stratum of cathedral town society I'd never known existed: Earnest students – the kind who look like Che Guevara and Janis Joplin, whichever era they are born in; elderly amateur intellectuals – the women with close-cropped hair and large red framed glasses, and the men with embroidered waistcoats and brown trainers; comfy young couples in conservative wear paired together like lovebirds; assorted old lecturers and young tutors from the university, looking harassed and twitchy from marking essays into the early hours; and the old codgers and their mates on the scrounge for a plastic cup of Rioja and as many cheese cubes as they could snaffle up. My author greeted them at the door and I milled around shaking hands and topping up the plastic cups. I couldn't remember when I'd last spent time with forty or so people who demanded nothing of me.

My author had appointed a stand-up comic – a friend who didn't expect a fee – to MC the event and launch the book. The comic rang a small bell and stood on a shelving stool.

"Fank you ladies and gentlemen. I note that all the wine has gone so you can fuck off 'ome," he said, and walked out of the door and into the street, at which a couple of Che Guevaras rushed outside, captured him and stood him back on the shelving stool. And that set the tone for the rest of the evening. The wine did indeed soon run out, but I gave two Janis Joplins fifty quid, and they came back with half a dozen bottles of something exiled from the New World. My author autographed and sold fifteen copies of the novel and listened philosophically as the old codgers lectured him on using the f-word on the first page.

As the guests left, I saw my author talking to three people I'd noticed sitting in the front row.

"Fiona," he said, "These are my beta readers – Gus, Pilar and Jonquil. I'm taking them to dinner at the Secret Garden. Why don't you join us?"

We locked up and walked through the cobbled lanes to the restaurant, where my author had booked a little nook off the main dining room.

"My secret. Magical things have happened in this

room," he said.

He'd mentioned before that the beta readers had been with him from the beginning of the novel. He'd recruited them from his circle of acquaintances, making sure that none of them knew each other. They'd receive draft chapters from him, with their email addresses blind copied so that they never came into direct contact. When they sent him comments, he summarised them and sent them out blind copied to the group. This was the first time any of them had met, which perhaps explained why they were sitting rather stiffly in the crammed nook pretending fascination with the menu.

"What was the incentive to keep reading?" I asked.

The beta readers looked up from their menus at my author.

"I promised them parts in the novel."

"And are you happy with your parts?" I asked the three.

The heavily bearded man in his forties between the two women – he turned out to be Scottish – said, "I'm not sure actually. Was I meant to be the truck driver?"

One of the women – again in her forties, trim, conservative, maybe a solicitor – blushed heavily.

"Something wrong?" I asked, and the third woman – younger, arty looking, unnaturally black hair – laughed heartily and said, "He was quite a performer, that driver."

"So," I said, "You were performing with ..." I gestured towards the solicitor lady, who smiled slightly and said, "It would appear so".

"And I'm the dyke?" the black-haired woman asked.

My author roared with laughter, and the trio followed suit in a slightly forced manner. Drinks flowed, and in a short time the nook was filled with the sound of clinking glasses and the aromas of very fine food. The owner,

Maxwell, looked in occasionally with louche expressions and more bottles.

"Now these two," my author indicated the Scot and the black-haired woman, "were my left and right brains. I could always rely on dear Gus to get right to the detail, like a scientist dissecting an insect ..."

"Well I am a scientist, you silly sod," Gus said.

"Just so. But Pilar, she'd read the same chapter and it'd be like a theatre review, from the heart, big florid adjectives all over the place ..."

"That's because I'm a drama teacher, darling!"

"And what about Jonquil?" I asked in the direction of the solicitor lady, but my real attention was on Gus and Pilar, who were now occupying enough of each other's personal space to suggest that the Secret Garden's magic was at work.

The party split into two, with the solicitor lady, my author and I settling into an earnest discussion about books, while Gus and Pilar ran their own sideshow. This entailed making comments on our discussion, which were directed to each other rather than the whole group. Thus an odd discourse of courtship proceeded alongside our literary discussion until Gus and Pilar retreated into their own gilded cage and we three were left, talk fading, gazing at the lovebirds.

My author made harrumphing sounds and dug into his jacket for his wallet. Maxwell appeared: "*L'addition, mes enfants?*"

"Just bring us the bill, you old fake," my author said, and Maxwell guffawed.

"We were at school together. He's as French as my foot."

Outside Gus said, "I'll be off then. It's just a quick walk

to the hotel."

Pilar said, "I'll walk with you".

"You're both staying at the same hotel?" I asked. They looked slightly bashful, and then linked arms and nodded. We watched them walk away, and then stop to kiss under a lamp post.

I turned to my author: "I thought they didn't know each other until today."

"Actually," Jonquil said, "You forgot to blind copy the emails once. We saw each other's addresses."

My author looked alarmed: "Oh my goodness. So they were pretending they hadn't met?"

"Actually no," she said. "I'm a good judge of people, and I don't think they'd been in direct contact until tonight."

"What, love at first sight, just like that?"

"It happens," I said.

"In books," my author said.

We walked Jonquil to the station and put her on the train to London, and then went back to the shop to vacuum the carpets and wash up. My new lover and I embraced and agreed to meet the next evening. As he walked away, I began to imagine richer possibilities for my life than I'd hoped for in a few years.

***

It had been five months since I'd visited Jack in prison. I hadn't been back to visit him: Not because I hadn't wanted to. In the first few months, I ached to see him, but I knew that Boris would have told Riswell Park to block me from visiting. But as the year wore on and the last of Jack's traces disappeared from the shop – I gave his linen jacket to one of the old codgers – my irrational hunger for the imprisoned bookseller had given way to a coolly rational yearning to know the truth about that day in March when Francis Benton and Errol Sparkes died. Rational did I say? I still had trouble discerning what motivated my yearning: To know the truth about a man I had thrown away my career for? To see justice done in a court of law? But what could I do? I was sure that Thea wouldn't see me again, and I wasn't going to chance my kneecaps by contacting Simon. I was a bookseller, hardly in a position to pursue some kind of private gumshoe quest for the truth.

The one thing I was clear about was that Boris Rance would answer for beating me up. I hadn't thought much about what I'd do with the recording of that morning in the woods, but as the weeks passed and I tended the bookshop back to health, a compartment of my mind constructed a sort of moral scaffold to prop up a resolution that I could live with: I excused myself for my pathetic infatuation with Jack on the grounds that I had been in a state of unresolved grief for Darren. As for my unprofessional behaviour in trying to shield Jack from the legal consequences of the law – handing back the file to Boris and sabotaging the interview – I calculated that very little harm had been done to the investigation, which was itself an unprofessional mess that would inevitably spill over anyway. I'd started the process by showing that Francis could have driven down to Elephant and Castle that morning, and that served as expiation for my stupidity. And Boris – he deserved whatever came to him for beating me with a golf club. As for Jack and Thea, I just didn't care anymore: If she chose to keep her mouth shut about Francis and he chose to protect her, they deserved each other.

With the exorcism of Jack the bookseller from Books by Birdswell, the shop became a little magnet for locals and tourists. I started to host book club meetings, book launches, and coffee mornings for the town's cosy literati, and I'd agreed to give a couple of talks in a creative writing course at the university. Even better, I could see the shop starting to provide me with an income that would reverse the drain on my savings.

Then two things happened. The first was that in October I found that my author had made me pregnant. While he was philosophical (he was philosophical about everything – what to have for breakfast, the price of books, an ant on the wall) I became someone else, a Fiona Salmon shifted off centre, a Fiona Salmon no longer exclusively focussed on unravelling the knotty strands of the last few years of my life, but curious to acquaint myself with the idea of a miracle inside my belly. The practicalities didn't seem insoluble: I could run the business with a child in tow, and my author philosophically offered to help out in the shop. I didn't pressure him – I wasn't sure I wanted him as a life partner, but I knew by now that he was a decent man who would take into account my wishes when I had worked out what they were. He'd been through fatherhood before. "Take it week by week," he said. "Your feelings will resolve as the baby grows."

The second thing was a letter from Thea asking me to visit her – she didn't give a reason, but wrote formally and courteously. The idea frightened me because of Boris's threat, but at the same time it was oddly intriguing. I lay awake sifting the reasons for my interest and eventually realised that I'd never considered Thea as a mother: A woman with children, yes, but not a mother – because I hadn't had an authentic innate sense of what being a mother was like. Now with life inside me, I realised that my view of Thea had been two-dimensional. I'd grown a third dimension, and so had she. There were things I wanted to tell her and ask her.

The next day I visited a solicitor with my audio recording. I had worked with her in my time as a detective, and I trusted her. The day after that we met with two granite faced male senior officers, who sat across the desk from us glowering and exhaling sour breath. In my written statement I listed the registration number of the four-wheel drive, the precise items of clothes that Boris and Simon had been wearing, the brand and number of the golf club, the genders, race, outfits and approximate ages of the other runners in the park, and the small plaster that Boris had on the top of his ear. I included time coded photographs of the bruises.

"You seem to have a photographic memory," one of the officers said.

"She's famous for it," my solicitor said.

She rang me two days later: "Boris Rance and his offsider have both been suspended. It might get rough for you yet."

20: A visit to Thea

"You look different," I said to Thea. The expensive choppy hairstyle was back, and she was wearing new jeans and a cashmere jumper.

"So do you," Thea said.

"I wish I could get my hair to do that," I said, immediately feeling foolish. My hair is like fuse wire.

She looked at my hair and frowned. "Yes, well I'm solvent again. Didn't you know? I've got a buyer for the house. Not the amount I wanted of course, but given the circumstances ..."

I wondered about Jack's place in this, but then I remembered that the agreement for the bookshop had borne Thea's name, not his. Was the house hers too?

The cottage looked more spruce, too. The old sofas had been replaced with new stuff – Ikea by the look of it, but bright and welcoming. The ironing board was gone, and the piles of essays were stacked neatly in shiny black in-trays on the shelf of a bay window.

Thea briskly made some decent coffee: "There's still a bit of morning sun at the back. If you're warm enough we can have it out there."

We sat at a sagging rustic bench on a deeply worn brick patio, looking at a forlorn orchard of scraggy apple trees. "My children's heritage," Thea said. Then she said, "Why have you come?"

"You asked me to come," I said.

"Yes, I did, but I'm interested in why you actually came.

You had a choice. You exercised that choice."

I pondered this question, and the way it had been delivered. I'd begun to lose the habit of talking tough in my transition to bookseller, but Thea's tone had stirred the cop in me. She had the manner of a district nurse, a house mistress in a boarding school – or at least how I imagined such people from films I had seen. I didn't see why I should answer and I said so, not rudely but firmly enough to signal that I wasn't to be made an idiot of.

"Suit yourself," Thea said. "But just so that things are clear between us, there are topics that are off limits. I'm not going to talk to you about either of the deaths, so don't bother asking."

I fell for it. "I'll be off then," I said, using the trick of the MC at the book launch. I'd walked halfway back to the car and was reaching in my bag for the keys when she said, "All right, no need for theatrics, I'll behave."

We both laughed – not easily – but it was something.

Back at the garden bench Thea said, "So you have the advantage. I invited you and I suppose I'd better tell you why."

"OK," I said. "In a minute. Can we just sit and drink the coffee? I'm tired after the drive." I'd been getting weary in the daytime, but I really needed a few minutes to work out how to approach this difficult woman. So much for the bond of motherhood.

A keen breeze ruffled the apple trees, bringing a distant whiff of something rural and sour. I slid a few inches along the bench to find some sun. I asked for a glass of water.

When Thea came back with the water she sat opposite

me and looked me up and down forensically.

"Do you always stare at your guests?" I asked.

"Sorry, it's a bad habit of mine, and I know that I sometimes seem rude. Can I ask you something? It's not my business of course," Thea said.

"I know what you're going to ask me and yes, I'm expecting a baby."

Thea allowed a distant smile. "I thought so. You look less – angular somehow."

"That's as much to do with the fact that I've given up punishing myself in the gym. I've put on five kilos. You can see it in my face."

"Punishing yourself? That's a strange choice of words. Have you done something that warrants punishment?"

I didn't answer the question, but I stored it away for later. In my internal ponderings, the word punishment often popped up in the context of the gym, but I'd never made the connection with transgression.

"I'm guessing," I said, "that your curiosity isn't just coffee morning chit chat. You're wondering if my pregnancy could be connected with your husband." She didn't respond, so I pressed on. "You're wondering if I got myself impregnated in some conjugal visit facility smelling of Dettol and equipped with wipes and a sterile bin?"

"I wouldn't have put it quite so coarsely," Thea said calmly. "But I did wonder."

"Have you ever been in a prison? Could you have a fuck in a painted brick room with a guard outside?"

Thea scraped the froth from the inside of her coffee cup and put the spoon in her mouth upside down. She had no inhibition about letting a conversation hang. I sensed a coldly mechanical intellect, a mind like an abacus.

At last she said, "That really wasn't worthy of you. You're a highly intelligent woman. Surely you can see that you're not going to rattle me by saying fuck?"

"We're not getting far, are we?" I said.

"Where do you want us to go?" Thea said, and this time I led the silence, holding her eye boldly. After thirty seconds or so she said, "OK, truce. I think I like you. Let's talk properly. Tell me about Jack. I gather that you've given him up. That's why you're here."

I told it briefly: My author, the success of the bookshop, my waning feelings for Jack, and my embarrassment at the memory of visiting him in prison and declaring my devotion for him.

"Well, thanks. At least I know I'm not competing for him." I couldn't decode the inference; was she being ironic, sarcastic?

"Anyway, I hope things work out with your author. What's his name by the way?"

I told her. "Oh him. Yes, I met him once at the university. Mature man, good looking. He was writer in residence for half a semester. His office was always full of swooning girls. And a few mature aged female students." I didn't react.

There was another long silence. A tiny beetle walked across the table and Thea tracked its path with a finger until it fell into a crack. She wore orangey nail varnish that would have looked slutty on me. The sun had moved and I shifted along the bench to catch the last rays of faint warmth. I heard sparrows, a dog very far away. Another faint waft of manure drifted past on a warm air current.

"I suppose you've got something else to tell me," Thea said.

"If you're interested, but then it could be off-limits, I

suppose," I said. It was a stupidly offhand remark, and I was tired of sparring with her.

"That's disingenuous. The difference between me and you is that I could get arrested for murder. You just got the sack, that's all. You can hardly blame me for being careful."

"I suppose I can't," I said. "But I didn't come here to interrogate you. When you wrote to me, I hoped we could straighten things out – about Jack. It's pretty obvious that you've intentionally isolated yourself from your husband to protect yourself – or him, or somebody, and you haven't got a clue what's happening to him."

"And why should you appoint yourself as my information bureau? And while you're generating wild hypotheses about me, my advice is don't bother. You'll never know what happened the day Francis died, and all your fishing and guessing is a waste of time."

"Fair enough," I said. "Anyway, you'll be getting your husband back soon. That's all."

"When?"

"Soon. I don't know exactly when." I took my phone out and found the audio recording of my beating. "This is the detective who got Jack arrested for murdering the old man. He's beating me up with a golf club because I exposed him."

Thea looked stony. As the track rolled, the muscles of her neck strained and she stared fixedly at some point a hundred miles away. The firm flesh of her face paled, the corners of her mouth stretched downwards and made deep grooves in her jaw. When the recording had finished, she suddenly stood up, shook her head, squeezed her eyes tight, opened them, inhaled and exhaled: "You've been brave. More courageous than I've ever been. Is the recording in the hands of the police? '

"At the very top. I went with my lawyer and made a statement. I think I'm safe. The Crown Prosecution Service will withdraw the charges against Jack and he'll be released."

"And that'll be it? What about Francis? If he killed the old man, what happens next?" Thea asked.

"Nothing. Jack's half-brother is dead, don't you remember? Sorry, off-limits of course. But when Jack gets out, you'd both better agree on a story. Don't think the CPS has given up on finding out how Francis died. And with Jack out of prison there'll be a few ambitious cops keen to get you or him or both of you in the frame for Francis."

Thea sat down again. "What makes you think that I'm going to be with Jack when he gets out?"

"Aren't you?"

"My business I suppose. I shouldn't have mentioned it."

"I don't think you ever mention anything that you shouldn't," I said.

Thea gave me a very long look. "Thanks for the warning anyway. There'll be a knock on the door one day. I just hope the children are at school when they come to get me."

She seemed to soften, and said, "Look, let me make you a sandwich. I can't send a pregnant woman away unfed."

While she prepared the food in the scullery I wandered into the orchard. The misshapen overgrown apple trees rustled like dowagers in faded brown taffeta. Small hard green apples rotted in the leaf litter. I seethed: An hour with Thea had yielded almost nothing, and where I had seen a crack in her shell – her remark that she might not be with Jack in the future – I had no idea whether her reply was genuine or a stratagem. I knew nothing about her as a woman, let alone as a mother.

I wasn't prepared to go home with nothing to show for my work.

As I finished my sandwich Thea looked meaningfully at her watch. "Don't rush," she said.

"I won't. I've got some questions to ask you before I go." I was in cop mode. I couldn't help myself.

"Questions?"

"Well, statements if you like. I'm going to tell you the various ways that Francis could have died."

"I can't stop you. There's freedom of speech in this country. "

I held her eye as I had before.

"Frank told Jack that he'd killed the old man but set Jack up for the murder, and Jack threw him over the balustrade."

"I like this game," Thea said unblinking. "Whoops, you should have said that I threw him over, or we did it together. That makes three hypotheses rather than one."

"Jack came back and found you in bed with Francis, and threw him over the balustrade."

"That makes four hypotheses."

"Francis had a brainstorm and threw himself over."

"Five." Not a blink.

"You and Francis set Jack up for the old man's murder, but Jack came back and worked out what had happened, and threw Francis over."

"Six, and of course under that scenario we can't add me as a possible suspect," Thea said.

"Not so fast. You could have said that you were

working with Francis under duress, and you decided you'd had enough, and so you killed him."

"All right, seven." Not a trace of emotion had passed over her face.

"Jack discovered Francis trying to rape you and threw him over the balustrade."

"Eight. I take it you're done? Wait a second, you forgot one."

"Really?"

"Francis was using the balustrade for tightrope walking practice and he slipped."

"Goodbye," I said but I wasn't quite finished. As we both stood up I approached her as if to embrace her, and her face showed a minute trace of alarm. I stopped short and brought my face uncomfortably close to hers and gently grasped her elbow. Very quietly I said, "Thea, it was the children. That's the key. That's why Francis died. I don't know why exactly, but I'm certain. You know that this is true". To my astonishment she drew me tight against her body in a swift embrace, broke free and strode back into the house.

It was early afternoon when I got home. My author had offered to look after the shop for the day so I spent the afternoon on the couch listening to Satie, leafing through glossy art books, and thinking about life with a baby. My author didn't figure in my imaginings, but I wasn't concerned. I roused myself to make some tea and toast around five. While the kettle boiled I stood on the front doorstep and watched a cat fruitlessly stalking a pair of ducks that had flown up from the lake in the cathedral grounds. It was chilly. I closed the door but left it unlocked, and took my snack into the sitting room. The afternoon had alternated between sunny breaks and little flurries of rain, and now the lowering sun sent horizontal rays through the window that lit up silvery motes of gently falling dust. I took my toast meditatively, thought about Thea, failed to rekindle the anger that had led me to enumerate the possible ways of Francis's death, wondered about the hug. I dozed a little, and had fond dreams where Darren was walking by a river and was transformed into a brown infant and back again. I woke to recall that my husband was dead, but without distress.

The garden gate clicked, and my author rang the doorbell in Morse code – dot dash, dot dash dash dot.

"It's not locked Tony. Come in."

"How are you?" my author asked.

"Content. Satisfied. Like a boulder's been lifted off me. Don't know why really, or perhaps I do. Was the shop OK?"

"It was a good day. The tourists had their wallets open. How was the visit to Thea?"

"Infuriating, instructive, complicated. I'll need to think it all through I suppose."

The fact that my author hadn't yet sunk into a chair and begun to muse on beauty, futility, destiny, the price of spring onions, climate change or whatever was currently preoccupying him, was a sign that he was uncomfortable.

"I have to tell you something, Fiona."

"That sounds grave."

"Well it is really, in some respects. Depends which way you approach it. Like everything we must weigh up ..."

"Better tell me," I said.

"I'm going back to my wife. And my children."

I said nothing.

"And my house."

Now he'd got it all out he sat down with his back to the

sunny window, so that his face was in deep shade. It struck me how, with his face obscured, it could have been Jack Walsingham or anyone else sitting there. Gazza, Hugh, just another bloke.

"I suppose I expected you would," I said without acrimony. "Not much point in you hanging around here, is there?"

A brief embrace and he was gone. In the last of the weakening sunbeams I lay still, ran my fingers over my belly and closed my eyes, my mind languidly searching for the dream with the river where Darren and the infant were.

PART THREE:
THEA AND JACK

21: A face from the past

I stood in the bay window of Forty Apple Trees watching Fiona's car pull away, regretting the way I had treated her. It was obvious that she had tried her best to be warm to me but I had sabotaged her efforts with my brusque manner. I meant it when I said I liked her, and I could imagine her as a friend. God knows, I need some friends in this forsaken lane with its forty decaying apple trees and its damp breezes. I avoid talking to the neighbours. I cannot take the risk of them working out who I am and gossiping among the locals, so that William and Zita are taunted at school for what their parents may or may not have done.

I meant it when I hugged Fiona, or I meant something at least: Thank you for being an adult that I can touch, even briefly? Thank you for the news you brought? Thank you for bearing a bully's blows so that my husband can be released? I am not sure. I am hollowed out, so that my responses are like a half-deflated balloon being distractedly tapped into the air at the fag-end of a party – flaccid, directionless, futile. I wondered how much Fiona really wanted to know what happened on the day that Francis died. On reflection, not very much perhaps. I suspected she had been ill, a breakdown of some kind – yes, she had to have been ill to behave with Jack as she had. Perhaps she had come to tidy things up with me and Jack, to close the chapter.

The late autumn sun faltered behind a clotty drift of cloud and I went inside to warm the house and prepare things for when the children came back from school.

***

"Thea. Lovely Thea."

"I guessed it was you. Now leave us alone," I said and slammed the door. A minute later I heard loud revving and smelt exhaust smoke in the sharp January air. I looked out and saw him standing on the pavement with one foot inside the door of a dirty white van gunning the accelerator. I opened the door and called out to him, "I'm phoning the police," but he laughed and turned up the radio in the van so that the street was filled with sickening bass thumps.

I beckoned for him to come back, and he cut the engine and the radio. "Just as far as the front door. What do you want? Why are you tormenting us?"

"I've come to visit my sister-in-law. At, what is it ...?" He looked at the carved wooden house sign, "The Windings, very classy."

"There's nobody of that description here. You've got yourself confused. I really am going to call the police."

"No, wait. It's you. You're my sister-inlaw. I'm Jack's long-lost brother Francis."

"This is outrageous. Just turn around and crawl back to whatever putrid heap you burrowed out of."

"Putrid? You've still got a lovely way with words, sister-in-law. Yes, putrid's how they treated poor Francis, quietly sent me off for adoption, forget Daddy's nasty secret. Look, do we have to have this discussion on the doorstep?

It's freezing cold besides anything else."

"It isn't a discussion. I'm calling the police right now."
I stabbed some random numbers on the mobile and held
the phone to my ear. "Yes, an emergency, police. There's
an intruder, I'm at ..."

But Francis laughed, pushed past me, and was now in
the vestibule casting his eye over the furniture and the
carpets with the demeanor of a second-hand dealer.
"You've done nicely, very nicely. How's my niece and
nephew?"

I grabbed an umbrella and swung it at his head, but he
grabbed the spiked end and twisted it out of my hand.
"Now, that's not very family-like, is it?"

"Don't you dare mention my family with that filthy
mouth!"

"It wasn't so filthy before. I seem to remember you
rather relished a bit of tongue ..."

I collected myself. He was as vile as I remembered him,
but now there was a sinister edge that I'd sensed but not
directly observed. I fleetingly analysed the circumstances
before me, and tried to recall what Jack had said about
him. He was a planner, otherwise he would not be here
now with a preposterous story, and with me at home
alone. He was also unpredictably violent – he'd knocked
Jack around, but I also knew that the unpredictability
would be on the part of the victim. The quick violence
would be a contingency, allowed for in a well-planned
strategy. While I could feel a cold sheen of sweat under
my winter clothes, the logical side of my mind calculated
that I was in no immediate jeopardy.

We stood and looked at one another, he with a
sardonic smile, I with what I hoped was an absence of
expression. I had to keep him in ignorance of my fear and

my next move.

"We'll wait to see what Jack has to say," I said. "He'll be back in an hour for lunch, but you must let me warn him."

I dialled Jack at the shop. "Francis has come to the house. I'm not in danger, and I'm not calling the police." I spoke over his shocked protest: "He has something to tell you. He says he's your brother, or half-brother." There was silence, and then Jack said, "I'll get someone to take over. See you in ten minutes".

I indicated a chair, and Francis sat down. I stood as far away as I could, ready to flee into the corridor that led to the kitchen and the back door.

"Any chance of a piss?"

"No."

"I'm busting."

"Your problem."

"I'll go in the van. Don't lock me out."

He let himself out and reappeared in a couple of minutes. "I keep an orange squash bottle behind the back seat just in case."

"I'm entirely uninterested," I said, and we remained in silence for five minutes, he looking at the pictures on the wall and I staring at him expressionlessly.

Then he said, "Of course he doesn't know, Jack that is?"

"He doesn't know and he isn't going to know," I said. Francis gave me a leer and said, "So we've got a confidence between us then," and I felt a squirm of nausea. I also needed the toilet, and I clenched my knees while we waited for Jack.

I was struck by Jack's composure when he came into the house. Considering that Francis had bashed him, blackmailed him and threatened the children, I would not have been surprised to see a man in a black rage. Instead he was calm and prepared.

"Some ground rules before we start," Jack said.

"Now look old son, let's get straight who makes the rules ..."

"I'm sorry," Jack said. "You're in my house, you've virtually imprisoned my wife, and you're about to spin me a rubbishy story to extort money out of me. And I've got a tyre lever from that white van inside my jacket. That is your van, I take it, the unlocked one that stinks like a urinal? I thought so. How would it go? 'The intruder came at me with a tyre lever, we struggled, I wrested it from his hand and hit him with it to protect my wife ...' Quite neat really."

Francis arched his eyebrows and mimed terror.

"So these are the rules for today: You tell your story, we listen, you leave the house and drive down to the cathedral and wait, my wife and I discuss your story, I walk down to the cathedral and tell you what is going to happen."

Francis looked at me with the faintest hint of query and I made an infinitesimal nod of my head. I had not the slightest clue what would happen next. He began to speak.

"The first thing I want to say is that I unreservedly apologise for my actions in relation to your family." My viscera shrivelled and my head whirled. The trite formulation warned of some grotesquerie that I could barely imagine. Jack stood with a face of stone.

"All my actions were the consequence of a ..."

"You sound like a priest caught with his hand down the choir boy's pants," Jack said. "Now speak normally, like the evil sod that you are."

Francis grinned and went on. "Yeah, that's best isn't it? Brother to brother, nice and casual. All right, I know I've caused you a lot of bother, but I did it for a reason. See, I've kept an eye on you and Thea the last few years, just checking how you were doing, you know. How you came into our money, moved out of London. It's my line of business, you see. I'm here, I'm there, I keep my eyes open ..."

"Just get on with it. We know about your line of business. You're a con man and an extortionist," Jack said.

"Slow down," Francis said. "You're right, some might say that's what I am, but you and Thea, that's different, that's family. It's not extortion when you want to get what's rightfully yours."

"This is absurd," I said. "Why wait so long? If you were Jack's half-brother, why didn't you contact us five years ago after the crash? You weren't at the funeral." I hoped my protests did not sound as half-hearted as they seemed to me. I was on quicksand.

"Exactly," Jack said. "Now let's get to the core of all this. I've heard you out so far. You say you're my half-brother. Show me some proof or get out."

"It's in the van."

"What's in the van?"

"The proof."

"Can Thea go and get it?"

"Yes, there's a brown envelope on the front seat."

I slipped out, and took the envelope from the foul-smelling van. When I came back in, Jack was holding the tyre lever.

"Thea, open it please."

I carefully opened the envelope – I never rip them

open – and pulled out a photocopied birth certificate. The mother's name was unknown to me, but there was Jack's father's name, occupation Doctor, and the address of the house we stood in. The birth was registered eleven months after Jack's. I handed it to Jack. He glanced at it and said, "You think I'm a fool?"

Francis said, "No, I know you're not a fool but neither am I. I wouldn't pull a stunt like this when you can order a copy for nine quid at the Government Records Office".

Jack looked rattled for the first time since he'd come in. "Even so," he said, "who's to say what really could have happened? There could be any number of ways that my father's name ended up here. And who says you're this person anyway?"

"I say that I'm that person, that's who."

"Well, I'm sorry. You're no part of my family."

"Ever heard of a Y chromosome test?" Francis said. "Three hundred quid. Do it yourself. Results in five days."

Nobody said anything. The floor creaked as Jack shifted his weight. I said, "What next, then?" I wanted Francis out.

"Back to the ground rules," Jack said, his composure regained. "You drive down to the cathedral and I'll be there in due course."

"There's one more thing. I've got nowhere to stay. I've been kicked out of my flat."

In Oxford, I thought. God knows what crooked arrangements someone like Francis negotiated to keep a roof over his head. Did he barter blackmail photographs for a free flat? I thought of the wretched Marjorie Smith at the Bathwell Trust. Anything was possible, I knew that of Francis.

"Not my problem," Jack said. "Now go."

The air in the vestibule seemed cleaner after Francis had gone. We bolted the front and back doors and went into the sitting room. I poured two large brandies.

"He's a monster," I said, but Jack made no comment. He sipped the brandy and gazed at the ornate plasterwork on the ceiling.

"He's going to ruin us," I said.

"Funny. All these years and I'd never realised that the ceiling rose was off-centre. Had you noticed, Thea?"

"Jack, he's so dangerous. This brother nonsense. It's a sick joke. We know how evil he is."

"Do you remember Aunt Florence?"

"What's Aunt Florence got to do with anything?" I said sharply. I needed to know what course Jack had in mind for Francis so that I could keep ahead.

"She was the arty one, all flowery kaftans, so different from Dad," Jack said. I could not imagine where this conversation was leading. I played along.

I said, "Yes, they were worlds apart. She liked her drink, didn't she? I don't think we've seen her since the funeral."

"It was the funeral I was thinking about. Do you remember how she got a bit loud at the funeral breakfast and called Dad some unfortunate names?"

"Yes, it was right here in this room. None of it made sense as I remember. Can we get back to the issue at hand?" I said.

"The issue at hand." Jack said. "Thea, this isn't exactly a tutorial discussion topic. It's fucking serious." My husband sighed, slid deep into the armchair, and gripped his brow with his big fingers.

"Look at my hands," he said. "They're trembling. It's not every day that I wield a tyre lever."

The house phone rang and I picked it up. It was Francis.

"Get a move on sister-in-law. I'm freezing my bollocks off down here."

"Just wait. Jack won't be long," I said, and put the phone gently back on the handset. "What shall we do, Jack? This brother nonsense is revolting. We just need to get rid of him."

"You mean lure him round the back of the cathedral and bash his head in? Tie him up in his van and run a hose from the exhaust into the window. Invite him in and give him poisoned fruit cake?"

"It's hideous," I said. "He can't seriously believe that we'll go along with the idea."

"Can't he?"

"Of course not." I spat the words out, as if trying to spit his memory out of my body. "A half-brother for pity's sake. And what comes next? A secret will? We hand over the house?"

Jack looked at his feet and spoke without lifting his eyes to mine. "The thing is, Thea ..."

"Yes. Tell me." I began to perspire as I had when Francis had burst in. I was ready to tell Jack about the events of so many years ago. I had my account ready for when the moment came. "Jack, I think I know what you are going to tell me."

Jack looked at me directly. "I hardly think so unless you're a mind reader. What I was going to say is that I do have a half-brother."

22: The man in the dirty white van

Jack wiped the tyre lever with a rag soaked in methylated spirits, and held it with a paper napkin. "I'll toss it into his van," he said. I watched him go, wondering how it had come to this. Two dried up human husks being blown here and there by a gust of dirty wind.

I had slowly grown to recognise Jack's emptiness during the passing of the years. With him it was his eras: The Cooling, the Warming, the Turning: One -ing after another, labels he would invent to parcel up periods in his life and to validate them with depth and complexity of feeling where there was none. The quirky jokes, the deadpan irony, the peppering of his his speech with obscure literary trivia – it was a veneer, burnished to a patina, the early performances applauded in his teenage years by his mother.

I had seen it for myself when I first met his parents at a dinner the mother had arranged at a restaurant in Bushey, neutral territory. The occasion was aimed more at seeing off the immigrant girlfriend than welcoming me as a potential daughter in law. She ignored me throughout the meal, fawning over Jack's witticisms and glaring at her mute husband. My own hollowness – and it took me years to see it – was more an urge to substitute reason for sentiment, to analyse instead of feel. I have learned to pretend to feel.

Jack returned in half an hour.

"Is he coming back? I have to pick the children up

soon."

"No, not today. He says he'll sleep in the van for tonight."

"For tonight? And what about the other nights? Jack, I'm scared of what you're about to tell me."

"It's not that simple Thea. Remember I was talking about Aunt Florence before?"

"Yes, I wondered what that was about. Go on."

"And Thea, do you remember how I took her downstairs into the consulting rooms after she'd made a scene upstairs?"

"Yes," I said. Evidently the day held more surprises.

"She told me that Dad had confided in her a few days before the crash. He said his illegitimate son had turned up."

"Go on," I croaked, gravel in my throat.

"He told Aunt Florence that he couldn't tell Mum – it would destroy her."

"That would have been typical of him. Your father thought that women belonged to some lower order that could only cope with housework. She always had to be the obedient Doctor's wife – spotless waiting room, copies of *The Lady* and *The Countryside* on the coffee table; sherry at six thirty and three-course dinner served at seven o'clock sharp."

"You're right," I said. "He belonged in the nineteen thirties. The thing was that Aunt Florence already knew about it. She'd known about it for years. She'd been teaching an art class – you know, a hobby course at the evening college, and during the break the students had been complaining about husbands. One of the women told them about a neighbour who'd just had a baby out of marriage to a doctor, and how she'd convinced him to put his name on the birth certificate. Aunt Florence did a bit of discreet investigating and realised that it was Dad, and she confronted him."

"But it's out of character. He wasn't the adultery type. But then children on the side do seem to run in the family," Thea said.

"You know how to stick the knife in."

"And you just slide it in gently," Thea said. "So why did he agree to have his name on the birth certificate?"

"I can tell you that. He told Aunt Florence that the woman was going to give the boy up for adoption. She was one of his patients of course, so he was potentially in enormous trouble. It seems that the woman agreed not to make any demands on him if he was named as the father. She handed him a time bomb. And the time bomb's in a dirty white van down the road."

"Sorry, Jack. There is someone who calls himself Francis in a dirty white van down the road. We're a long way off establishing that Francis is your half-brother. What about this chromosome test?"

"That can wait for now. In fact, I doubt if we'll even need it. We had a good talk down by the cathedral. Francis knows things that he could only have learned from Dad. He says that after he contacted Dad he accepted him as his son and wanted to make amends for abandoning him ..."

"You mean he confronted your father and threatened to blackmail him? How can you be so gullible?"

"Hear me out, Thea. He knows things about the family."

"What things?" I said sharply. I hid my trembling hands in my lap, and focussed on breathing calmly.

"Things he could only have learned from Dad – my

birthmark, the racy novels that Mum wrote and tried to hide from Dad. It's weird."

I tried to speak but could not. I had been on the point of telling Jack on the evening of Christmas Day when I had almost been sick in the gutter. Could I have been plainer, telling him I imagined the face of a man who I was supposed not to have seen? But how could foolish Jack have possibly made the link between my peculiar outburst and the unimaginable reality? And what else had Francis prised out of me during our squalid couplings in the reptile house?

I composed myself, put back on the efficient Thea mask. "Time to get the children. You're sure he won't be back today?"

"He promised me."

**

The drive to the school took me past the cathedral, but Francis's van was not to be seen. I had never liked the cathedral town, never liked its smug tidiness, the air of entitlement among the burgers and their wives who motored out to the golf club for Sunday lunch. Leaving London had been a foregone conclusion for Jack, not an option for me. We were certainly struggling to survive, but much as I would complain about the cramped flat and the scrimping budget, I had no real desire to leave Kilburn with its rowdy pubs and familiar shabby markets and rainbow population. But how could I resist? For Jack it was 'obvious', it was 'common sense', it was 'best for the children'. To object was to be blind, to have no sense, to be neglectful of Zita and William. When I confided in my mother, she was astounded that I was hesitant about moving to a 'grand house in the country' and Jack being a 'proper businessman'. I had quietly resigned from the university and tipped my career into the bin, destined to sporadic casual tutoring in the windy ex-Polytechnic on the fringe of the cathedral town at the behest of a faculty administrator who barely knew my name. Who needs philosophers anyway?

The next day was a Saturday, and I arranged to drive the children to Camden Town where we would spend a day with my parents while Jack ran the shop. I was thankful to leave behind the menacing cobbled lanes of the town centre, and to strike out along the ring road between clean green fields, sweeping round the broad roundabouts that led to the motorway. William struck up a song and we three warbled down the black shiny strip of tarmac to blessed, grimy London. My parents insisted that we stayed the night, and I called Jack at the shop.

"Yes, good idea. Things are complicated at this end."

"You've spoken to him again?"

"Well, yes, but I don't want to ruin your weekend. Let me look after things here and we'll all be together on Sunday evening."

I watched William and Zita playing with their grandparents in the battered sitting room. Charlotte played separately, but just inside the circle of grandparently love. My parents' love for the children was unconditional, uncomplicated, unsullied and totally reciprocated. It was my sole touchstone, the only thing of pure and faultless value in my life.

I borrowed a coat and scarf from my mother, took a mug of tea into the little walled garden at the back of the terraced house and, out of sight, wept the bitterest tears of regret at the danger we had put the children in through our rash grown-up games. I mopped my face, finished my tea, and went back in.

"Mum, I'm popping out to the shops. Do you want anything?"

"Bring something nice for the children if you can."

"I'll have a good stroll while I'm at it – get some exercise."

I walked the twenty minutes to Kentish Town Police Station, envying the scarved shoppers, yearning for their lives, however difficult. Surely none of them would be going home tomorrow to the foulness that awaited me. I rehearsed my account as I walked, debating with myself where to start, what to put in, how to project myself, how to project Jack, how to explain why I had waited until now. My resolve to confess toughened as I walked, until I began to sense flutterings of elation at the prospect of telling my secrets. I visualised the police officer at the counter – a man, I did not want a woman – and he would be big and bluff-faced, listening with concern and sympathy like an older brother, carefully writing in a fat notebook with a maroon cover, a listener, a kind man.

But there was no confessor waiting for me, just a queue of scruffy supplicants and a sign proposing a hotline number. I stood in the grimness of the ironically named Holmes Street as drizzle began to soak my shoulders and I considered – against all my instincts – praying.

My inchoate prayer was rewarded with the toot of a car horn. A dirty white van pulled up beside me. I was not at all surprised that he had followed me to London.

"Hop in and we'll have a cuppa somewhere."

"I'm not getting into that filthy van."

"But you'll have a cuppa?"

"I don't have any choice."

"Stay here while I park this thing and we'll walk up to

the main road."

I began walking towards Kentish Town Road and by the time I had reached the end of Holmes Road he was waiting on the corner.

"You had me worried for a minute then, Thea. Still, good thing you can't find a copper when you want one in this particular case. The Met's gone to the dogs. No wonder there's so much crime these days."

I pointed to a coffee shop and we went in. He ordered what looked to be a litre of coffee foam, a supermegaccino I think it was called. I had Earl Grey. I waited for him to speak.

"I never forgot you Thea."

"Why did you pick on me all those years ago? You did target me, didn't you? It wasn't just random?"

"I did. I picked on you on purpose. I wanted what my brother had. What they owed me."

"You wanted me as part of his chattels?"

"No, it wasn't like that. First of all, I just wanted a life like his, wife, children, some kind of future. But when I saw you I ..." He faltered. "I fancied you."

"Fancied me? What, fancied me like a greyhound? Fancied me like a set of golf clubs? Anyway, there was no money in those days. Jack's parents were still alive. You couldn't have had his life or his future. You couldn't just bundle his life up and put it in a van."

"There wasn't any money, sure, but there was you, but you're not getting my meaning. I really fancied you."

"I see," I said. "I think we might be talking about lurv, like in the pop songs ... you wanted me to be your lurv. You lurv me. I fall in lurv with you. It's all lurvely. Stop messing me around."

Francis sucked on the huge coffee cup. He wiped a

foam moustache away with a napkin and looked at me balefully. "Don't take the piss. I mean it. It's you I wanted all the time. I do love you."

"You're sadder than I ever imagined then. Anyway, let's be realistic about this. You might have fooled Jack with a few bits of information you're not supposed to have, but that doesn't mean anything. I don't believe you're Jack's half-brother. Why would you have set up your own brother for blackmail? Is that what a brother does? You're a calculating criminal. We know what you get up to – that poor man being photographed while he was being whipped. And what about ..."

His hand shot out like a ferret and gripped the muscle above my knee. "What do you know about whipping?"

"The old man told Jack about it. He told him he went to the house on the wrong day ..." I stopped, feeling the grasp of his hand, watching his eyes become lethal slits. He squeezed harder, but I stared him out, feeling tears springing to my eyes from the increasing pain.

"What else do you know?"

"Is this how a lover behaves?" I hissed, and he relaxed his hand and looked down. "I have to go now."

I snaked home through alleys and back streets, but I was sure that he knew where my parents lived.

**

The inquest five years ago had found that Jack's father's car had accidentally crossed the centre line of the road and hit the lorry head-on. Driving conditions were appalling because of the fog and freezing sleet, and both the lorry and the car were driving at excessive speed. Now I knew Francis was behind the accident, and I wondered when Jack would work it out.

23: Porter of hell gate

The autumn evenings are long here at Forty Apple Trees. My precious children are in bed by eight thirty, and I generally mark my ration of tedious university essays for an hour before taking to my bed with a brandy, a novel, and my memories of the summer when Jack and I became the unlikeliest of criminals. Invariably the novel drops from my hands and my mind turns to the day before our wedding anniversary when I picked up Sir Percy Bushmore's wallet and relieved it of a wad of crisp new bills.

It had nothing to do with money. Certainly I had known that the shop was only marginally profitable. Jack was no businessman, but it suited both of us to pretend that we were doing fine. Once a month he would 'walk me through the books', and I would accept his assurances that we would 'turn the corner' in the next quarter, knowing in my heart that each three months brought us nearer to a frank confrontation with the real facts. Jack had always been one to cut corners. If there was an easy way he would take it, and ignoring the plight of the shop was easier than making the effort to fix it. I kept on spending – not extravagantly, but not modestly – knowing that the credit card bills were nibbling at our cash reserves. In moments when I was honest with myself I conceded that it would be a relief to reach a crisis point when we would have to give up Books by Birdswell, sell The Windings, and move back to London.

I must have used up millions of highly trained brain cells in trying to understand that moment on the path by the lake. The expensive wallet, the driving licence with the Chancellor's patrician image behind a plastic window, the crisp cash: All that went through my mind by the lake was "Why not?" And the price I paid was an endless mental loop of tape asking the question "Why?" But I took the cash, threw the wallet into the water, and then taught an ethics class, not without a frisson of excitement at the feel of the notes stuffed into my jeans pocket. The impetus for taking the money must have been something deep in me, something I could sense but not articulate: Perhaps it was an amalgam of frustrations; my futile career; the house which never lost the cold aura of Jack's dead parents; Saturday mornings – 'my time' – mooching in the shopping mall of the New Town; Jack's posing as a literary gourmand, and his blasé attitude to the realities of profit and loss.

I looked forward to our anniversary dinner mostly with guilt. Jack reveled in the fussy attention we received at The Secret Cottage, but I found the place pretentious and outrageously expensive. I would have preferred toad in the hole at one of the pubs on the Birdswell rather than being fawned over by Maxwell and his boyfriend. The night before the dinner, I undressed for bed and scanned my wardrobe for something to wear at The Secret Cottage, but the rows of dresses and skirts and tops looked as stale as I felt. I got into bed and gently pushed Jack away.

The next day I woke up feeling unsettled and edgy. Being a Saturday, the morning was mine and I took the bus into the New Town twenty minutes away, with the nine hundred pounds in my jeans. My edginess gave way to a kind of euphoria at the thought of spending the money: It was not the quantity – nine hundred pounds was negligible in the wider pattern of things. It was the idea of doing something entirely against the predictable grain of my life.

The dress was just serendipity. It could have been an antique map of the world, a rare bottle of wine, a pair of celebrity designer shoes, a box at the opera. I just happened to walk past Jules Hector and see it in the window. The magenta and grey sheath was seductive, exquisite, gorgeous. I calmly handed over the banknotes while my heart hammered inside my ribcage.

Jack hung around in a fizz of anticipation watching me dress that night until I kicked him out. Against my expectations my excitement at the evening began to mount: A complicated mix of feelings that evoked first experiences – the first glass of champagne, the first time in a small plane, the first time naked with a man in a bed. The Secret Garden felt new, different; I felt new, different. I sensed the eyes of men on my back as Maxwell walked us across the restaurant to the half-private niche. We drank far too much and I was emboldened to tell Jack about the money. He was of course stunned. I said something like feeling like a child riding a bike downhill without brakes. I was slightly irritated that he wanted to know the exact particulars of the crime scene. The details were irrelevant. This was Thea, housewife and university tutor, turned criminal and blatantly wearing the slinky proceeds.

When we tipped ourselves into the taxi, Jack had got over his scruples about the where and the when of the theft. He caressed me boozily on the back seat and I had to surreptitiously pull his hand out of my knickers when the driver stopped and asked for four pounds twenty. It had been a long time since I wanted to make love to Jack, and I told him to hurry up paying the babysitter. By the time he came back I was fighting off vertigo and a desire to be sick. I remember struggling to take off the dress without damaging it, but the rest of that summer night is lost in a drunken blur.

***

By the time I had snaked my way back to my parents' house in Camden I was soaked through from the dirty January drizzle. The children – nut brown Charlotte included – were lined up on the sofa bracketed by a Greek grandparent at one end and an Irish one at the other, apparently wedged in hard. Each grandparent held a big bag of crisps which the children, mesmerised by a horror film on the TV, mechanically dipped their fingers into. I went upstairs, towelled my hair dry, peeled off my clothes and tossed them into the clothes drier in the bathroom. I sat on the toilet and breathed in the fug of warm damp air and my mother's coal tar soap until somebody knocked. William said, "I want a wee," and I quickly dressed and let him in. The innocent child looked at me bashfully and I closed the door and went downstairs.

There was no singing on the way home from London that night. I chewed the inside of my cheek until it bled, and the children went to sleep as the car gobbled up the wet black strip of tarmac. We swung round the big roundabouts and then plunged into the narrower streets that led to Cathedral Row. Jack had heard us arrive, and opened the door. We led William, Zita and Charlotte upstairs and got them ready for bec.

While Jack had a last word with the children, I went downstairs in the big kitchen, where I set out two plates and laid out a supper of cheese and pickles. I put two frozen half baguettes in the microwave and looked for some wine. There was none in the kitchen so I walked into the little pantry area that led to the guest quarters where we stored our wine supplies. The former consulting rooms had their own outside and internal doors separating them from the main house, and we often left shopping and deliveries there until we needed to bring them in. I rattled the internal door handle – it often stuck – but it would not open. I sensed Jack behind me.

"I've locked it," he said.

"Locked it?"

"We've got a guest staying," he said, and my stomach dropped.

I refused to undress when we went upstairs. "We're all going to a hotel. I can't believe what you've done. I'm utterly disgusted at your deception."

"He can't get into the main house and he can't get in through the front door," Jack said.

"You'd planned it when we spoke on the telephone today. How could you not tell me?"

"He's just staying for a week or two. It's complicated. Anyway it's too late to find a hotel."

I reflected on this, as well as one or two other matters. My marriage to Jack, however shaky, would be a wreck if Francis exposed our relationship. And what other ghastly unravellings would follow? I had a nauseating vision of being escorted to a police van while my children were bundled into a car by social workers.

"I want you to sleep in the corridor outside the

children's rooms. I'll stay here in the bedroom." I took a couple of golf clubs from the back of the wardrobe: "Here, one each."

Jack took a golf club and a duvet and closed the door behind him.

***

I was woken the next day by joyous shouts from the back garden. Jack was asleep in the corridor grasping the steel end of the golf club. It was seven o'clock and hardly light, and the children's bedrooms were empty. I ran downstairs to find the back door open, and the children playing football with Francis in their dressing gowns. There was a faint drizzle falling, which made the children's gowns glisten with tiny diamonds of moisture.

"Any chance of a cuppa for Uncle Francis?" he said, tossing a cigarette end into the flower bed.

"Uncle Francis is staying with us for a holiday," Zita said.

"A winter holiday," Charlotte said

"Get inside, all three of you. Keep away from him!"

The three faces looked up at me in confusion and disappointment. They turned to Francis, who made pretend sobbing noises that made the children giggle. I roughly bundled them inside the house, and locked the back door. A few minutes later I heard the van revving up. I opened the front door, and saw Francis speeding off, leaving the smoky stink of a clapped-out engine lingering on the wintry air.

"He'll be gone all day. He says he has projects." It was Jack. Like me he was still in yesterday's clothes. His eyes were red and he looked wan.

"I need to open the shop," he said.

"I'll get these three ready for school," I said.

"Good idea."

We retreated to our separate tasks, both trying to find some normality in mundane routine. With school outfits and paraphernalia assembled, and having roughly groomed myself sufficiently to face the Monday morning school parking crowd, I hustled the sullen children in the car. Jack left on foot at the same time, but we said nothing to each other. When I drove past him he walked with his eyes on the pavement.

Zita said, "Uncle Francis is nice, isn't he?" I ignored her, perhaps for the first time in her life.

***

Despite the events of the night before, Jack and I began the evening on civil terms. He looked so wretched when he came home, that I hugged and kissed him. The children gazed up in melting wonder.

"I wasn't expecting that," he said, and collapsed into a chair. The children climbed on him like spiderlings, and I made him a gin and tonic, then another. We all played card games after dinner; the house rule was no screen time after 6pm. We put the children to bed and settled on the big chintz couch in the sitting room. I had just freshened up the G&T's when there was the sound of the van outside and the clunk of the heavy side door to the guest quarters.

"Is the internal door locked?" Jack asked.

"Locked and a wooden wedge jammed under it."

"If a man were porter of hell gate, he should have old

turning the key," Jack said.

"Hamlet, isn't it?"

"Macbeth."

"I didn't really get the meaning. There seems to be a word missing."

"Well," Jack said heavily, "There's nothing missing. It means that if you were in charge of the door to hell, you'd get old in the job because there are so many people who have to be let in".

We sat and considered this. Me especially.

"Jack," I said. "I was thinking through what you said about Aunt Florence ..."

"Francis turning up a couple of days before my parents died?"

"The person who calls himself Francis."

"My half-brother."

"The person who calls himself your half-brother. Oh Jack, are you so disingenuous? Can't you see how this man is feeding off your need for ..."

"Need for what?"

"Need for, I don't know. Just forget it."

"Yes, let's. I'm not in the mood for psychoanalysis. Let's get this out in the open – the crash, my parents dead."

"Your father," I said. "He never occurred to me as suicidal."

"Nor me, but then he never occurred to me as a man who'd have an affair with a patient. God knows what went on behind that stern face."

"And Francis, whoever he is, where does that leave him?"

"It wasn't his fault – not directly anyway. He confronted his natural father; it must happen all the time.

How was he to know that his new-found dad would wipe out himself and my mother by driving into a lorry?"

I could not help myself: "I called you disingenuous. But it's worse – you're willfully resistant to the truth that's staring at you!"

"What truth?"

"That the evil scum sitting in our guest quarters – brother or not – threatened to expose your father and drove the man to suicide and murder."

Jack slumped into the chintz. I knew that he knew. With Jack you have to wait until he has cut every corner, and finally has to take the long road that leads to the inevitable destination.

"I'll work out a plan," he said. "A good one – tomorrow."

24: Red Indian for something

But Jack did not come up with a plan the next morning. Plans were my job – the analytical one, the intellectual one who could turn 'ectoplasm', as Jack called my academic sources and references, into comprehensible schema. His sole original contribution to the plan to get the bookshop back in the black had been to suggest that we get our lawyer to set up mutual powers of attorney: "If either of us goes to prison, at least the other one can sign cheques and keep things running." So while Jack had earned a B+ for that idea, the morning's effort was definitely an F.

Francis's van coughed away up the street just as we were getting up.

"So what am I supposed to do while you're at the shop?"

"I don't know. Take the children to school, come back home, have a think about all of this."

"And what will you do in between selling prodigious quantities of books?" I asked.

"Well, I'll think about it too and when I get home we'll pool our ideas and come up with a plan – a joint plan."

"Marvelous," I said. "We can issue a joint communique with five key points and a roadmap. I'll call the UN Secretary General."

"Come on, easy goes."

"Jack, there's only one plan. We have to get rid of him."

Jack gave me an odd look, finished his coffee, and

headed for the door.

"Jack," I said, nodding towards the children.

"Oh yes," he said, and swiftly hugged the bewildered darlings before leaving.

I was home from the school drop by nine thirty. I had no classes to teach so I changed into trainers and a tracksuit, ran down to the cathedral, turned into the park, and pounded my way to Parsons Wood. There was a light drizzle that stung my eyes and frosted my clothes. A few hardy young mothers were pushing babies along the asphalt paths in thousand-pound carbon-fibre Everest-grade prams. I turned onto the footpath along the Birdswell, and splashed through duck poo and wet nettles until I began to smell hot scones and coffee from the cafe in the cathedral annexe. The verger, wrapped in scarves and smoking a pipe, waved to me – Jack had introduced him to me when we were out walking one day. I remembered that he was the bearer of the news about the cathedral books contract. I didn't wave back.

At home I stripped and stood under the shower for a long time. I wrapped myself in a big bath sheet and went into the bedroom. I stood in front of the full-length mirror and let the towel drop.

"Hmm. Very tasty."

"How the hell did you get in here?" He was in the bedroom doorway. I bent down to pick up the towel with one hand, covering my backside with the other.

Francis gave me a look of pity: "That lock wasn't much of a challenge. Not for someone like me. Don't worry, I'm not here to ravish you. Get dressed so we can talk without me being put off by the thought of what I just saw. And no phone calls." He held up my mobile and the two portable house phones.

"You piece of slime. All right, we'll talk. Go down to the kitchen and I'll join you in a minute."

Francis was sat at the table doing a cryptic crossword from *The Guardian* when I came down. I remembered there was a stack of old newspapers in the separate quarters.

"You can do that?"

"Nearly finished," he said. "See, you've got the wrong idea. I'm not educated – unlettered, you'd say – but I'm smart. I've picked up a lot. You could get to like me again."

"I never liked you. I had what must have been a total mental brainstorm, and you took advantage of it. I betrayed my husband and you've got me in a trap."

"Takes two to do the reptile house tango. I seem to remember some very convincing zoo noises from you in the throngs of passion. That doesn't sound right – it's throes, isn't it? Oh, hang on, maybe you picked up a degree in acting on the way through your career. Maybe you were pretending."

"Get to the point, Francis. What do you want?"

"I want to live here with you and my brother and the children. Like a family. We'd have lovely Christmases and birthdays with cake and soup and the central heating on in the winter, and we'd all buy presents for each other."

"Jack's not your brother. What do you really want?"

"I just told you. And I am Jack's brother – to Jack anyway."

I was beginning to panic. None of what he said made sense, and yet he seemed sincere. It was like a paradoxical code with no key: The gauche sentimentality, the sinister undertone of blackmail, the oblique threats, the brazen duplicity.

"And how long do you think this twisted *ménage à six* would endure?"

"Ooh French. I must learn a few phrases like that. Till death do us part, I suppose," he said without a trace of irony or sarcasm.

"And how do you and I fit into all this?"

"We revive our old ... friendship, and when opportunity arises we ... take advantage of the situation."

"Don't be coy," I said. "You want to screw me when Jack isn't around."

"Make love, not screw."

"Like you made love – sorry lurv – to that poor cow Marjorie Smith?"

Francis sat up straight: "You know about Marjorie? You're even cleverer than I thought. Jack doesn't deserve you. Me and you – oh, let's talk like people who can do *Guardian* crosswords – you and I could do fantastic things together. With my contacts, my little projects, and your brains and charm – my God, we'd become millionaires."

"OK, Francis, you're having a nice bit of twisted fun here. What else do you want?"

"Half the house."

"I thought so. You can leave now. Go down to the guest quarters or clear off in that urinal on wheels and let me think."

"Another nice little chat this evening?"

"Jack will be here."

"Well, yes. I thought you might invite me for dinner so I could have a proper talk with my brother. Say eight o'clock?"

I said nothing, but I knew I had no choice. And I knew

there was only one solution.

***

The children grumbled when they were shunted off to bed at seven thirty.

"We want to see Uncle Francis," Zita said.

"He's fun, not like Daddy," William said, prodding the limits of indignation.

I suppressed a raised voice and took them gently to their rooms, promising delights on the next day.

"It seems weird, but I'm quite excited," Jack said when I came down and started making a salad. I wondered how Lucretia Borgia would have handled things. Cantarella on the cucumber?

"I'm astounded that you've kept this brother business to yourself these last five years. Didn't I deserve to know about it?"

"I wanted to say something but I didn't want it to turn into a big hoo-haa."

"Big hoo-haa? Is that Red Indian for something?"

"You would have started looking up the records, trying to find him, stirring things up ..."

My heart bounced as a wave of rage flooded me, and I slammed the flat of the knife on a ripe tomato, splattering myself with red.

"Jack, not a word more. Not a word."

"But we have to talk."

I breathed deeply, mopped the juice off my front.

"You know how it was for me at home, Thea, when I was a kid. Me, my father, my mother, big silent rooms, cold stares, everyone being civilised and restrained and proper. I really envied the boys who had brothers. I remember being sent to my room after dinner to do my homework – it was where William sleeps now – and how I'd so much wish I had someone to share my microscope with. I had a friend called Tony who had three brothers and two sisters. They lived in that council estate near the quarry, all crammed into this little house. Tony's dad had built a kind of mezzanine floor in the back bedroom and the four boys slept on different levels."

"Sounds horrible."

"No, it was great. Their mother never went in the back room, it was such a mess. They did what they liked in there – kept hamsters, made camps, looked at girlie magazines, took their dinners up there."

"Ugh. Animal droppings, masturbation contests, dirty plates."

We both laughed. I couldn't remember the last time. But I had to turn the conversation back before Francis arrived.

"It's really important to you, the idea of a brother?"

"I hadn't realised how much till now."

"And where do I fit into all this?" It was the second time I had asked the question in thirty-six hours.

"Where you always did, Thea. My wife, but perhaps now we can be more of a family – no, that's not right – a bigger family – and you can have a brother in law and the children can have an uncle."

"And what of the things that Francis has done to you and me, his family? Threatening our children?"

"Thea, I'm not a fool. He's got a bad streak – we've seen it. But let's give him a chance to explain himself."

***

I heard Francis exit the guest quarters through the side door and knock on the front door. Jack brought him in.

He was wearing a shiny brown suit and carrying some decent looking flowers.

"You didn't need to dress up," Jack said. "Drink?"

"I'll have what you're having." We all sat down in the lounge with big glasses of claret.

Ten minutes of other-worldly conversation proceeded: The decor, the price of petrol, prospects for the bookshop. The bottle of wine quickly emptied and – with misgivings – I fetched another.

"I'll leave you two while I finish the food." I refilled their glasses and stepped into the vestibule, where the thick carpet muffles any footsteps. I stood silently by the lounge door, which was slightly ajar, and listened. I heard the odd word – they seemed to be talking about music – and then the hi-fi began to play something I recognised. The Thompson Twins? It was fruitless to listen anymore and I went to the kitchen.

After five minutes, I opened the lounge door and got a blast of the lyrics from *Stay With Me*, and the two men stood up and came towards me grinning, belting out the words and swaying.

"For pity's sake, shut up and come and eat."

I spotted the children sitting on the top stair, and said to Jack, "Put them back to bed!" The brothers in booze swayed up the staircase singing, and the children scuttled to their rooms giggling.

Dinner was The Jack and Francis Show. As the wine glasses emptied and my carefully prepared dinner was used as a sponge to soak up the alcohol in their stomachs, the two men guffawed and frolicked, grew sentimental and maudlin, scaled the heights of absurdity and silliness, and scoured the depths of vulgarity. The hilarity kept returning to Uncle Clive's 'death'. How many times, I wondered, could they use the word 'clock' as a verb? After dessert, I became the focus of their glee, with Jack making slightly risqué hints about our relationship and Francis looking me up and down like a piece of female horseflesh. Francis brought this nasty chapter to an end by digging a spliff out of his jacket pocket, and the two men smoked and giggled. I eventually relented and I was soon laughing foolishly, but then I started to cry and excused myself.

I curled up in bed, the smell of roasted meat and marijuana in my hair filling the fuggy hollow under the sheets. There was muffled banging and laughing as the two men cleared up the mess downstairs, then eventually the clunk of the guest quarters door, and Jack's heavy footfalls on the stair.

"Still awake? I thought that went very well."

"Weird definition of well," I said. "I feel sick."

"Not used to the old weed, probably. How many years has it been? The smell brought back so many memories."

"Jack, what next?"

"I go to sleep. That's what's next."

"Don't be cute. We have to get rid of him. Tomorrow."

"Tomorrow's tomorrow. Let's sleep on it."

"Spare room please. Or go and share the room with your brother. You could get a guinea pig and eat rice crispies and watch porn," I said.

25: Three's a crowd

The *ménage à trois* struggled along for a week. Francis went out each day – to 'work' he called it – and came back each evening, joining us for dinner. The atmosphere during dinner was forced and surreally civil, even more so if the children were about. I quietly warned them not to speak to Francis, and not to be alone with him in any of the rooms. At nights Jack locked the internal door to the guest quarters after Francis had had his meal and gone downstairs.

On the Friday evening, after the children had been sent to play in their rooms, Jack questioned Francis about the visit to his father.

"How did you track him down?"

"I always knew I was adopted – my father threw it in my face all the time. Called me a runt and a waste of valuable space."

"Your father being Mr. Benton?"

"Yep. Well, we never got on. My mum tried hard but she wasn't a strong person. One day there was a big bust up and my father – Benton that is – went upstairs and brought down an envelope. His exact words were 'This is who you really belong to. Get out of my house'. I would have been about twenty-two. It was my original birth certificate. The one I showed you."

"So did you look for your real parents back then?"

"Crikey, no. I was too busy making a career for myself."

"Your career, yes of course."

"You know, buying and selling, this and that. I more or less forgot about it until about six years ago."

I could not read Jack's demeanor, but I knew that Francis was lying.

"So you decided one day to find out about your real parents? It must have been so difficult for you. Such an emotional wrench." I stared hard at Jack, willing him to give me a look, a wink, something to help me understand what was happening.

Francis seemed to be warming to the idea of a heart-to-heart with his new brother. "Yes, it was emotionally challenging, but it was a bridge I had to cross."

Steady on Francis, I thought. These clichés are bordering on bathos. You'll get caught out. Jack has read many more books than you.

"So you found my father – our father – pretty briskly I suppose. But what about your mother?"

"God rest her soul, she'd passed on before I found her."

"And when you went to see Dad," Jack said, "He must've been absolutely stunned. What did he say?"

"Well, when he'd got over the shock he was very nice. He wasn't a warm man, I could tell that, but he was genuinely moved to meet me. He told me a bit about his life but we had so little time. I'm just sorry that I only knew him for that short while."

"Between you meeting him and the crash, you mean?"

"I was devastated when I read about it in the news,"

Francis said. "Gutted."

Jack did not blink. Just sat back contentedly and said, "Extraordinary, two brothers find each other. You just turned up on the doorstep one day when I was out. Good thing Thea was in. She must've thought 'who the hell is this character?' But she probably recognised you. There's a resemblance between us. Thea would have seen it, wouldn't you, darling?"

I gulped and said something indistinct. Jack gazed affectionately at Francis and said, "Listen, what are your plans? You said you'd just need a couple of weeks of accommodation".

Francis made a cupid bow with his lips, and rolled his eyes upwards. I did not know what impression he was trying to convey, but it just looked foolish.

"Ah," he said. "Bit of a problem turned up."

"Problem?" Jack asked.

"I need a bit longer. Month perhaps."

"No problem at all," Jack said. "That's fine with us isn't it Thea? And it'll give us more time to catch up."

***

When Francis had gone to his quarters, Jack and I cleared away the dinner things. He seemed distracted but not unhappy. When I tried to talk about Francis he fobbed me off with "This needs a lot of thought, Thea. I have to work some things out in my own mind". I was furious, frustrated, shut out, excluded from the game, not even understanding if it was a game. Detesting myself, I told him to go to hell and he slept in the spare room that night, and every night after. I lay wretched and confused, my mind simmering with morbid shadows and hideous possibilities. I mourned the loss of my integrity, my spirit, my morality, the person I was before I picked up that wallet. I ached with despair at the thing that my husband had become: A man whose hollowed out feelings had been filled with some bizarre and dangerous brew. Most of all I was crushed with guilt and remorse that my precious innocents – and I included the dear nut-brown Charlotte – were associated with this vile, infected, plague-rid piece of inhumanity called Francis.

***

I woke on the Saturday sick and exhausted.

"No sport," I said to the children. "Would you like to go to Granny and Pappous for a few days? There's a bank holiday on Monday. You can stay till then."

The children started to pack, while I called my parents and explained that I was overwhelmed with work. As always, they agreed. Jack was already at the shop and I had not heard any noise from Francis. I peeped through the drapes at the front of the house. The dirty van was there.

By ten we were ready to leave, when Francis knocked on the front door.

"Quick cuppa? I'm out of milk."

"No, I'm busy. I'm taking the children to London."

The children had seen Francis and started to dance and chant 'Un-cle Fran-cis, Un-cle Fran-cis'.

"We have to go kids. Now, quick."

"Un-cle Fran-cis, Un-cle Fran-cis"

"Come in you bastard," I hissed. "Five minutes."

I made him a cup of tea while he invented a ball game in the kitchen, flicking a washing up sponge in random directions while the children tried to grab it. I heard a noise in the vestibule and realised that Charlotte was gone. She reappeared and said, "There's a pretty lady at the door".

"Are you selling something?" I asked. It was a dark woman, lovely, intelligent looking. Indian, Caribbean? I wasn't sure.

She held out a police warrant card: "Detective Sergeant Fiona Salmon. I'd like to speak to Mr. Walsingham please. Is he home?"

I was starting to hyperventilate. I hung on to my composure. "No, he's working late tonight. What's this about?"

Francis came up behind me and opened the door wider.

"And you would be, sir?" the beautiful detective said.

"Just a house guest. Why don't you give us your card and Jack can ring you?"

I returned from dropping the children off in London in the evening, but nobody was home. Jack had left no message or note. The white van was outside, but there was no sound from downstairs. I crept around the side of the house in the darkness and looked through the gaps in the curtains of the guest quarters. The rooms seemed to be empty, and there were no lights on. I went back inside and tapped on the internal door to the guest rooms. No answer. I silently unlocked the door and walked through the rooms in my socks. Francis was evidently using the side bedroom; there was a neat pile of clothes by the bed and a packet of cigarettes.

I looked around the familiar room. Even in the gloom I could ascertain the contours of the bay window, the line of the skirting boards, the shape of the drapes. I had supervised the renovation of the old surgery, and I knew every nook and angle of the room. On an instinct I stretched up and reached behind the heavy pelmet, where

I knew there was a little cavity where the builder had neglected to cover an old duct. Inside was a small book – an address book. I didn't know what I expected: A stash of heroin, a roll of banknotes? But I knew that Francis would have found a hiding place. I slipped the book into my jeans and quietly went upstairs. Half an hour later Francis walked unsteadily down the side passage. He knocked over a flower pot, scraped his key against the lock until it turned, and the door slammed.

I went to bed but could not sleep. I heard Jack let himself in and quietly use the bathroom. I lay in bed willing him to come in, but he went to the spare room and shut the door. With the children in London I felt bereft, and my anger at Jack faded to a sort of sentimental stew of melancholy laced with self-pity. I recalled the weeks after we became criminals, the nights when Jack was aroused like an adolescent by the thrill of what we were doing; and my own struggle against my instincts, my failure to match his ardour, my frozen feelings, my play-acting the amateur detective to smother my fear of what we were doing. But then there was the day I went to meet Marjorie Smith, when I sensed just a little of the frisson of the invisible criminal. I had carefully justified to myself why I had to trick Marjorie into telling her sad truths, but when it came to the confrontation I felt – against my rational, philosopher's psyche – bold and crafty and powerful. I was almost boastful when I played the recording to Jack that evening.

My thoughts turned to my husband. Yes, our marriage was a clump of flotsam to which we four – five with little Charlotte – clung. Could Jack and I steer ourselves back to some safe landing, some way back to love and respect and pleasure and – most of all – an absence of the fear for my children that invaded every cell of my brain? I did not know. My husband had become unrecognisable in the last week, joshing with the foul Francis and swanning complacently round the house as if a maiden aunt was spending a few days with us. I took a sleeping tablet, and blackness descended.

I woke up late the next morning with my eyes gritted and a rank taste on my tongue. Jack was gone, and there was no sound from the guest quarters. Francis would have left hours ago to do whatever he did all day. I took a very long hot shower, and went to the kitchen in my dressing gown. The clock said 8.55. It was a silly thing that Jack had bought for my birthday when we were students, with the numbers and the hands running anticlockwise. I remembered the inscription he had had engraved on the back: Here's to the next four million minutes – J. I suddenly wanted him with me. I rehearsed a little conversation: Let's wind the clock back (I would point at the silly clock), let's get back what we had all those years ago (I would tousle his hair), let's sell the shop and the house and move up to Forty Apple Trees (he would give me that ironic, slightly querulous raise of one eyebrow).

Then the house phone rang and it was Jack's mobile.

"Thea, hello, everything fine there?" The voice was warm, affectionate.

"Yes. Are you at the shop?"

"No, I didn't open it today. I got a call early this morning from the old boy – the Major – asking me to come down to his place urgently."

"That's odd. Is that where you are?"

"No, I've just left there. When I arrived, he wouldn't let me in. He said everything was fine. I'm having a coffee at Elephant and Castle station right now."

"Are you going straight to the shop?"

"No, damn the shop. Let's drive out into the country and have a pub lunch. I'll be home around half ten."

"Hurry back, Jack."

I went back to the bedroom and turned on the small hi-fi we never used. There was an old Pet Shop Boys CD in there and I turned it up loud – *Being Boring* I think was the track that came on first. I would dress up for lunch. I scanned the wardrobe and pulled out the magenta and grey dress, still in its dry-cleaning bag, unworn since the first charged weeks of our criminal careers. Hardly a dress for a pub lunch, I thought, but I slipped it out of the plastic and put it on. I did a swirl in the mirror, put on a pair of dangerously high heels – I had bought them on a whim and they were unwearable – and did another swirl. Such a small thing, that scrap of dress, but so potent. I was about to take it off when *Being Boring* faded out. During the brief interval before the next track I heard a knock, and turned to see Francis on the landing. He was in pajamas.

"Shit, Thea. I can't wait any longer. Let's get out of here, leave that loser with his books. I've got enough cash to keep us going till you can get rid of him."

I tried to sound very calm: "Is that the plan?"

"Yes," Francis said, and took a few steps towards me.

"Stop, just stop, don't come in. I'll come out to you. We could go to the front bedroom," I said. The next track began on the hi-fi.

Francis looked at me with what I suppose might have been tenderness, or the nearest he could get to such a feeling. He wiped his eyes and I saw tears. I was unmoved.

"There's something else," he said. "The kids. They'll

come too. I'll make a fantastic dad."

My insides were a seething bag of acid. My brain was black with hatred.

"You can have me," I said. "We'll make it work. Jack won't know. Look, I'm wearing this dress. It drives him wild. You can have what he has."

I approached him. I could smell the rankness from inside the pajama jacket. I swallowed a pellet of vomit. I couldn't touch him. He backed against the balustrade, breathing hard. He pulled down the pajama pants and his doughy penis sprang free. He said, "Get on your knees". I glimpsed a silhouette outside the glass of the front door below – Jack was home!

"I can't kneel in these shoes," I said. "I'll have to stoop. Ease yourself up onto the balustrade." He placed his palms on the rail, and hoisted one buttock onto the rail. I bent into a kind of curtsey with the ludicrous shoes digging into my flesh like torture irons. I looked down at his dangling feet and judged the force and the angle I would need to take both his heels and flip him backwards.

"Get up there properly," I said, and he eased the other buttock onto the rail. I saw the glistening drop on the end of his penis and could only think of venom oozing from a fang.

"Hold on, my bollocks are squashed," he said. He took one hand off the rail to free his red testicles, and his centre of gravity shifted just enough for him to fall backwards.

The dance music pounded away in the background as his neck snapped against the top of the hallstand twelve feet below. And that is how, in a sense, I killed Francis.

26: A meat pie and *The Sun*

They let me out a month before Christmas. I signed for the possessions I had on me when I went in: Clothes, wallet, keys, phone, and then I was out of the gates and looking down across the wet Northamptonshire fields to the motorway a mile away. It was raining. The phone was flat of course.

I walked down to the bus stop and waited with the women and children who had been visiting their men. I had just over two hundred pounds in my wallet. I asked a woman where the bus went to, but she only spoke something Eastern European. She looked down at her daughter – a girl of about eleven – who named a railway station I'd never heard of.

The only visitors during my ten months on remand had been my brief (twice), Fiona Salmon (once) and Mr. Nussbaum (I'd repelled him four times and he'd given up). I hadn't received a letter or a phone call from Thea, for which I was grateful; although I ached to see my family I was relieved that my wife had avoided any contact with me that could implicate her in Francis's death.

At the railway station I tried the cash machine, but it ate my card. I bought an on-the-spot ticket home for a prince's ransom in cash. The ancient couple in front of me held up the queue for twenty minutes while they loudly debated with the ticket seller over rail cards, magazine coupons, and hearing aid batteries, and I missed the train. It was midday and I hadn't eaten since breakfast time, so

I bought a lukewarm pie full of greyish meat paste, and *The Sun*, the only newspaper left on the stand.

After three tricky connections the train slid into the quaint old station behind the market square that flanked the cathedral. The pie repeated on me, and my clothes felt sticky. I bought a deodorant and a packet of chewing gum and popped into the public toilet, the one where Francis had made his first blackmail demand. I squirted an icy blast of deodorant into my shirt, cleaned the surfaces of my teeth with a wet finger, and chewed a big plug of gum. I walked home, practising some possible opening lines but I gave up. All I wanted was to embrace Thea and the children, and have a cup of tea with a saucer.

The Windings looked different. The little garden in the front was scruffy and unweeded, and the rubbish bin sat in a mess of take-away cartons. I felt a dagger of remorse. My poor Thea, burdened with keeping the family functioning and the house in order while I wasted ten months in a prison cell. But I looked again and saw cigarette butts among the take-away boxes and – surely not? – a knotted condom. I put my key in the lock but it wouldn't turn. I knocked.

"If you're selling something we've got no money so bugger off." The door had opened a crack and a young woman with long greasy hair peered out. She was standing up in a sleeping bag, and the vestibule emitted a warm fuggy smell of unwashed bodies and stale food.

"Where's Thea? This is my house. Who are you?"

"Your house? You'd better come in then."

I stepped inside, and the girl hopped down the corridor in the sleeping bag. She shouted up the stairs.

"Randy, some old bloke down here. He says this is his

house."

There was no reply, so the girl asked me if I wanted a cup of tea. I said yes, and followed her as she hopped into my kitchen, in which every surface was covered in filthy plates. A big black cat sat on the stove chewing on a cold sausage in a frying pan.

"Who's Randy?"

"He's the bloke who has the lease. We rent rooms from him," she said.

"We?"

"Students, you know, at the uni."

"And what are you studying?" I asked. The girl had given up looking for clean cups, and was making a roll-up.

"Philosophy and fashion marketing."

"You must know my wife, Dr. Thea Walsingham. She teaches philosophy."

The girl took a long drag on the roll-up and looked into the distance.

"We had her at the beginning of the year and then she left. Shame, she was brilliant. Most of the others couldn't care less."

I must have looked very downcast because the girl held my hand and asked, "Are you her husband, did she get ill or something? Look, I can find a cup. You can have some tea. I'm Rune, by the way".

"Ruin?"

"Rune – you know ancient runes, druids and all that."

I mumbled something and excused myself. The girl hopped up the stairs and I let myself out, but I tiptoed to the garage and put my hand into the crevice under the tile. Francis's phone was still there and I put it in my pocket.

If I didn't have a house, perhaps I still had a shop. Thea

and the children must be living in a cheap rental flat somewhere, with the income from The Windings making a surplus. Thea would be running the shop. She'd know how to make an income from odds and sods.

But the shop was unrecognisable: Buzzing with customers, festooned with abstract hanging art, a maze of book racks laden with glossy titles, a robed storyteller in a corner surrounded by half a dozen toddlers while their mothers chatted around a coffee machine. My two old codgers were snaffling the free biscuits. The man was wearing a linen jacket that I was sure was mine. They spotted me and the woman said, "You're back, more's the blooming pity. This new girl's smashing".

"For a coloured person, that is," the man said, and they both gave me 'and that's all we've got to say' looks.

It was Fiona at the counter – my counter – plumper now than she'd been when she'd paid me that mystifying visit, bookish-looking. I approached her, stood by the counter. She was bent over inscribing something in the frontispiece of a book with a calligraphy pen. When she looked up and saw me the pen jerked and a blot of ink welled up on the paper.

"You're out, Jack. I was expecting it any day."

"What are you doing in my shop?"

"It's my shop now."

"Why is it your shop?" I was talking like a four-year old.

"Because Thea sold it to me."

It didn't make any sense whatsoever. I was in my shop and a detective was at my counter writing in fancy calligraphy 'Happy birthday Neville from your darling Peg' in a book about Second World War battle tanks.

"What are you writing?"

"A dedication. We gift wrap and inscribe messages for the customers. It's a free service. I've mucked this one up now. I'll have to cut the page out and sell it at a discount."

"Is there a chair?" I asked. I was tired and I could smell myself.

Fiona called to one of the toddler mums.

"Lena, can you look after the shop for half an hour?"

She led the way out saying, "Lena runs one of the book clubs," as if I knew what she was talking about.

We went to the Dog and Goldfish, and Fiona bought me a double scotch. She had a pineapple juice: "No alcohol, I'm expecting." I must have looked confounded because she said, "Just sit back and I'll fill you in. You must be exhausted and completely confused".

And so it came out. The footsie during my interview, the abrupt change of investigator, her shot husband, her illness – her words were, "I just went mad with grief but I began to think that was normal and so I didn't know I had to get better". Then the business about her boss Boris – I remembered the bull-faced peasant – and how she'd got him suspended.

What was disarming was that she seemed to know me well, but I'd met her just twice before.

But I wanted to know about my family. Bugger her love for books and all this stuff about finding the flaw in my case. If she hadn't made a catastrophe of the interview I might have got out a bit quicker.

"Yes, all right, but where is Thea living? I went to my house and it was full of dirty students."

"She's in the Cotswolds. I've been to see her – twice."

Something clanged in my head as 'Cotswolds' collided

with an image of my grandfather's house.

"You mean she's at Forty Apple Trees?"

"Yes, she sold the house, got a fair price under the circumstances."

"What circumstances, and how do you know so much about my affairs?" I was getting querulous.

"It was a murder house, Jack. She had to sell it because she was broke, but you can't get a decent price when there's been a violent death."

"Who said anything about murder? What has Thea told you?"

Fiona sipped her juice and looked down.

"Jack, she told me nothing, even though I used a few tricks to find out what happened on that day."

I visualised the scene – this canny ex-detective sparring with a philosopher who could spin skeins of truth from a knitting bag full of warm air.

"Is she well?"

"She's better than she was. I'd say much better."

"And since you seem to be an expert on my wellbeing and my financial standing and my wife's state of mind, did you evince any clues about how she feels about me?"

"She wants you home," Fiona said, "But you're becoming sarcastic and nasty. I got beaten up because of you. A word of thanks wouldn't go amiss, but I don't expect anything of the kind". She got up and left.

I confess that I stayed in the Dog and Goldfish all afternoon and got maudlin and mawkish. I was very hungry, and alternated pints of bitter with bags of crisps and pork pies. My teeth felt furry and my stomach was windy. The barman wouldn't listen to what I was trying to say about the unfairness of it all and even barked at me, "Sit down or piss off." At around 5pm three men came in and ordered pints of lager. They were detectives – men in baggy-kneed suits who should be with their wives and children rather than hanging around in the pub at home time. I recognised one as the smarty pants who had taken over from Fiona. They clocked me (I think that's the word they'd have used) and muttered among themselves, and then the one I knew came over and said, "If I were you I'd piss off".

"You're the second person who's told me that this afternoon," I gurgled. My fingers were greasy with the jelly in the pork pie, and I'd spilt beer in my lap. The man went back to his colleagues and ignored me.

It was futile to try to travel to Forty Apple Trees that night, so I swayed through the cobbled lane and across the council car park, and found myself outside a cheap modern hotel, sporting motor racing motifs.

"I'd like a room for the night."

"Can I please sight your credit card sir?"

"Don't have one. Machine took it."

"I'm afraid, sir, that the management requires all patrons to proffer a valid credit card ..." He made the indefinite article rhyme with 'hay'.

"Proffer. What the fucking hell is 'proffer'? Here, let me 'proffer' you some money. Let me proffer some proper fucking banknotes and then you can proffer me a room and make a profit and stick it up your sodding proboscis."

He must have been a black belt in something because I was on the pavement in two seconds with a sore arm. I launched myself in the direction of The Windings and stumbled through my front gate. I knocked and a man opened the door. He had a big beer belly under a tight T-shirt that said 'Hey Big Spender'.

"I'm Rune's uncle. She said I could stay the night."

He grunted and pointed to what used to be my sitting room. I went in and lay on an air bed in the corner. I guessed that Rune slept on the mattress in the other corner. The walls were stuck with posters of bruised-eyed anorexic singers, and there were piles of clothes and books and handbags and shoes on every flat surface. I turned off the light and lay on my back. Across the ceiling in stick-on luminous stars was the phrase 'you are what you emagine'. I winced.

Familiar bird twitter woke me and I rolled over to touch Thea, but the plastic air bed squeaked as the skin on my back rubbed against it, and my hand touched a stiff object. I grasped it and held it up in the dawn light. It was a sticky vibrator with whisps of carpet fluff attached.

Rune was in whatever night garden students of philosophy and fashion design haunt. She didn't stir when I stepped over the piles of junk and crept out of my house like a thief.

27: There isn't any normal any more

It was mid-afternoon when I got out of the taxi.

"Don't they bleeding tip where you come from," the driver snarled as I watched him count out the exact change. After my ruinous train journey, I'd had six pounds left, and I sat in the taxi anxiously watching the meter. It stopped at four pounds forty and I handed over a fiver.

"Plus ninety pee surcharge."

"Surcharge?"

"Rural surcharge. I've got to drive back to town now. This is the countryside, mate, not bleeding Piccadilly Circus."

With that unpleasantness over I stood at the threshold of my grandfather's house, a place I'd never dreamed I'd visit again. The signs were propitious. William and Zita rushed out and I bent down to hug them, and they cried and so did I. After a little while they withdrew, Zita saying, "Why are you smelly, Daddy?" William asked for a present.

Thea had been standing at the doorway. She looked mouthwatering in jeans and a cashmere jumper.

"Come in, Jack," she said and embraced me coolly. I squeezed her bottom but she eased away and into the house.

"Phew, Zita's right. You are a bit whiffy."

There was an atmosphere of domesticity and comfort in the old place – bright furnishings, apple-pie cooking smell, school bags spilling pencil cases and drink bottles.

I wandered around to see what Thea had done to the place, eying especially the big bed in the front room.

Meanwhile the household carried on as if I weren't there, Thea chivvying the children over their homework, making snacks, rinsing glasses, taking washing from the line outside.

"Daddy, what was it like in do boy?" William asked.

"Dubai, silly," Zita said. "Daddy went to work on a camel. Daddy, was the camel smelly?"

"Children, let Daddy relax. He's had a big journey and he wants to relax. Jack, go and have a shower. You'll find some of your clothes in the front bedroom."

"Dubai?" I mouthed across the room.

"*Tu veut que je leur dis la vérité?*" she asked.

My schoolboy French wasn't up to replying in kind: "All right, Dubai. Yes, Zita, the camel was very smelly."

That seemed to please the little girl, and I was released to take my shower. I emptied the tank of hot water, rotating slowly under the shower head in privacy for the first time in nine months. I discovered trousers I'd forgotten about in the old wardrobe my grandfather had built into an awkward nook between the chimney breast and the window. There was the sweet pleasure of a drawer full of thick, new underpants. I'd existed in prison on a couple of pairs and they'd become stretched and baggy and stained. I felt renewed, taut, brisk, secure in well-fitting underpants and a clingy roll neck sweater.

Thea and I hadn't yet had a conversation out of earshot of the children, and as the afternoon went on I began to suspect that she was avoiding talking to me in private, or even one to one for that matter. At last the children were in bed, and I sat at the kitchen table with a glass of wine while Thea busied herself with what seemed to me domestic trivia, sorting baking tins into square and round, polishing jelly moulds.

"Just sit down please, Thea. We have to have a grown-up conversation at some point."

She poured herself some wine and sat down stiffly.

"So you arrive from prison as if you've been down to the shops, and we all return to normal?"

"No Thea, it can't be normal. There isn't any normal anymore. Us here at the cottage, the house sold, some twisted ex-cop in my shop. If you want normal perhaps we should talk in Latin and stand on our heads with sticks of celery in our ears."

"You know what I mean. There's a lot of hurt between us. It won't just go away in ten minutes."

"Hurt?" I said, "Hurt is spending nine months in a bunk with a stranger farting and wanking all night. Hurt is not knowing if you'll spend your life waiting for the day when somebody shoves a sharpened toothbrush handle in your kidneys. Hurt is not seeing your kids, not knowing even where they are." My voice was rising.

"I'll tell you about hurt," Thea said quietly. "Hurt is becoming a nobody, a pariah, the woman in the murder house. Hurt is having to take the children away and teach them a pack of lies. Hurt is not being able to speak to a living soul about what happened. Hurt is not knowing whether your husband will come back before you're sixty."

"We can talk about it now," I said. "Let's talk. It'll do us good. That day, when he attacked you ..."

"Your half-brother, you mean?"

I stopped. Thea looked at me and said, "Go on then".

"I just meant, well, we need to understand what happened on that day. He toppled over the balcony, didn't he? You must have been trying to hold him off ..."

Thea looked into her glass.

"Yes, I suppose it was something like that. And did you want to talk about what happened to the Major?"

"No really," I said. "I mean, all that's been cleared up or I wouldn't be here now."

We both took big draughts of wine and I topped us up. We didn't look at one another. I spoke to the tablecloth, asking, "And what about the house and the shop?"

"I sold them."

"Sold them? How? I was part owner."

"We have powers of attorney. It was your idea. You made a big fuss about it, how we'd have to keep the family functioning. You weren't around and I needed the money."

"What for? You could have run the shop and done a bit of teaching," I said.

"I needed it for the children. It's all in a trust for them. In case we ... in case the police ..."

I saw it then of course. Poor Thea, not knowing whether I'd be freed, not knowing when she might be arrested.

"And your parents are the trustees?"

She nodded.

"That was good work," I said, and she looked at me with a hint of affection for the first time.

We hadn't eaten, and so Thea produced a simple meal that I lingered over, concentrating on the sheer sensuality of eating at my own pace in my own room with my own wine, and a beautiful woman at my side. When she cleared the table, she touched my shoulders lightly and I dared to think that bright days might be ahead.

But at bedtime she was stiff and aloof. I said, "What's

wrong?" and all she would say was, "There's been enough for one day. There are things to talk about tomorrow. It'll wait".

I slept until lunchtime the next day and woke with a bursting bladder. The bathroom in the old house had been installed decades ago under a government grant, and the builders had simply whacked the plumbing on the back of the kitchen wall, and cut off half of the sitting room for the bathroom. I passed Thea, who was lying on the sofa speaking on the phone, and I mouthed 'busting' as I hopped past. As an ocean of urine spurted into the bowl, Thea's side of the conversations drifted into my consciousness. I realised that she was talking to Fiona Salmon, and that my name was being mentioned in affectionate terms. When I came out she was saying, "Yes, I'm not surprised. He'd had an awful day. OK, talk soon."

I raised my eyebrows in query.

"Nobody, just a friend. Any plans for today? The kids won't be home till three." We went upstairs to bed, and it was sweet.

Afterwards Thea asked me, "Those weeks, when you behaved so oddly, all that joshing and joking with ... him."

"What about it? He was my half-brother."

"Really?"

"Does it matter?"

"Of course it bloody well matters," Thea hissed and sat up in bed to confront me. I fondled her delicious breasts but she snatched my hand away and pulled a sheet around her. "It matters because I went through two weeks of hell living with that monster while you two took the piss out of me! I'm owed an explanation!"

I hesitated. Of course I'd been initially stunned by Francis's story, but it hadn't taken me very long to realise that he wasn't my half-brother; he was such an obvious imposter and opportunist. But I'd sensed something else wrong about the whole setup – me, Thea, Francis. There was a faintly bad smell, but where it came from and what was rotting, I knew not. How had he known about Aunt Florence and indeed talked his way into my father's presence? Who'd told him about my mother's novels, my birthmark?

"Well," I said, "I did have doubts."

"Just doubts?"

"Strongish doubts."

"Strongish? Is that a real adjective?"

"Strong then," I said.

"That's good enough for me," she said. I blinked. That was it? Thea unwound the bed sheet and I was happy again. Or perhaps not entirely. I'd behaved pretty oddly that week, and she did deserve to know why. But deserving doesn't mean you necessarily get what you think is due. Sometimes it's better not to know things.

We went to a pub for lunch and again I gloried in the food: Cheesy tepid bitter and a toothsome pie with turnips and lamb. By God, well-cooked food was a gift to be cherished. I watched Thea delicately separating the cubes of meat from the pastry, taking a sip of cider with each mouthful, concentrating, planning the next forkful, both of us absorbed in the sensuality of a simple meal again.

But there was a barrier, invisible but palpable. We were polite and courteous with one another, tender in a restrained way. I had a ball of something vaguely tense in my chest, the same anxious feel I had in the prison showers, naked and looking over my shoulder. I wondered if I should say something to provoke my wife on the way back from the pub; we'd stop the car, she'd get out and walk into a field, I'd follow and she'd shout at me to go away, and I'd yell at her, and we'd bellow out all our bitterness and end by clutching one another with wet cheeks and stinging eyes.

But we carried on politely eating, and by the time we arrived home the children were due to be collected from school. I welcomed the chance to escape the strain of what seemed to be developing into the opening salvos of a cold war. I got William and Zita into rubber boots and woolly hats, and took them outside to help me restore the orchard. I gave Zita a rake and William a blunt saw, and we sloshed around in mud and wet leaves until Thea called us in for dinner.

My second evening of freedom didn't go quite like the first. With the children in bed we started amicably enough with a cup of coffee in the sitting room. We sat side by side on the sofa and Thea wriggled down, stretching her legs out and putting her feet on the coffee table.

"Jack," she said, not without warmth, "What was it like having them think that you killed the Major, when it was really Francis? You must have been desperately bewildered and frightened".

I didn't say anything, just shrugged and made a downturned mouth.

"Jack, we need to have – what did you call it? – a grown up talk about it."

I tried a different version of the shrug.

"Jack, speak to me. Don't give me that face. It looks ... insincere, shifty ... What's going on?"

"Nothing's going on," I said. "I'm just not quite ready to talk about it."

"'Not quite ready to talk about it. Not quite ready to talk about it'. Now what soap opera have I heard that on before? Jack, that's not your way of talking. We're supposed to be intelligent people."

I sat and sipped my coffee, not sure what expression I should make next. I tried out a few but what I ended up with must have been pretty weak because Thea snapped: "Jack, you look like a constipated vicar. Now tell me why you don't want to talk about it."

I made my decision: I would lie to my wife. And I had to be careful.

"It was the weirdest day, Thea. Of course I had no idea that Francis was the killer at that point. I only found that out when my brief told me I was getting out. I mean, Francis was lying dead in his pajamas when I got back from Elephant and Castle. I never imagined for a microsecond that he'd left the house that morning. But you're right. I was totally bewildered and frightened. Those detectives grilling me for hours and hours."

"And what did you tell them?"

"As little as possible. Just said I'd had a worrying call from the Major, I drove down there, he was OK, and I came home. I had to say that there was a connection with Francis – otherwise how would I know the Major? But I made a point of saying that you weren't connected to any of it. I needed to keep you and the children as distant as possible, especially because of ... the other business."

"Don't remind me of all that," Thea said. "But what did you think would happen at the trial? Weren't you worried that you'd be convicted?"

I was thinking in fifth gear. I had a stab at this: "Well, strangely enough, I was terrified up till the moment that Fiona turned up – she's told you about it I expect?"

Thea nodded.

"Somehow," I said, "that bizarre meeting gave me

hope, a light at the end of the tunnel". Watch it, I cautioned myself. Keep the clichés in check. "It seems so strange, but she spoke with such conviction that I absolutely knew that I'd get out," I said.

I could see Thea softening. Evidently, Thea and Fiona had an understanding. More than an understanding? I had a momentary flash of the three of us, white on brown on white ... and stuffed it back in a mental hidey hole somewhere for later use. Unlikely. Impossible. But still, Fiona must have confessed all and been given absolution. My story dovetailed with the facts as Thea knew them. My wife leaned against me and graced me with the faintest kiss.

"Shall we watch the telly?" she asked. "It'll be rubbish, but it'll do us good."

We watched a reality show about a verruca clinic, which helped take my mind off the question that was burning a black hole in my brain: Why was my wife wearing a Jules Hector dress and shoes like a Birmingham shop girl on a Saturday night when my bogus half-brother fell to his death with his cock hanging out?

I snuggled up and kissed my wife on the cheek.

"What'll you do tomorrow?" Thea asked. "I suppose you'll have to have some sort of plan?"

"I'd just like to look at the sky for a few moments," I said, and took a thick jacket from the hall stand.

It was sooty black in the front garden, but as I stood breathing in the dank bitter smell of wet nettles and rotting hollyhocks, my eyes grew accustomed to the lights on a distant hill – the road snaking through the woods from the motorway turn off – and to the east, the whitish glow of a town on the horizon.

Tomorrow? I didn't have a clue.

28: The man with currant bun eyes

The next morning, a Saturday, I asked Thea, "Do we have any money?"

"Not much," she said sniffily. "Do you have any?"

I sat and nibbled guiltily on my toast. I could see a pile of essays on the sideboard, and wondered how many 'good arguments' and 'evidence weak here' my breakfast had cost. I'd offered to help mark some essays years ago when Thea was overwhelmed with work. After reading a few I'd suddenly remembered a ceiling that needed painting.

"When you say not much, how much not much?"

"About enough to last us until just after Christmas. The rest is in the trust."

I kept quiet. There was a barely disguised challenge in her reply, along the lines of 'after Christmas it's down to you'.

"I could get a job," I said.

"You could."

I finished my toast and said, "Could I have some money please?"

"Yes, look in my bag and you'll find some in the red wallet."

I took a tenner and went for a walk along the lane, then struck off on a footpath that wound up the hill to one side of the orchard. There had been a silvery frost in the night, and the ruts in the mud had frozen hard. Halfway up the hill I stopped and looked down on the cottage a quarter of a mile away. I saw Thea carrying a basket of washing into the back garden, followed by Zita and William. The trio stationed themselves in front of the washing line with their backs towards me, Thea in the middle. William handed the items of washing and Zita handed up the pegs. I could faintly hear their chatter, or at least the higher pitched voices of the children. The little task was harmoniously completed in a few minutes, and I felt bleak when they went back inside. I unclenched my right hand, which had been rolling the tenner in my pocket into a tight tube.

I couldn't bear to go home to the ambiguity of whatever passed as our marriage. I walked on, ignoring the bank of leaden cloud that was moving in from the coast. I was wearing a thick knitted cardigan, an old matted grey thing that I liked to watch TV in. Soon the beads of drizzly mist soaked through and met the sweat coming from under my shirt as I toiled up the slope.

I didn't know the area around Forty Apple Trees well, but I figured that soon I would meet a road that led to a village that had a row of shops with a café that sold warm buttered scones and tea. At the top of the hill I saw the motorway below and realised that the path threaded down through a field that abutted the stream of lorries and cars heading north – no sign of a village. Two cows stood staring at the traffic. A solitary tree stood halfway down the slope, and I stumbled down the fifty yards of glutinous mud path to shelter under its canopy. The rain was now of the steady soaking kind that the Cotswolds specialises in. But my spirits lifted ever so slightly when I saw a burnt-out car, nose down in a ditch behind the tree. Judging by the weedy shrubs thrusting through the rusted-out wheel arches, it must have been there for years. I crawled inside and crouched on the pressed metal platform where the back seat had been, just out of range of the rain dripping from the glassless frame of the rear window.

I sat there for a long time. There were no intrusions: No murmur of prisoners' voices, no TV reality show blaring from a cell, no bells and buzzers, no sounds of Thea washing dishes, no chatter of the children, no customers leafing through the paperbacks. And it came to me that this was the first time I had been truly alone for a year – perhaps for many years.

The idea crept into my mind like a sewer rat. I shoved it down into the muck but it manifested itself again, almost visible like a thing with yellow teeth and blank eyes. I shivered on the cold metal seat, wiped my brow with a sooty hand. One of the cows had made its way patiently up the slope and now stood in the rain ten yards away sagely looking towards me. A gallon of urine gushed from its rear. I tried to think of anything but the hideous notion that was forcing itself into clear consciousness.

Thea and Francis. Francis and Thea.

Perhaps during those days when Francis had moved into The Windings, I'd maintained my sanity by simply shutting out the possibility. Perhaps the idea was so monstrous as to be inadmissible. Sitting in my wet cardigan, I reached into my memory and replayed fragments of loops from my tortured nocturnal thoughts in the spare bedroom: The things that Francis shouldn't have known about my family, the sense that Thea and Francis shared some understanding, the words that Thea had spat out that night under the lamp post about visions of a man she'd never seen, the suspicion that Francis had been at least indirectly responsible for my parents' death. I'd spun these into a web of hatred for Francis and Francis alone, this frightening man who'd infected my family, this rotten con man who I knew I had to kill. I wasn't a killer, I'd sworn to myself, just a man driven to the last shreds of dignity.

And in prison, with Francis dead, I suppose it had been easier to slam the door on the grotesque idea, even it meant drowning the memory of Thea on the balcony in the grey and magenta dress and Francis smashed to death in his pajamas below.

I was shivering quite violently by now. I squeezed out of the filthy car, and staggered past the cow and down to the barbed wire fence by the low muddy embankment at the edge of the motorway. I grappled a path under the barbed wire, and came up bloodied and mud stained on the other side, teetering a foot away from the carriageway. The traffic presented a solid hurtling force of matter and sound, but a vehicle separated itself out and pulled into the hard shoulder two hundred yards ahead of me.

A figure got out of the car and walked towards me. It was a man in a green wax jacket and a tweed cap. As he came nearer I saw currant bun eyes and a face wreathed in deep kindness and concern. It was Mr. Firth, Business Development Officer at the Cathedral sixty miles away.

They patched up my cuts in Casualty. Mr. Firth telephoned Thea and left me to continue his journey to see his sister in Cardiff.

"I do feel that Christ may have had a little to do with my decision this morning to drive to Wales," he said, giving my shoulder a gentle squeeze as he departed. How I envied him his simple goodness.

I managed to convince the anxious young Iraqi doctor that I was sane and didn't need to see a psychologist, and by the time I had signed some forms Thea was in the waiting room with the children, who watched me solemnly.

I went to bed for the rest of the day, my first Saturday at Forty Apple Trees. Thea left me a tray of lunch things and went out again with the children. Apparently, Saturday sport had continued in my absence. But I could not eat. I could not formulate a thought that was not suffused with the vision of Francis mounting my wife like a goat. The afternoon crawled on and my putrid imaginings expanded in detail and depravity until I leapt from the bed, threw myself onto the floor and did fifty press ups.

Thea and the children clattered into the house in the afternoon. Thea shushed them, and when she looked in on me I pretended to be asleep.

I came downstairs after the children had been put to bed, and we watched another reality show, this time about working in a human resources office. I sat at one end of the sofa and Thea at the other. After half an hour she turned the volume down and asked me, "Are you feeling better?" but I just nodded.

We both watched the silent screen for a few minutes, and then she said, "Jack, I've done something abominable."

"We don't need to talk about it," I said.

"Jack, I almost destroyed our family."

"Thea, it was me who did that."

"No, before, all those years ago ..."

"Yes Thea, but I wasn't innocent either. We both did ... things."

"Things," Thea said. "Funny how we can reduce the most profoundly awful events to mere things: I did a thing, you did a thing, two minuses make a plus, the things cancel each other out. Everything goes back to normal."

"That's a bit on the deep side for me," I said.

"Come on Jack, don't play dim. It's how we protect ourselves from going mad, how we try to redeem ourselves."

I thought about this: "You mean you can correct a wrong by doing another wrong rather than doing something right?"

"In a way, but then you have to live with it, and you have to weigh up the moral balance. Let's say that there is a mortal threat to someone close to you – someone who utterly depends on you ..."

"You mean your husband or wife ..." I asked.

"Well, perhaps. Your children too."

A break was forming in my foggy thoughts. The vision became clearer, or at least the edges of a vision.

"So," I said, "You might be justified in doing something awful?"

"You might. But none of this is clear cut."

I groped to comprehend what she was saying. Was it possible that Thea had redeemed herself by killing Francis? Was is possible that she had seduced him on his return from Elephant and Castle, and pushed him off the balcony when he was distracted? Was it possible that she had redressed the hurt that she had caused me by squashing the life out of the cockroach that had crawled over our family?

Well, it was a thought, and when Thea turned the sound up on the TV, I slid over to her side of the sofa and massaged her foot until her eyelids fluttered and she fell asleep.

At the end of the human resources program a jarring newscast theme woke my wife, and she sat up in her drowsy pulchritude. I think she looked at me fondly. She said, "I'd better check on the children," and went upstairs. She was a long time in their rooms. I knew she liked to sit and watch them sleeping.

I went to bed and started on a crime thriller I'd found under the sofa. Thea undressed and slipped in beside me.

"You didn't kiss them goodnight," she said.

"Not to worry. I'll see them in the morning."

I read my book for half an hour but when I turned out the light she was still awake.

"Jack," she said, "Can we not talk about it again — all that business?"

"Business? Oh, you mean the falling?"

"Falling?"

"Yes," I said, "That January, it felt as if everything were falling down".

She breathed in the dark and then said, "Yes, I see. The Falling with a capital T and capital F?"

"If you like. It's handy to label a period in your life sometimes."

"Yes, sort of saves having to talk about the detail ..."

"Or think about the detail ..." I added.

Thea went to sleep but I stayed awake for a long time. Tonight I could imagine a life with Thea. I dared to think that she loved me and that the evidence for this might have been the crumpled man in blue pajamas at the foot of the stairs.

29: Rural bliss

But the scales of moral equilibrium (I coined the phrase over a cup of cocoa one night) were still wavering. I was a newcomer to ethics, but I was getting the hang of the whole idea.

I'd started applying for jobs in my old field – chemical engineering – but with Christmas drawing near there wasn't much going. If I was honest with myself I'd have admitted that my expertise was woefully out of date and that I made the effort mainly to please Thea.

So with the whole of December at my disposal I set about digging vegetable beds with the vague intention that we'd be self-sufficient in food. I'd get some hens perhaps, and even buy a goat. And perhaps in a year or two I'd be harvesting bushels of apples from the forty trees in my possession.

As I worked in the open air with my honest tools and hearty mother nature under my boots, I pondered the idea of confessing to Thea about my part in the old man's death. But I was reluctant. The moral balance of my hypothesis that Thea had killed Francis – and it was only a hypothesis of course – relied on the notion that Francis had killed the old man. As I hacked with my axe at a buried root, or grubbed out a stand of blackberries, I formed the idea that for Francis to have deserved to be murdered, he would have to have been guilty of a decent stack of offences. For Thea, it wouldn't be enough just to seduce and corrupt her – but I calculated that she could feel redeemed if Francis himself had been guilty of murder.

And that, of course, was the whole basis for the collapse of my case: Thanks to Fiona Salmon's work, Francis had been ostensibly the last person to see the old man alive, and was therefore – although conveniently dead – the prime suspect.

I had to keep my mouth shut, not to protect myself, but to protect my wife from ethical jeopardy. I felt deeply sympathetic to Thea because of her admittedly hypothetical dilemma. Halfway through December we'd reached a point of companionable ease in one another's company. On an especially cold afternoon she brought two nips of whisky into the garden, and kissed me affectionately after we'd thrown them back. I was falling into a confused but exciting variety of love with her; she was brave martyr, reluctant murderer, devoted mother. To think otherwise was too revolting.

One afternoon I uncovered a buried drain, and was worrying the old bricks with a pickaxe. I sensed Thea behind me and turned to see her crying. I embraced her and smeared mud on her jacket.

"I need to know something, Jack."

I knew what it was. I knew that my beloved spinner of ectoplasm, my dearest doctor of philosophy – actual philosophy – must have tortured herself contemplating that morning in The Falling, hoping against all hope that the man she had murdered – hypothetically of course – had murdered the Major, and forcing into the remotest corner of her mind that I could have been responsible.

"Thea, I need to say this just once. I did not kill the Major."

She stopped crying and said, "Of course you didn't. I

just needed to hear you say it. I'm sorry".

"Thea, we'll never speak of it again. Look, I'm starving doing all this work in the fresh air. Can you make me a bacon sandwich?"

She went inside and I considered the question neatly closed. This ethics business wasn't too difficult once you'd had a bit of practice. I don't mean to be flippant or superficial of course.

***

I called a few old contacts in the baby wipe business, but it wasn't encouraging. For one, nobody really remembered me.

"Jack Walsingham? Weren't you in accounts?"

"No, that was Jack Waters. I did all that work on tear strength."

"Wasn't that John Whatmough?"

"No, he worked on lubricants."

"Look I'm sorry John ..."

"Jack. I'm Jack."

"Yes, Jack of course. Look the business isn't what it was. There's a lot of imported stuff around since you left ..."

And on one occasion I was remembered, but for the wrong reason:

"Oh yes, I remember you," the voice said ominously. "Murdered somebody. Bugger off."

I dropped a few hints to Thea about my likely poor prospects but she didn't seem too concerned. I'd been fixed up with an ATM card, and been pleased to see that the remaining funds weren't quite as low as she had led me to believe; but the money was finite, and even with the parsimony that we practised there would be a reckoning.

We agreed that we'd invest a little money in cultivating the land. I dug in potatoes by the middle of the month, and I was laying out beds for carrots and peas and onions after Christmas.

"How about you, Thea? What are your work prospects?" I asked just before Christmas.

"Not so good really, Jack. All I'm good for is marking. The nearest university is thirty miles away and I'd be competing for scraps with all the young PhDs. Let's get Christmas out of the way and then we'll make some plans."

***

One day, late in the afternoon, a car pulled into the drive, and Fiona Salmon got out. Thea embraced her and they went into the house. I carried on breaking up a bed of sticky clay, exhaling white breath in the chilly saturated air.

"Come in and talk to Fiona," Thea called from the doorway.

The ex-detective looked different: Fuller in the face and with a slight bump below her chunky jumper. Thea made tea, and I sat opposite Fiona. We made small talk about the shop – what was selling, what wasn't, the book club, the old codgers.

"Sell much Isherwood these days?"

"I think I was the last sale. But guess what?" Fiona said.

"Tell me."

"The book club are reading *A Dance to the Music of Time*."

"It'll take them five years to get through it," I said.

We laughed, not naturally, and Thea laid out the tea things.

"I haven't thanked you, Fiona. For getting me out," I

said.

She looked at me with what I thought might be the slightest doubt, and then Thea said, "We're so grateful Fiona. You were so courageous."

Fiona said, "And I haven't apologised, Jack."

"For what, a daft infatuation? You couldn't have been in your right mind!"

"There's not the slightest doubt about that!" Thea said.

"Anyway," I said, "congratulations on the ..." I looked at her midriff.

"Baby," Fiona said.

"I'd better get that carrot bed dug."

After an hour Fiona came out. The two woman embraced, and then Thea stood by the door while Fiona came down the garden path to say goodbye. She leaned towards me to brush my cheek with hers and whispered, "I damn well hope I was right about you Jack".

I shivered and whispered back, "I didn't kill anybody".

When she had gone, Thea brought a quivering chunk of warm bread pudding out to me.

"That's kind of you," I said, leaning on the spade and negotiating the pudding with muddy fingers.

She was wearing a green wax jacket and looked rurally enchanting, a red English bloom on her half-Greek cheek. Her rubber boots had a smudge of clay on each toe.

"She didn't drive all the way here for a cup of tea," I said.

"No, you're right Jack. She came to warn us."

"I expected it. How long have we got?"

"She's not sure, but this is just a lull. They'll come after us once the business with her boss is settled. Fiona thinks her phone's being tapped."

"That's why she drove here then. To tell you in

person," I said. I didn't want my bread pudding anymore.

"And she's heard things. They're starting from scratch with both cases – Francis and the Major. Both of the inquests came up with open verdicts."

"So maybe a few months?"

"Maybe longer, maybe a year. They'll want the case to stick like glue. They'll want both of us."

"Superglue," I said. "It's not just, is it? What harm did you ever do?"

"And you, Jack. You're not a bad man."

"Bit of a twit sometimes."

"Give me a kiss."

30: An old-fashioned look

The night before the Major and Francis died I came home late. Thea was in bed and I let myself into the spare room. I turned down the ringer on my phone, and fell into dreamless slumber almost instantly. I woke in blackness and checked the phone: 4.21. I went back to sleep, but this time there was a sequence of repetitive nasty dreams: Black babies with golden tails swam in a fish tank in a cottage where I was on holiday with my parents. I'd lost William and Zita, and then I was on a boat with them on a warm day, and then a storm struck and they were washed into the water ... I struggled not to cry, struggled to understand if this was real or a dream, crawled out of the dream into real life, and lay there in utter relief that the children weren't dead.

I became aware of a vibrating sound that stopped abruptly. The light on my phone blinked off. I picked it up and checked the screen: 7am, message waiting.

I recognised the scrapy posh old voice at once: "Terribly sorry to bother you Jack, but it is most awfully urgent that you come here right away. I'm in a shocking fix and I've nobody to help. Please come."

I rang back but got the engaged tone. Tried again with the same result. Listened to the message again: He sounded panicky and weak.

I slid out of bed and into yesterday's clothes, splashed my face in the kitchen sink downstairs, and quietly left the house. The cold January morning air shocked me into sensible consideration as I strode towards the station. I couldn't afford to leave any ends untied; the Major's troubles could only be connected with Francis, and the sooner I knew what was going on the better. The commuter train to London was packed, and smelt of halitosis and shower gel.

The door of the Major's flat was ajar, and it was cold and damp inside. The old man was lying on his front in stripy pajamas.

"Have you dragged me down for a bit more play acting?" I said.

The Major made a little bleat.

"Get up for God's sake. I suppose this is Francis's idea?"

Another bleat. I knelt down and saw the cheap mobile phone in his hand. He whispered something and I put my ear to the side of his head.

"Awful bloody pain in my head. Gone black."

"What's gone black?"

"Left eye. Pills. They're on the top shelf, Francis," the Major said.

"This is Jack, not Francis."

"Terribly sorry, Jack. I rang Francis too. He didn't answer so I left him a message."

I looked around the room. I guessed he had a crippling migraine if he was asking for pills. Or a stroke? I'd heard how you test for stroke so many times, but couldn't remember – something about smiling, or was it counting to five? I couldn't see any pills on the shabby shelves.

"Which shelf?"

"Use your bloody eyes, man," the Major said.

I looked up at the huge clock, and for just a second I visualised smashing it down onto his skull. I luxuriated very briefly in the image of the old fool's brains splashed on the floor.

But there was something behind the clock. It looked white and flat. The pills? I pulled a spindly chair across the room and stepped up so that I could get a clear view; the white thing was just an old faded matchbox.

"Quick you bloody fool," croaked the Major.

His feeble bleating angered me, and again, for a fraction of a second, I contemplated grasping the monstrous clock with both hands and braining the old conman with it. But the chair wobbled, and all I could think of was avoiding falling and breaking my ankle. I reached for the edge of the shelf to steady myself, missed, and grabbed the edge of the huge timepiece instead. It slipped from my hand and tipped off the shelf, and I watched in sickly dread as it dropped onto the Major's head.

I stood transfixed by the super-saturated colours of the wound and the fluids, by the other worldly nature of the scene, by my own calm. What, I thought, would Lincoln Rhyme make of the theatre of crime? What did I need to do next to secure my safety? And then I remembered that the Major had said that he had telephoned Francis.

I thought swiftly. The only thing I had touched apart from the clock was the chair, which I wiped with a tissue after returning it to its place. I glanced at the clock, but I didn't have the stomach to wipe it. I might even introduce suspicious smears in the gore. I backed out of the room and walked down the steps, and then turned in the direction of the station. A hundred yards down the street I passed a side road, and saw Francis's white van parked half a dozen cars down. I slipped behind the mouldy remnant of a privet hedge and watched Francis, his back to me, pulling a burqa over his head. I strode on.

Me officer? Just been visiting an old friend in a jam. Turned out he was fine, so I'm off home now. See anyone acting suspiciously? No, nothing at all. That's how it would go. And sooner or later the thousands of cameras that tracked the movements of every Londoner, wherever they went, would turn up the fact that the last person to see the old man was a blackmailing, violent thug with a taste for disguises. Well, it took a bit longer than I'd expected.

I called Thea from Elephant and Castle, and suggested we had lunch out in the country. She sounded pleased. The train back from London was almost empty – just mums with small children, the odd pensioner with a large print library book. I walked home with something approaching optimism. I wanted to embrace my wife, tell her that things would be settled soon, tell her that our family would survive the ghastliness that we'd brought down on our own heads.

When I opened the door, there was disco music playing from upstairs and a bundle of something blue and white on the hallstand. Had Thea had something delivered? A duvet? And then I saw my second corpse of the day, and there was Thea on the landing in the grey and magenta dress and very high heels, pale and trembling.

"Did he attack you?" I called to her. "Are you alright?"
Thea nodded.

"Thank God. Let me come up and see how you are."
"No, stay there."

She must have been in profound shock.

"Did he lose his balance?"

Thea looked at me glassily and said nothing. She slowly bent down, took off the high heeled shoes, and went into the bedroom. She came out barefooted and walked slowly down the stairs. She made the familiar paddle hands and said, "Just leave me for a moment".

"I have to call the police," I said.

Thea nodded.

"Say nothing. Absolutely nothing. Say nothing. I will look after everything."

Thea went into the kitchen. I looked around. Francis's neck was obviously broken. I looked at his genitals and felt queasy. His mobile phone was on the floor; it must have slipped from the breast pocket of his pajamas. I picked it up, switched it off, and opened the front door. The street was empty. I took the side passage to the back garden and went into the shed. I wrapped the phone in plastic and duct tape and pushed it into a crevice between the roof tile and the rafter of the shed. It took no more than a minute.

I went back inside, turned off the Pet Shop Boys and called 999.

***

We had a splendid Christmas here at Forty Apple Trees. The garden looked neat and organised, and poised for a bursting out of good English vegetables in the spring. I almost didn't have the heart to get rid of the Austin Princess – William and Zita wanted to use it as a planter box – but a man with a hoist truck and a hearty Cotswolds daughter hefted the thing off the bricks and took it away. On Christmas Day William and Zita phoned Charlotte in London. She was sent back to her mother after I was arrested, but she'll be visiting us soon.

We spent New Year's Eve at home. It being the season for fresh starts and weighty resolutions, we put the children in front of the television with a bag of pork scratchings, and retreated to the kitchen for a serious talk about what we would live on. We had a vague discussion about chemical engineering and essay marking, but the fact that one or both of us could be back in prison a year hence took the sharp edges off any solid plans we came up with.

"We'll talk again tomorrow," Thea said.

"Yes, there's always tomorrow. Bed, I think."

While Thea shepherded the sleepy children through the bedtime ritual, I poked around in the little flatpack desk we had squeezed into the corner of the lounge. I remembered that one of my old baby wipe colleagues had been fractionally less pessimistic than the others. Why not give him another call when work resumed after the New Year holiday? Wedged between some papers was a little address book that I didn't recognise. It seemed to be full of gibberish.

Thea came back in: "I'd forgotten about that. It's Francis's. I found it hidden in the guest quarters."

"What is it, do you think?"

"Haven't a clue," Thea said.

***

One of the advantages of being a bookseller is that – assuming your bookshop is a flop – you have lots of time to browse. I'd been particularly fascinated by a work on the Bletchley Park code breakers, and a close inspection of the notebook convinced me that the gibberish was encoded. It took me just a couple of minutes to work out that it was a simple substitution code. Francis hadn't even bothered to group the letters into strings of five, so the encoded forms for 'road', 'street', 'david' and 'john' practically leapt out of the page. As for the numbers, well they were obviously sums of money. These were Francis's human bank accounts.

I struggled with my conscience, but not too manfully: Hand the address book in? But it could do more harm than good. The man who was being whipped, for example: What if the police investigated him, and his wife found out? And Francis's crimes had already been committed. I couldn't uncommit them. Why not just collect the cash and put the victims out of the misery of the phone call that they knew would come one day?

So a few days later when I was alone in the house, I retrieved Francis's phone from behind a loose brick in the toilet, plugged it into a charger and turned it on. The names in the contacts list matched the decoded names, and I wrote them down. I drove to the petrol station and bought a cheap pay-as-you-go phone with cash. I called a number at random from the list.

"Hello, Matthew here."

"Matthew," I said. "I'm an associate of somebody you know." I'd rehearsed.

"What?"

"Matthew, I believe you're holding some assets in trust for the person in question."

It was quickly arranged with Matthew for Saturday, when Thea would be taking an early train to London with the children for a day with her parents.

"Sure you don't want to come?" she asked.

"Better not. I really need to get some job applications done," I said, feeling despicable.

Matthew lived in Brighton, so I drove down and scouted round for a suitable place. I rang him again from the car.

"The Portslade Cemetery. Know it?" I gave him the grave name and location and told him to put the cash in a bouquet of flowers. "Matthew, that's the end of it. You won't hear from us again, OK?"

But I almost lost my nerve in the cemetery. I sat on a bench a hundred yards away and waited till a portly man in a tweed jacket sidled up to the grave, laid down a bouquet and scuttled off. I looked around but couldn't see anything that might conceal a CCTV camera. And then I thought, what would Francis have done? He'd have taken that extra precaution.

There was another bench next to mine, on which sat a woman of about thirty in a dirty anorak and muddy trainers. She was scratching her arm and one heel was drumming on the asphalt.

"How'd you like to make thirty quid quickly?" I asked, being careful not to turn towards her again.

"Fuck off, perv."

"Fifty."

"Wassit I gotta do? I'm not a tom, mate."

"Just by that big tree next to the path. There's a bunch of flowers. Go and pick it up and meet me outside the gate and I'll give you the money. Don't look at me."

"Make it 'undred."

"Seventy-five."

In ten minutes I was on the road with next month's housekeeping in the glove box. I stopped at the motorway services and went to the toilet. Inside the cubicle I took out the SIM card and flushed it away, then wrapped the phone in toilet paper, crushed it with my heel, and tossed the remains into the litter bin. The fry-up kiosk sold me a package of oily chips and something that looked like pieces of crisp-fried vomit, and I ate them off the passenger seat as I sped home.

Thea called me from the station just as I came off the motorway.

"Be there in five minutes," I said, marvelling at my timing.

The family piled in and Zita said, "Daddy, the car stinks!" Thea balled up the greasy food wrapping and said with tenderness, "That's what happens when we leave you alone for the day – you eat like a soccer hooligan!"

I privately stewed in my shame, producing a stream of false jaunty chat while the children went on about the pong.

"Smells like a monkey was sick," Thea said, and the children began to catalogue all the possible varieties of animal vomit they could think of.

"Donkey sick with HP Sauce," William said.

"Rhinoceros sick with duck poo," Zita proposed.

"Enough," Thea said.

But by the time we arrived home, I was tortured with remorse. I loathed myself for the ease with which I'd manipulated the wretched Matthew.

"Damn," I said, "I forgot to get milk. I'll pop out to the petrol station".

Night had fallen when I stopped the car outside the church two hundred yards past the petrol station. I turned off the car lights and sat watching for passers-by. Nobody was around. I put Matthew's envelope on the floor of the porch and opened it. Using the tips of my fingernails I slid the banknotes out and pushed them under the door.

"We had milk," Thea said when I came back. "You didn't need to go out."

"Just as well – when I got to the garage I realised I'd

left my wallet at home. I'll be going out in my pajamas next." This, I promised myself, was the last lie.

***

It's been a year since the night I ripped Francis's address book to shreds and flushed it down the toilet. A couple of days later I was struck down with flu – real flu, the one that puts a hot pile driver in your head and turns your muscles to pain-racked blubber. Thea said afterwards that in my delirium I told her what happened the night the Major died.

"What did I say?"

"That you were there but the old man died by accident."

"Did I say that I wanted to kill him?"

"You did."

"I was a whisker away."

"But," Thea said, "you didn't kill him. You can't feel remorse for a momentary intention you didn't fulfil. If we did that we'd all go mad".

"That's philosopher talk."

"Just someone trying to get things straight. Let me bring you some tea."

When she came back she said, "Is there a question you want to ask me now?"

"You know the question. It's really whether you're ready to answer it," I said.

"Then I'll answer. I'll tell you how Francis died." And so she did.

***

Over the next few months we absorbed the grim symmetry of the deaths and the ambiguity of our parts in them. We came to an accommodation with ourselves and with one another. Eventually I had the courage to confess to Thea what I'd done down in the cemetery in Brighton.

"I guessed you'd been up to something. I didn't want to know what," she said.

"But you must have put the pieces together. That's what you're good at, Thea."

"I suppose I did."

"How can you bear to be with me?" I asked.

"You can't separate the two sides of a coin."

***

Just as the money was running out in the spring, one of the baby wipe pals called me with the offer of a fill-in contract for somebody on maternity leave. It was a fifty-mile round trip to work by bus and train, a salary just short of risible, but an escape from digging cabbages and watching for a police car to turn into the drive. When the new mum's husband was offered a job in Singapore she resigned, and the company said they'd keep me on. I'm still there.

And we're still free. Fiona has been up to see us and thinks we might be safe. The county police force is presently mired in that huge bribery scandal that has been entertaining the country for the last six months, and seen most of the senior police echelons sacked or transferred. Fiona told us she'd talked to her old colleague Simon, who was getting ready to pack up and emigrate to New Zealand.

When I was offered the permanent job, I hired the teenager from the cottage next door to baby sit, and I walked with Thea the two miles to the local pub on a perfumed summer night. We polished off giant meat pies, black forest cake, and a bottle of something reasonably drinkable. Rolling home contentedly under the moon, our stomachs were tight as kettle drums.

"Why don't you dig out that magenta dress later if you've still got it?" I asked, but Thea gave me what her Irish mother would call an old-fashioned look.

THE END

About the author

I used to be a Professor of Linguistics, but these days I write novels and short stories. I was born in London but I've lived in Sydney, for most of my adult life. You can learn more about my books at stuartcampbellauthor.com

I love to get feedback on my novels. Readers' comments motivate me to keep writing, and help me to spread the word about my work. If you enjoyed *An Englishman's Guide to Infidelity*, scan the QR code below to tell me what you liked. You can write an essay or just a few words! Thank you very much – Stuart.